Forged in Secrets

Forge Brothers Security
Book 2

Kendra Warden

Chapter 1

Donald

Three Months Before

Donald Fairman grimaced as he looked down at the phone resting in his palm.

He let it ring once, and then twice, unsure whether he was eager or terrified to hear what the man on the other end had to say.

There was so much riding on this. What would he do if things didn't work out?

He shook his head and reached out to tap the

green button before bringing the device to his ear.

It was always better to know. One way or another.

"I take it this couldn't wait until I was on the plane?" he asked by way of greeting.

He glanced out the window as he waited for a reply, taking in the glimmering lights of downtown Austin. It was beautiful out there. Paradise, really. As much as he tended to wax nostalgic about the snowy weather he'd experienced growing up, he had to admit that the Texan climate suited him just fine.

"Sorry, Don. I thought you'd want to know right away," the man said. There was a teasing tone to his friend's voice, a near-guarantee that he'd like what he was about to hear.

"It's fine. Everyone's long gone for the day," he said, giving the open floor plan a final visual sweep, as though someone might have returned to grab a forgotten wallet or set of keys in the last five minutes. "Just tell me so I can confirm my plans."

"The acquisition is officially going through."

The words waited a moment then, suspended in time as Donald considered the implications. It was the news he'd been waiting for, yes, but that didn't mean it would be a simple matter going forward. Oh well. There was no time to second guess anything now. Things would work out. They had to.

"Anyway," the man on the phone continued. "We announce publicly in three weeks."

Donald gripped the phone more tightly, noticing a slight 'click' as his wedding band met the hard plastic of his protective case.

He wasn't sure if he'd ever be ready to stop wearing it, even though his wife had already taken her ring with her to her grave.

"Three weeks is cutting it too close," he said. "I have funds to move. Not to mention the meetings, and everything I'm going to have to do to try and hide the paper trail we're about to leave behind. And I'm leaving for China on the thirtieth."

"We don't have a choice."

"Did you try to talk to them?" Donald asked. Somewhere on the street below, he heard the faint sound of a driver blowing his horn. Real life always felt far away when he was up here. Especially now.

"Of course I did! The board wasn't having it. The accounting department is already upset that this chaos is all going on mid-quarter."

"Okay," Donald said, letting out a breath. "I'll make it happen."

"Three weeks."

Without another word, the line went dead.

Donald smiled to himself. He'd half expected to be reminded of what he owed. Not that he would have complained about the exorbitant fee he had agreed to pay in installments in exchange for information on the acquisition.

It was worth it, and a whole lot more.

But making sure he kept everything nice and legal, now, that would be a bit more of a challenge. Still, it was nothing he couldn't handle. He'd been in business a long time. It was amazing how many invoices could be categorized under the single title of 'consultant fee.'

Another horn screeched below.

Donald stared down at the street as two men got out of their now banged-up cars and began yelling at each other, their words silenced by the thick glass.

Real life–in the form of past-due stamps and scowling IRS agents–was coming for him, and for everything he'd built.

But AveroTech would survive in the end. He'd make sure of it.

Chapter 2

Grace

"Why do we even have this chair?" Grace asked, picking at the velvet upholstery with the end of a manicured fingernail. "It's horrible."

"Because your mother would notice if we burned it, Miss Hinton," the security guard said, not bothering to look up from the newspaper he was reading.

Grace stifled a giggle. She liked the new guy so far. Even if he insisted on calling her by her last name.

Before she could make any further comment, she heard the walkie-talkie on the man's belt crackling to life. "Grace's ride is here."

"Thank you," she said loud enough for the man on the other end to hear, getting to her feet and sending the chair scraping across the marble floor of the foyer.

The security guard muttered something from behind his paper. She could hardly blame him for his disinterest. The Hinton family's mansion was well-secured with high fences, sturdy gates, and cameras every few feet. For the most part, all her parents expected of their hires was that they stayed awake for their entire shift, just in case.

She hitched her tote bag up on her shoulder before striding out toward the driveway, her heels clicking as she went. Spring had come at last, and she had dressed for the season in a coral wrap dress that she hoped would accentuate her blue eyes.

Benjamin Forge's nondescript sedan was already waiting in the horseshoe-shaped driveway. As she opened the passenger door and sat down, she caught a few bars of a Beastie Boys song pouring from the struggling speakers.

"This music is horrible," she said cheerfully as she pulled her seatbelt across her chest. Ben stuck out a finger and hit the power button, engulfing them in silence.

She couldn't help but to admire the cords of thick muscle in his forearm.

Despite the fact that he was the resident tech nerd at Forge Brothers Security, he spent more time in the gym than any of the other guys, and it showed. The man was massive.

"No way," Ben's twin brother, Asher, chimed in from the back seat. "I never would have let you ride shotgun if I thought you were going to trash my playlist. Intergalactic is in my top ten!"

Grace glanced over her shoulder.

"I thought you were a gentleman who wouldn't ever make a lady sit in the back."

"Yeah, a lady," Asher said, feigning puzzlement. "You've basically turned into a man at this point, working with us for so long."

Grace reached back and swatted Asher's arm as hard as she could. He pulled away laughing as though he'd been struck by the mighty force of a mosquito's fist.

Ben chuckled and shook his head.

"Okay, I'm driving, and we're listening to Paganini. Both of you could stand to listen to some real music."

"Hey, that's not fair, bro. I ate a panini, like, two days ago," Asher said.

"It's Paganini," Ben grumbled as exuberant violin music filled the car. Turning down the volume, he shifted into drive.

"Yeah, it's Paganini. You uncultured swine," Grace added, feigning a hoity-toity British accent.

Who this Paganini fellow was was anybody's guess, but she didn't often pass up the opportunity to make fun of Asher.

She caught the hint of a smile on Ben's lips, and the sight of it made her heart leap a little in her chest. Despite being surrounded by the constant foolery of his brothers, Ben tended to be serious most of the time. Drawing a smile out of him wasn't always a small feat, and she was pretty good at it.

"I give us ten minutes before Gabe calls and yells at us for being late," Ben said after a moment, pulling out onto the road and picking up speed.

"I'll take that bet," Asher chimed in from the back seat. "Grace?"

"Oh, be nice," she said, shaking her head and giving them what she hoped was a stern expression. "He just wants to keep the family together. I know first-hand how hard it is to get all of you Forge boys in one place at the same time."

"Like herding cats?" Asher joked.

Grace laughed, resting against the back of the seat as Ben passed a slow-moving truck on the highway. She always liked to watch him as he drove, the solemn way he always kept both hands on the wheel and checked his mirrors, as though he was bearing precious cargo.

She didn't want him to catch her looking, however, so she turned to Asher in an attempt to distract herself.

Despite being Ben's twin, the two men could hardly look more different. The only feature they seemed to share was their choice of slightly-scruffy facial hair. Both of them were tall, but Asher was compact, bordering on skinny. While Ben had dark red hair and green eyes, Asher was blonde, with blue eyes a little paler than Grace's own.

Her plan to stop staring at Ben worked. Within a few minutes, Asher had managed to draw them both into a spirited debate about which breed of dog Forge Brothers Security should adopt to serve as their company mascot.

By the time Ben pulled into the parking lot at the Trinity Medical Center in San Antonio, they had narrowed the contenders down to German Shepherd, Chocolate Labrador, or–Grace's suggestion–a King Charles Spaniel.

"You know Gabe is never going to go for having a dog in the office, right?" Ben said, waiting for the car in front of him to make its turn.

"Let the women handle this," Grace said. The fact that Ben didn't seem to oppose the idea was half the battle won already. Gabe, the oldest

Forge brother and unofficial leader of FBS, was a softy at his core. Usually.

"You owe me five bucks," Asher said as Ben pulled into a parking space and turned off the car.

"No way," Ben said. "It's been seven and a half minutes, I checked."

Grace rolled her eyes.

She'd already forgotten about their little bet, but she should have known better than to assume that her friends would have. The Forge boys excelled at turning anything and everything into a competition.

Still, if she was a gambling woman, her money would have been with Ben. Gabe did have a bit of an obsession with punctuality.

"But we're at the hospital already and he never called!"

"Doesn't matter, it still counts," Ben said with a chuckle. "You lose."

"I think I have to side with Ben on this one," Grace chimed in.

She climbed out of the passenger seat and adjusted the hem of her dress as she waited for the others. The sunlight felt warmer now than it had even a few minutes before, back at her house. She looked forward to what was sure to be a gorgeous day.

"How shocking," Asher said. "Grace, taking Ben's side, whyever might that be..."

Grace stole a glance at Ben, trying to read his reaction to his twin's little comment, but he wouldn't meet her eyes. Instead, he began walking faster, striding toward the hospital's sliding front doors. She tottered after him on her heels, deciding that, for the moment, she wasn't going to think about her feelings.

Or his. Especially considering that she had no real reason to get her hopes up.

Today was about Ben and Asher's cousin Reilly, his wife Lauren, and their twin girls. Lauren had delivered them early, and they'd had to spend a week in the NICU. Finally, they were healthy enough to meet the family.

Grace smiled at the thought as she followed Ben and Asher. Despite the fact that she wasn't related to the Forge family, her role as FBS office manager had grown into something almost as deep as their bond of blood.

"Let's get going," Ben said gruffly, pausing as they caught up to him.

Just then, a phone began to ring.

"Ha!" Asher crowed.

"Hold on," Grace said, following him into the hospital's reception area as she shoved a hand into her large purse in search of her phone. As always, it managed to elude her for several seconds before she finally got hold of it.

"It's not Gabe, actually," she said, glancing at the screen. "Sorry, Asher. Hey, Dad, what's up?"

She tucked the phone into the crook of her neck as she ushered Asher and Ben forward. Whether or not Gabe called to yell at them, she didn't want to be late.

"Baby, I have some news," her father said in her ear.

Something about the tone of his voice made her stomach clench.

"It's Katie Fairman. Her father just called me. She had just headed off for spring break on South Padre Island."

Her father paused, releasing a sigh.

"She's gone."

Chapter 3

Grace

Grace could hardly believe what she was hearing.

"What do you mean, she's gone?" she said, unable to keep the edge from her voice. "When did this happen?"

"Her best friend had a late dinner with her around ten last night. She says that Katie wasn't feeling well and decided to take a cab back to their hotel. She offered to go with her, but Katie insisted she was fine. It's the last time she was seen."

"Last night? Do the local police know?" Grace asked, swallowing down several more questions as she began to pace back and forth.

"They've been looking into it," her father said. "They checked the security footage at the hotel. No sign of Katie after she left for dinner that night."

He paused again, and she could almost imagine him wiping a hand over his brow, trying to decide how to phrase what he had to say next.

"Anyway, the police seem to think she just ran away. They told her dad that she'd probably turn up in a few days."

Grace's jaw tensed. "Of course that's what they think. Typical. I know Katie, and she wouldn't do that. I know she wouldn't."

This was a nightmare. She hadn't seen Katie in several years, but she couldn't imagine her taking off and worrying everyone like this.

"Well, tell Donald I'll call him, all right?" she continued. "We'll get someone on this. I just have to talk to Gabe."

She tried her best to ignore Ben and Asher's curious glances as she and her father said their goodbyes.

He sounded as worried as she felt. Mr. Fairman was one of her dad's closest friends, and they'd gotten even closer ever since Mrs. Fairman died of cancer quite a few years ago. She had no doubt that her father would do anything he could to ensure Katie's safe return home.

"What's going on?" Ben demanded as soon as she'd thrown her phone back into her bag.

"We're needed on a case?" Asher added.

Grace glanced between them as her eyes began to fill with tears. All of a sudden, the day ahead seemed more frightening than beautiful.

"A family friend of mine, Katie Fairman, has disappeared. She was on spring break," she managed to choke out. "And I just know something terrible must have happened. I know it's not exactly our usual security work, but we need to help her. I need you to help me talk to Gabe."

Her words hung in the air as several people entered the hospital behind them, shooting her

18

pitying glances as they passed, probably assuming she had just received bad news about a patient.

Ben took a couple of steps in her direction. She opened her mouth, expecting some argument, but instead, she found herself pressed up against his broad, warm chest.

She stiffened for a moment, not quite processing what was happening.

Benjamin Forge was absolutely not a hugger.

Despite her confusion, she felt a shiver coursing through her as he ran a hand gently across her back.

"Don't worry, Gracie," he said.

He hadn't called her that since they were about seven years old.

"We'll find her. It's going to be okay."

She wanted to think of something to say in response—she would have settled for a sentence or two of vaguely comprehensible English—but before she could, yet another ringing phone demanded her attention.

She suppressed a sigh as Ben pulled away, crossing his arms over his chest, retreating into his usual standoffish posture.

"Yo," Asher said, answering his phone.

Grace could just make out Gabe's voice. He was saying something about one of Reilly's twins having an important checkup with a cardiologist in a half hour.

"We have a good excuse this time," Asher said after his older brother paused his scolding. "And we'll tell you all about it after we see the twins, okay?"

Grace didn't want to wait, but she could hardly argue the point. Reilly had enough to worry about right now. He didn't need to overhear any shop talk.

Asher hung up the phone and gestured toward the hallway behind the reception area.

"The hospital is only letting a few people in at a time, and everyone else has already headed back to the office. Gabe said he's waiting in the cafeteria with Dad. "

Ben let out a grunt. "I wonder how that conversation is going."

"The two Gabriels butt heads all the time. I'm sure they won't let the arrival of new life stop them," Asher said.

She hoped that Gabe and his father could remain civil for Reilly and Lauren's sake, but she wouldn't be surprised if they were bickering as usual.

Gabe Sr. had a clear idea of how to live his life.

Faith first, family second, work last.

Like all of the Forge boys, Gabe Jr. had been raised with the same set of priorities. Unfortunately, ever since he'd walked away from the family agriculture business and founded Forge Brothers Security, Gabe Jr. had put work first more and more often.

Not that Grace could judge.

Especially when it came to her own faith.

She shook her head as she followed Ben and Asher deeper into the labyrinth of the Trinity Medical Center. There was no point in beating herself up over her struggle to hear God's voice.

Not today.

Katie Fairman was in trouble, and she was going to do everything in her power to find her.

Ben

Ben drew a deep breath as they approached the door of the maternity ward. Somewhere within, he heard the cry of a newborn baby, and found himself hanging back as Asher strode into the room.

He was acutely aware of the fact that his burly size could be intimidating, and though logically he knew that his cousin Reilly's twins weren't old enough to fear him, he couldn't help but to feel out of place.

"You coming?" Grace said, beaming at him as she leaned against the doorframe. "I'm sure the twins are excited to meet their...second cousin?"

He nodded. "Something like that."

As he followed her toward Lauren's room, he couldn't help but to replay the last few minutes over and over in his mind.

He shouldn't have hugged Grace.

Though his brothers constantly teased him about her supposed crush, he wasn't so sure she thought of him as more than a friend.

Not that it would have mattered if she did.

He'd already sworn to himself that any kind of romantic relationship was out of the question for the foreseeable future. He'd been down that road before, and he wasn't interested in shooting himself in the foot twice.

That was apart from the small fact that he and Grace were pretty much polar opposites. He respected her, sure, but she drove him completely insane, and he was sure he annoyed her just as much.

It would never, ever work. And he had no intention of letting her get hurt by pretending for even a second that it could. If she did have feelings for him, they would pass. She'd find some handsome guy who drove a Tesla, played golf, and didn't buy his t-shirts in packs of five at Walmart.

And that would be that.

"Hey, guys," Reilly said, interrupting his thoughts. Recovering quickly, Ben extended a hand before engulfing his cousin in a good old-fashioned bro hug.

"Congratulations, man. I can't believe you're a dad, let alone twice over."

"I'm still not sure I believe it," Reilly joked. "I'm already in love, though."

"What are their names?"

"Clara and Josefina. Josefina after Lauren's abuelita." Reilly said. "She can't really leave the nursing home, but we hope they'll be healthy enough to bring them to her for a visit soon."

"I'm sure she'd love that," Ben said. He'd heard quite a lot about Lauren's grandmother. She'd practically raised Lauren, and though she suffered from dementia and didn't always know what was going on, he was certain she was happy that her granddaughter had turned her life around.

When Reilly had met Lauren just a year ago, she'd been running drugs for the Iron Prophets down in El Paso. Forge Brothers Security had helped her to escape gang life, and had made sure that both she and her abuelita got a fresh start here in San Antonio.

The fact that she'd married and had children with the man who'd helped to free her was probably icing on the cake.

"She's going to love the girls," Reilly agreed, glancing over at his wife. "And Lauren just wants to show them off to the whole world."

"Rightly so."

Ben followed Reilly's gaze to the other side of the room, where a large window let in the cheerful morning glow. Lauren and Grace were sitting on a green pleather couch, curled up with several hospital-issue pillows, and Asher was standing nearby with a twin girl in each arm.

Ben couldn't help but to stare at Grace as she chatted animatedly with Lauren.

Unlike everyone else, who had no doubt made a beeline straight for the adorable, brand-new babies, Grace had focused on the new mom.

Despite his better judgment, he felt a rush of admiration for sweet, thoughtful Grace. She always knew how to bring her light to the person who needed it most, no matter where she was or who she was with.

Still, even as she joked and laughed with Lauren, her blonde hair gleaming in the sunshine, he could see the worry hiding beneath the surface.

Ben clenched his fists for a long moment before releasing the pressure.

As soon as they finished with their visit, they'd talk to Gabe about her missing friend, and he'd make sure to back Grace up. He hated to see her looking so anxious.

"It's my turn, Asher," Grace was saying, getting up from the couch and reaching out to take one of the wriggling bundles. Reilly took a seat next to his wife, planting a gentle kiss against the side of her head.

Ben watched as Grace looked down at the little girl in her arms, smiling and cooing to her as though no one else in the room existed.

After a moment, she looked up at Ben, the peaceful smile never faltering on her lips.

"Hey, why don't you take the other one off his hands?" she suggested, tilting her head in Asher's direction.

"The *other one* is Josefina," Asher said, feigning offense.

Lauren laughed. "Actually, you have Clara."

Before Ben could wonder how on earth she could tell the two babies apart, Asher was shuttling little Clara into his arms.

"Sorry," Asher said to the baby. "You get heavy after a while."

"She weighs nothing," Ben retorted, shifting Clara into a better position as her eyes fluttered open for a moment and then closed again. Ben felt like more of a giant than usual as he watched her sleeping peacefully in his arms, her chest rising and falling with the inhale and exhale of her tiny lungs.

"Aren't they perfect?" Grace asked, taking a couple steps closer with Josefina cuddled up against her chest. "It's always so amazing to me that God lets us take part in the work of creating. Like, He created the universe from nothing with only His words, and yet He allows men and women to come together and bring new human beings into the world. It just blows my mind."

Her eyes seemed to sparkle with excitement, just as they always did when she talked about Jesus.

Ben clamped his mouth shut before he managed to say something completely stupid.

He watched as Josefina clutched Grace's manicured index finger with one of her teeny hands. Grace would make a wonderful mother.

He cleared his throat.

"Yeah, it's pretty cool," he said curtly. "I think we need to get going, though."

"Oh. Right. Here, Reilly," Grace said, handing Josefina over to her dad with a pinched smile. Ben followed suit, passing Clara into Lauren's arms just as she started to fuss for some milk. "I'll be praying about the appointment with the cardiologist."

He saw a flicker of something behind Grace's eyes.

Disappointment? Sadness?

Ben felt a pang of guilt. He hated to shut her down like that, but he didn't really have a choice. He couldn't go soft now. Not if it meant letting her get too close.

In the end, they'd both end up hurt.

And it would be all his fault.

Chapter 4

Grace

The smell of chicken soup assaulted Grace's nostrils as she followed Ben through the doors of the hospital's cafeteria. She hadn't had a chance to grab breakfast before leaving her house that morning, but even though her stomach was beginning to rumble with hunger, she couldn't bring herself to waste any time ordering food.

She'd loved meeting Clara and Josefina, but even as she'd fawned over the adorable newborns, her mind was elsewhere.

She remembered holding Katie Fairman as a baby, though she herself had only been six or seven years old at the time. Katie's father, Donald, had been friends with her parents since college, and the two families spent a lot of time together during Grace's childhood.

She'd always wanted a sibling, and Katie had been the next best thing.

Though they didn't talk very often these days, with Katie off at university and Grace busy with her job at Forge Brothers Security, she still felt protective over her stand-in little sister. Every minute that passed only increased her fears that something terrible must have happened to her.

The two Gabriels sat at a table beneath a window, and Grace was struck by just how similar the men looked. Both were wearing button down shirts and jeans, and both had their elbows resting on the table with two plain white coffee mugs in between. She had no doubt that both coffees were black.

That was where the similarities ended, however. Gabe Sr.'s hair had long since gone gray, and his eldest son's hair was still inky black, setting off his blue eyes.

Grace felt Asher jab an elbow gently into her side as she began to walk toward them, and she paused.

"They're not fighting," he said between his teeth.

He was right.

The two men were leaning toward one another, their postures friendly. They were discussing how they couldn't wait to show the twins the farmhouse where the Forge brothers had all grown up and Gabe Sr. still lived.

She heard Ben letting out a sigh at her side. She hated to break up a rare truce between father and son, but Katie's safety was more important. There was no time to waste.

"Hey, guys. What is it that we need to discuss?" Gabe Jr. asked as they walked over, leaning back in his chair and crossing his arms against his chest.

"Let me guess," the older man said, a wry smile tugging at his lips. "Work."

Grace stepped in front of Asher and Ben. The Forge family patriarch may have taken issue with how much time his sons dedicated to their company, but he had always had a soft spot for her, and she wasn't afraid to exploit it when necessary.

"Yes and no, sir," she said quickly. "It's a family friend of mine. She's in trouble."

"Say no more," Gabe Sr. said, getting out of his chair and raising his worn hands in surrender. Even though he owned a multi-billion dollar agricultural company, he was never afraid to do the dirty work, even now that his sons were urging him to retire. "I'll get out of your hair."

Grace let out a sigh of relief as Gabe Sr. said goodbye to the men in turn before finally enveloping her in a warm, leather-scented embrace. She made a mental note to invite herself over for Sunday dinner soon. If she could drag any of the other Forge men along, all the better.

"So what's going on?" Gabe said once his father had left the cafeteria.

Grace told him about the call from her own father, making sure to tell him how useless the local police had been thus far. Gabe was a hound for justice, and she knew he hated to see any victim being denied the help they needed, whatever the reason.

"Katie is a junior at the University of Texas in Austin, studying business," Grace added. "But she's a bit more of a target than a random college student might be. Her father, Donald Fairman, owns a company called AveroTech. They're very wealthy."

Gabe glanced down at his phone, his fingers tapping at the screen. Knowing him, he was taking notes.

"I know AveroTech," Ben chimed in, tapping at a table leg with the side of his foot. "They were huge in the early millennium, but I haven't seen them in the media much lately. I wonder how they're doing."

"If they're tanking, it could be related," Asher added.

Gabe said nothing.

"She wouldn't run away," Grace said. "I know she wouldn't. I haven't spoken with her a lot in the last several years, but she's always been responsible. Especially since her mother died.

She and her dad are really close. She wouldn't scare him like this."

Gabe shifted in his chair, but before he could speak, Ben cut in.

"We need to accept this job," he said. "I know it's gonna be tight with our current caseload, especially with Reilly on paternity leave, but we'll just have to make it work."

Grace sent up a silent prayer of gratitude that Ben had spoken up for her, just as he'd said he would.

"I'm thinking, all right?" Gabe said after a minute had passed, rubbing at his temples with his fingers.

Grace bit her lip. There was a lot going on for the company right now, she knew. They'd just tied up a case involving Cameron Forge's now-girlfriend–and in-house paralegal–Bristol, and there would be a lot of court dates ahead for half of the staff.

And that was just the tip of the iceberg.

"Just because you're the founder of FBS doesn't mean that you're the only one who gets a say,"

Ben argued, his gravelly voice taking on an edge. "It's not like we all voted to make you the boss, Gabe."

"Cool it, bro," Gabe warned. "Look. It's a bad time for us, but you're right. If it's a friend of the Hintons, we're gonna just have to make the time."

"Thank you," Grace said before Ben could add anything else. "Katie is the only family that Donald has left. I know he'll appreciate any help we can give."

"We'll get it done," Gabe said, his eyes lingering on Ben a few seconds too long as he smiled at Grace.

Gabe's de facto leadership of FBS caused conflict now and then, but she knew that deep down the rest of the boys would agree that everyone trying to be in charge would be a disaster. Gabriel Jr. could be tough, but he always tried his best to be fair. She just hoped that he'd continue to let Ben's cranky comments slide.

She couldn't figure him out.

First he'd hugged her. Now he was risking a fight with his older brother to make sure that her friend was taken care of? It wasn't like him.

If she didn't know any better...

No. She wouldn't entertain the idea that he might be feeling something. She didn't need a distraction right now.

Especially not one that would lead to nothing but heartbreak.

"Sorry, Gabe," Ben said, not meeting his eyes. "I was out of line."

"You're forgiven," Gabe said. "But since you're so invested in this case, you're going to be the one heading down to South Padre to investigate."

Ben

"You want me to go to a spring break hotspot with a bunch of college kids?"

Ben couldn't help but to chuckle at the absurdity of the thought. Gabe had to be joking to get back at him for questioning his leadership of FBS. He had to be.

"You need to work on your field op skills," Gabe said with a shrug of his shoulders. "You can't just live in your nerd cave. Besides, if Katie's disappearance has anything to do with her father's work at AveroTech, your expertise might come in handy."

"And I can come and help you," Grace added. She sounded positively thrilled about the idea of tagging along on his own personal nightmare trip.

"You aren't an operative," he protested. "And how exactly do you expect the office to function without you to keep things running?"

He gave Asher a pleading glance, hoping that his twin would offer some backup.

"I'm sure we could survive without her for a few days," he said, winking at Ben. "Besides, Grace knows her way around a gun."

"Nevermind a gun," Gabe said, rolling his eyes. "Now you guys have got me thinking. Hmm. Grace knows her way around a beach, and knows how to talk to college kids and get information. Something Ben is going to be abysmal at."

Gee, thanks.

"He's not wrong," Asher added, grinning.

Traitor.

Ben cringed. His chances of getting out of this seemed to be slipping further away with each passing moment.

"What if Katie Fairman was kidnapped or something?" he protested. "Knowing how to shoot a target at the firing range is one thing. Being trained as an operative is another. Any number of things could go wrong."

"The police think she just ran away," Grace said, turning to Gabe, who was once again stroking his temples, lost in thought. "If they're right, maybe chatting up a few college kids will be all it takes to figure this out."

Ben glowered at Grace. She was the one who was convinced her friend was in mortal danger in the first place, and now she was trying to convince Gabe to let her have a nice vacation while playing detective. Unbelievable.

"Ben, you may be out of practice, but I have every confidence that you'll be able to handle this operation," Gabe said at last.

He paused, and Ben felt hope swelling in his chest. Maybe this wouldn't be so bad. He could go by himself and look for Katie, and when he wasn't investigating, he could enjoy the air conditioning at the hotel and ring up a suitably hefty room service bill to send home to his big brother.

"And Grace is a fantastic office manager, but it would be good for her to round out her skills with some field work," Gabe continued. "Unless you don't think you can handle keeping her safe while you're on the island?"

Asher coughed, suppressing a laugh. Ben ignored him and met Gabe's eyes, trying not to notice Grace's hopeful, puppy-dog expression.

"I can handle it fine," he said before he realized that he'd just stepped into Gabe's trap.

Darn it. His brother knew how to manipulate his competitive side way too well.

"Perfect," Gabe said, reaching for his coffee and taking a long sip. "It's settled. The rest of us will handle things back here in San Antonio. It's gonna be tight, but we can make it work. So long as Grace keeps her phone on in case someone needs help."

"You got it, boss," Grace said, getting up so quickly that her chair skipped against the floor. Two other people sitting in the far corner of the cafeteria glanced over at her for several long seconds before returning to their breakfast. She didn't seem to notice them as she hefted her purse up on her shoulder and started walking toward the door, heels clacking as she went.

"Um, where are you going?" Asher called out after her. "Don't you need a ride home?"

"I'm gonna take an Uber to the office. I have flights to book," Grace said. "I'll text you when I have the info, Ben. See you soon."

Ben watched as she walked away. Grace always managed to be both the most chaotic and most ruthlessly efficient person he'd ever met.

"Well, that's that, I guess," Gabe said, downing the dregs of his coffee. "I suggest you go home and get packed, Ben. Asher, I'd appreciate it if you could come straight to the office with me. We have some work to re-assign."

"Will do," Ben said, shaking his head to himself as Asher clapped a hand against his shoulder, giving him an exaggerated wink.

"Might be nice for the two of you to get some time alone to get to know each other better," he said.

"We know each other just fine," Ben said.

"I think Grace is looking forward to it," Asher said. "Look, man, she's obviously into you. I don't get what your problem is."

Ben ignored him and moved to leave the cafeteria.

When it came to women, Asher was hardly one to be giving out advice. Most of his past relationships–if he could even call them that–had lasted mere weeks, if not days. Which wasn't surprising, considering how many of them got their start when the bars closed for the night.

To his twin's credit, however, for the past several years he'd largely stayed away from partying and women. He'd even started attending church from time to time, and kept a Bible on the dining room table of the house he and Ben shared.

Ben muttered goodbye under his breath and began winding his way through the endless halls that led back to his car.

Asher may not have been a moral paragon, but neither was he.

Not by a long shot.

If he was going to be stuck bringing Grace along on this job, he had to be careful. He couldn't risk her getting the wrong idea about where the two of them stood.

She deserved someone better. Someone who would pray over her every night and take her to church every Sunday. Someone who didn't let his doubts tear at the weak threads of his faith.

Someone who was nothing like him.

Chapter 5

Grace

"We seriously couldn't have waited to leave until morning?" Ben grumbled beside her as he adjusted the flimsy neck pillow the stewardess had handed him a few minutes earlier.

Grace looked out the window, watching as the various airport workers skittered around on the pavement like oversized ants dressed in high visibility vests.

"It is morning," she said cheerfully as she turned to face the aisle seat again. "Technically."

Ben rolled his eyes. "Three AM does not count as 'morning' to anyone remotely sane."

"Gabe gets up at four-thirty every day," Grace pointed out, pretending to shudder in horror.

"Yes. My point stands," Ben said. He glanced down at his lap and adjusted the thin fleece blanket, but she could see the hint of a smile.

"I know it's early," Grace conceded. "But my friend is missing. Every hour counts, and there wasn't another flight until seven."

Ben sighed. "Not to mention that it's already Wednesday–technically–and we really do need to have some time to question possible witnesses before they leave at the end of spring break."

"Exactly," Grace said, taking her tote bag from her lap and shoving it under the seat in front of her. Once they were airborne, she hoped to get some reading time in. There was no way she was going to be able to sleep. Far too many competing worries swirled in her mind.

Out of the corner of her eye, she watched as Ben stuck earplugs into his ears and closed his eyes. He remained like that for the next several minutes, looking up only to listen intently to the safety speech.

At last, the engines began to rumble more loudly, and she felt the plane beginning to taxi down the runway. She was about to make a light-hearted complaint to Ben about wanting the window seat if he was just going to sleep the entire time, but the expression on his face stopped her.

His eyes were clamped shut, his mouth was a firm line, and she could see beads of sweat beginning to dot his forehead.

"Are you okay?" she asked as they began to pick up even more speed. Ben's hands were gripping his armrests as though he feared he might be sucked out of the plane the moment he dared to let go.

When he said nothing, she asked again, leaning in closer so that he could hear her despite the earplugs.

"I'm fine," he replied, the words pinched.

Grace felt the floaty feeling in her stomach as the plane took off, the nose of the craft pointing into the sky in what always felt like an impossibly steep angle.

She wasn't afraid of flying.

Not any more. Not since Indonesia. Those dark memories had a way of pushing aside a lot of the anxieties that used to plague her.

How could a 'what if' be more terrible than what had already happened?

As the engines continued to rumble, and their altitude increased, Ben's terror became more and more evident. He was so pale that he looked almost green.

Grace plucked the motion-sickness bag from the back of her seat and set it on Ben's lap.

His eyes flew open.

"I told you I'm fine," he snapped at her, letting the bag fall to the floor as the plane at last began to even out. He didn't make a move to pick it up, his knuckles white as he continued to clutch at his armrests. "Can you just mind your own business for once? Please?"

Grace felt her face growing hot as a couple of the other passengers glanced over at them from across the aisle. Even though Ben was being a jerk, she hated to imagine that anyone else would think less of him due to his outburst.

Ben was not the sort of person who expressed vulnerability lightly. For him to be forced onto a plane with her, where she'd see first hand just how terrified he was, had to have been quite a blow to his pride. Her trying to help had clearly made things worse.

After a few more minutes had passed, the seatbelt light went off, but she made no move to unbuckle. Instead, she retrieved her e-reader from her bag and attempted to get lost in a new romcom novel she'd downloaded for the flight.

She was midway through chapter one when she felt the plane lurch beneath her.

The device tumbled from her hands and out into the aisle, but she didn't see where it had landed before another shudder rocked the plane.

She heard several shouts and the sound of other people's belongings clattering against the floor. Over the intercom, the pilot was calmly reminding everyone to buckle their seatbelts, but she scarcely heard the words.

Ben was leaning forward against his lap, gripping his head with his hands. Something between a groan and a cry escaped him, sending a frigid chill straight through to her heart. She had never heard him sound this scared, and she doubted that his brothers had, either.

She decided to risk being yelled at again as the plane continued to bounce through the sky. Her own heart was thumping in her chest, but whatever fear she had was eclipsed by the utter horror that Ben was clearly experiencing.

She rested a hand against his back.

"It's turbulence," she said, hoping she sounded more confident than she felt. "Don't worry about it. The plane can take a lot of bumping around."

She barely got the sentence out before another stomach churning jolt sent the plane rushing downward. Grace heard more screams, along with the sound of more belongings clattering to the floor. Out of the corner of her eye, she could see that several of the overhead storage compartments had swung open, sending yet more luggage tumbling through the unstable aircraft.

She was too scared to open her mouth to scream now, let alone speak. She pressed her eyes shut for several long seconds, trying to think as the plane continued to jostle her in her seat. The pilot spoke with a shaky voice once again, but she couldn't hear him through the commotion.

"God, help us!" Ben cried out, his voice ragged with fear.

His words seemed to pull her back into reality.

Whatever happened now, she was a child of the living God. She could trust him with this life and the next.

She reached toward Ben, leaning as close to him as she could while restrained in her seat as someone's thick paperback narrowly missed her head.

To her surprise, Ben removed his hand from his armrest and accepted hers, holding her so tightly that she feared he might shatter her bones.

She looked over at him. Tears were running freely down his cheeks, and it seemed he had collapsed into himself, paralyzed with the agonizing, consuming fear of death.

Ben had struggled openly with his faith in God for years. Everyone at FBS knew it.

And yet it was he who had reached out to the Lord in this desperate moment.

The least Grace could do was to form the words of a prayer for them both.

"Heavenly father," she choked out, the words coming in stops and starts as the airplane bounced through the sky. "Help us. Please, bring us and every soul on board to solid ground safely. Lord, have mercy on us."

More shouts of terror. More cries.

Until suddenly, everything was quiet.

The plane's engine whirred calmly as they flew at a steady altitude. Grace closed her eyes again, forcing her lungs to draw in air. She heard the speakers overhead cracking to life as the pilot spoke, assuring them that everything was okay and that they were not in danger, and reminding everyone to keep their seatbelts fastened.

Her heart continued to pound as her adrenaline rush slowly subsided. At last, she realized that Ben's hand still gripped her own.

"Ben," she said, blinking away tears that she had only just begun to notice. "Are you okay?"

He looked over at her, but his deep green eyes did not quite meet hers, as though he was embarrassed for just how afraid he'd been.

Before she could reassure him, however, he slid his hand out of her own and unbuckled his seatbelt.

"They said to stay buckled up!"

"I'm sure people got hurt. I have a duty to help them," he grunted, getting to his feet and beginning to push past her and out into the aisle. She watched as he kicked aside several carry-on bags, sandals, and cell phones that sat on the floor.

She drew in a breath and looked around. Outside, the sky was pure black. The eerie quiet of the plane had slowly begun to fade as people spoke to their loved ones. At least four people that Grace could see had tears rolling down their faces as they sobbed.

She wanted to go to them, to see if she could provide any comfort, but two stewardesses had begun making their way down the aisle, telling everyone to stay put and asking who needed medical assistance.

"Sir, you need to return to your seat," one of them said to Ben. He was kneeling in the aisle several feet away next to an older man who had clearly hit his head against the chair in front of him. His forehead was smeared with blood, and Ben was using someone's cardigan to staunch the bleeding.

"I'm a trained first responder," Ben said firmly, not looking at the woman. Instead, he was directing the injured man to follow his fingertip with his eyes.

"Sir–"

"Other people on this plane need help. Are you going to keep wasting time harassing a law enforcement officer or are you going to do what you can to assist them?"

Grace flinched at his words.

Ben Forge had been a police officer once upon a time, before Gabe founded FBS. But he'd been fired for reasons she had never quite figured out. She knew that it had had something to do with his attempt to protect his former partner, and that afterward he'd broken up with a woman he'd been dating, but that was all. She had been away on a mission trip at the time and had missed most of the drama.

The sole time she'd asked him about it more recently, he'd made it very clear that he wasn't going to share the details with the likes of her.

In any case, he was no longer a cop, and Grace didn't appreciate the fact that he'd lied.

On the other hand, he was right.

She looked around at the scene. Both stewardesses were assisting several passengers each, and another man had joined them after grabbing two red first aid kits from the front of the plane.

She sat back in her seat and checked on the tightness of her seatbelt. Now that the adrenaline had fully subsided, she felt completely drained of energy.

By the grace of God, no one appeared to be seriously injured, but she could imagine the battle she'd be facing to get Ben onto the plane home after what they'd just experienced.

She smiled to herself as she watched him affix a bandage to a teenage boy's badly scratched arm.

Despite everything, she couldn't help but to hope that this trip could be the start of something good.

Even if Ben didn't realize it yet.

Chapter 6

Ben

Ben grasped the wheel of the rental car, steeling himself before turning the key in the ignition.

After the nightmarish turbulence they had endured, he couldn't quite seem to relax. Every nerve was on edge, waiting for another horrible bounce or bump that wouldn't come now that they were back on solid ground.

Or worse, for Grace to bring up how afraid he'd been.

She'd survived something far worse than any turbulence back in Indonesia, and yet there she was, taking charge of the situation and trying to hold them both together. He should have stepped up and been a man, but instead, he'd practically cowered beneath his seat.

He couldn't let his fear continue to paralyze him. Katie Fairman was missing, and every minute counted if they were going to find her.

The mental image of a young woman suffering hardened his resolve. He had a duty to put his own worries aside and to take care of her, just as he'd done with the injured passengers on the plane once the immediate danger had passed.

Still, as much as logic told him that he had to start driving them the rest of the way to South Padre Island, his body was uninterested in operating a motor vehicle. All he wanted to do was rest until he fully calmed down. Even the forty-five minutes Grace had spent in the airport bathroom putting on makeup and doing her hair hadn't been enough time for him to return to normal.

Fortunately, she didn't seem to have noticed that he was stalling. Grace had taken out a tube of mascara and a large poofy brush, and was apparently putting the finishing touches on her look in the passenger side window of the SUV they'd rented.

The minutes ticked by in silence, but to his relief, it wasn't as uncomfortable as it could have been.

Grace hadn't brought up how scared he'd been, or how he'd grasped her hand for comfort like a blubbering child reaching for his mother.

No, as always, the woman seemed almost lost in her own happy world, humming to herself as she dotted some kind of loose powder across her pert, tanned nose. No matter what Grace had been through in her life, she always found a reason to smile. It was honestly incredible.

Ben's jaw tightened as he looked away again, planting his gaze firmly on the logo in the middle of the steering wheel.

He hoped that Grace wasn't planning on telling everyone back at FBS about his fear of flying, but he couldn't bring himself to ask her not to. It was too embarrassing.

A loud yawn shattered the quiet. It took a moment for him to realize it had been his own.

"Do you want me to drive?" Grace asked, looking over at him with a puzzled expression.

"No," he said quickly, reaching for the keys sitting in the console and inserting them in the ignition. "I'm fine."

"That's a relief," Grace said, reaching for some metal instrument that she used to curl her eyelashes.

"Why, because you won't have to risk having to parallel park?" he teased, glad for even a small distraction from the lingering tension in his body.

He heard her scoff as he turned the key in the ignition and put the SUV into drive.

"I can parallel park, thank you very much," she said. "As a matter of fact, I just think it's more–" she paused, biting her glossy pink lip as she searched for the right word "–fitting for the man to drive."

"You know, some people might call that sexist."

"I call it chivalrous," Grace said, tossing a tendril of her blonde waves over her shoulder as he joined the other vehicles filing out of the parking garage. "I would have much rather lived in a time when men held open the car door for you and walked on the outside of the sidewalk."

"I chivalrously guarded the bathroom when you disappeared inside for a million years," he pointed out.

"You were asleep when I finished!" Grace retorted, not bothering to hide her smile.

As Ben drove off the airport grounds and out onto the highway that led toward the island, they fell into their usual routine. Grace chattered incessantly, and Ben listened, punctuating her comments with the odd teasing remark.

By the time they pulled up in front of the Mistflower Resort, he finally felt calm. He'd never admit it to her, but being around Grace's bubbly personality had a way of reminding him that the world wasn't always as dark as he sometimes believed.

Then again, they were here to solve a missing person's case, which was part of his problem.

Working as a police officer and then in private security had a way of shoving the most wicked tendencies of mankind firmly in his face.

"Where is everybody?" Grace asked, snapping him back to reality as he pulled into a parking space near the front doors of the main building.

"I thought it would be slammed with people," Grace continued, climbing out of the SUV with a giant tote bag slung over her shoulder. "I'm sure we're at the right hotel. Most of the resorts on the island are mid-tier, but Katie Fairman can afford the best."

Ben lifted a hand to his forehead and squinted against the sun as he looked for signs of life.

It looked like the best, all right.

He glanced around at what he could see of the luxury resort complex. Each building had hacienda-style red clay roofs and walls adorned with gleaming pale stucco, and the area was landscaped neatly with local flora. Behind a row of palm trees, he could see a gigantic blue swimming pool.

Despite his general dislike of sun, heat, and sweaty bodies being near him, the water looked inviting. Even though it was barely a reasonable hour for breakfast, it was already getting hot.

"I'm not surprised the spring break crowd is still sleeping off last night's bender," he said, joining her as she headed toward the main lobby doors. "But I thought there'd be a cop car or two."

When they reached the front desk, it was clear that the local law enforcement was taking this even less seriously than Ben had assumed. The clerk had not even realized anyone was gone, but finally, after a bit of arguing with a security guard, she'd agreed to give them the number of the room Katie and her best friend, Jade, were staying in.

"Why isn't Katie's father here?" Ben asked as they exited the elevator on the fourth floor, their footsteps silent against the thick burgundy carpet.

"He's stuck in China. Apparently there's some big business deal going on that he can't get out of."

Ben raised an eyebrow. If he had a daughter, and she was missing, he'd find his way home from Antarctica.

Before he could say as much, however, the room marked 217 came into view.

"No police tape," he said flatly.

"Well, it's pretty clear the cops don't care," Grace said, raising a hand to knock on the door. "I'm not surprised that they–"

Before she could rap against the wood, the door swung inward, revealing a petite blonde woman with giant sunglasses and a tiny chihuahua on a sparkling purple leash.

"I specifically told them no room service," the woman said, speaking slowly as if suspecting that Grace and Ben might not speak English. "I don't need some maid stealing my Love bracelets. I prefer to hire my own help."

Ben cast a confused glance at Grace. He had no idea what a Love bracelet was, or why this woman thought that they were some kind of co-ed hospitality duo, but none of that mattered. The Mistflower Resort had clearly reassigned the room. Any usable evidence about Katie's disappearance would be long gone.

Without another word, the woman closed the door with a pointed slam before dragging the dog down the hallway.

As soon as she disappeared into the elevator, Grace knelt down in front of the door, examining the slightly worn bit of carpet as though some Sherlock Holmesian inspiration might suddenly strike her. Ben half expected her to pull out a magnifying glass.

"I asked for another room once the cops looked it over," came a voice from behind him. "At least I got an upgrade out of this. Silver lining, or whatever."

He spun to face the woman who had spoken, immediately realizing that she must have come through the side stairwell door. She was tall, with silken ochre skin and black hair that reached nearly to the middle of her back.

Grace got clumsily to her feet, using the doorframe to support her weight.

"You must be–"

"Jade. Jade Gorsky," the woman said with exaggerated sweetness, extending a slender hand for Grace to shake. Ben noticed at once that her smile didn't quite reach her piercing brown eyes. "I'm Katie's best friend. And the last person who saw her before she was trafficked."

Grace

"Wait. You think Katie was trafficked?" Grace asked Jade, stepping back from the hotel room door and moving to stand next to Ben.

She felt sick.

Katie going missing was bad enough, but the thought of her being sold was too terrible to contemplate.

"There are rumors that a big ring is operating on the island," Jade said with a shrug of her slender shoulders. "It would make sense that they took her. She's a nice piece of...well, you know."

Ben's body tensed beside her as the young woman began to chuckle. Grace couldn't stop her mouth falling open in surprise at Jade's nonchalance.

"Let's say I don't know," Ben said, his deep voice filled with warning. "Why do you think human traffickers would be interested in taking Katie Fairman?"

"What are you, gay or something?" Jade said, laughing again. "You've seen her, right? She's banging hot, and she's obviously rich. They probably figured they could sell her to rich guys for top dollar."

Jade rolled her eyes as she spoke, and Grace gritted her teeth, hoping that Ben would contain his temper long enough to finish the conversation. It was incredible how quickly such a pretty girl had become ugly in her eyes.

"I don't know what kind of men you spend your time with," he growled, "but I don't make a habit of ogling women."

"Whatever," Jade said.

"Anyway," Grace cut in quickly. "Can I get your number so we can check in with you later? We'll have more questions once we get a chance to speak with the police."

Ben shot her a grateful glance.

"Sure," Jade said, giving her the number as Grace typed it into her contact list.

"I doubt they'll be much help," Jade added. "They just think she ran away. They wouldn't listen to my idea about her being trafficked, either."

Grace suppressed the urge to give Jade an eyeroll of her own. If she'd given the police the same breakdown of her human trafficking theory as she'd given the two of them, it was no surprise they dismissed it.

With an exchange of terse goodbyes, they watched as Jade Gorsky sauntered toward the elevator, her black rubber flip-flops smacking against the carpet.

"You think there's anything to Jade's trafficking hypothesis?" Grace asked as soon as she was gone.

"Maybe. While we were waiting for our flight yesterday, I poked around some local news websites. I saw some reports that a cross-border trafficking ring may be operating in this area, but I'd like to see what the police have to say about it."

Grace rubbed her hands up and down her arms, trying to stave off the sudden chill prompted by Ben's words. It was hard to reconcile the beauty of the island with the danger that seemed to be lurking in its shadows.

"Jade didn't exactly sound upset about the possibility of Katie being taken," she said as they began to head back toward the lobby.

"That whole interaction was beyond bizarre," Ben agreed.

Neither spoke for a while as they wound past groups of spring breakers who had woken up and were now crowding the halls. Grace found herself looking down at the ground as they passed yet another model-thin girl.

She'd never been particularly self-conscious about her appearance, but she knew there was no way her looks held a candle to half of this particular spring break crowd. At twenty-seven, she suddenly felt old.

"Thanks for cutting our interrogation short, by the way. I know I'm not the best Christian in the world, but I don't appreciate being accused of leering at potential kidnapping victims."

Grace felt heat rising to her cheeks as she averted her eyes from yet another neon-bikini-clad torso. She shouldn't be leering either, even if it was more for the sake of foolish comparison than lust.

Still, she was glad that Ben Forge just wasn't really that kind of guy. It made her like him even more. Not that she was going to say as much out loud.

"No problem," Grace said.

Ben's intense green eyes met hers, lingering there for longer than was necessary.

"All right," he said, breaking the spell. "Let's go see what she told the police."

Chapter 7

Ben

"There's a not-zero chance that somebody barfed on that chair," Grace pointed out a little too cheerfully.

Ben lifted his arm from the pleather armrest he'd been resting on with a grimace. "Lovely."

He lifted that morning's newspaper closer to his face, trying to see if he could find any useful local articles that might bear on their case while they waited, but he couldn't focus.

Grace was probably just messing with him, but

now he couldn't stop thinking about the possibility of puke. Gross.

"I prefer the resort," Grace added. "This place needs a new decorator."

"I'm pretty sure that the North Pier police department did not hire a decorator to set up their lobby."

"You say it like it would be stupid if they did," she retorted. "My father always says that presentation is everything, no matter what the business is."

Ben read the same sentence in his article a third time as Grace continued to talk. The piece was about a teen girl who had been propositioned for sex in South Padre Island's entertainment district, prior to the start of spring break. Not that he was retaining much more information than that.

"Hinton Logistics is the most boring sounding company ever," she continued, "but our brand story is really strong. Our PR team actually won an award for it a few years ago."

Ben let out an exaggerated sigh and tossed the paper onto the shabby end table beside him.

Truth was, Grace's near-constant chatter was kind of endearing, not that he'd ever let her know he thought so.

"You do realize the police station is not a company, right?"

Grace shook her head and gestured toward their feet. "Doesn't matter. The same principles apply. I mean, look at this place! The windows are filthy, the furniture is ancient, and there's nothing welcoming about coming in here. First of all, if this station wants to convey trustworthiness and competence, they need to get rid of this giant, hideously ugly–"

A door swung open nearby, and an unfriendly-looking man entered the room.

"–er, crime wave," Grace stammered.

Ben stifled a laugh, kicking at the edge of the green and orange patterned carpet she had been gesturing toward a moment prior. He didn't know or care much about aesthetics, but Grace had a fair point. The thing really was ugly.

"Yes, our idyllic island is well known for its high levels of crime," the man said flatly, offering Grace a raised, bushy eyebrow. "I'm Detective

Hayles. I'm told you're friends of the girl who allegedly disappeared from the Mistflower Resort."

"That's right," Ben said, getting up from the potentially barf stained chair and extending a hand for the man to shake. He introduced himself along with Grace.

"I'm also a certified private security operative," he added, looking into the man's grizzled blue eyes in hopes of gauging his reaction. Back in San Antonio, Forge Brothers Security had a good relationship with the SAPD, especially their liaison, Allie Parker. But their interactions with other law enforcement agencies tended to be more hit or miss. "I'm hoping you can provide me and my colleague with some basic information on the case."

The detective nodded, his expression revealing nothing.

"Can we speak in private?" Grace added.

A few minutes later, they were seated in an equally ugly–though much cleaner–office near the back of the station. Detective Hayles pushed his glasses up on his nose as he flipped through a thin file folder that had been resting on his desk.

"So. Katie Fairman, age twenty," he started, squinting at the page of tight, handwritten notes.

"We got a call to the non-emergency line on Tuesday morning from one Donald Fairman. Apparently, his daughter's best friend Jade Gorsky had not seen Katie since they finished dinner together around ten o'clock on Monday night."

Detective Hayles tossed the folder down onto his desk.

"So... that's it?" Grace asked.

"That's it," he said, nodding. "Took the report myself."

Ben frowned. "You didn't question Jade any further? She gave no other details about that night?"

"I've been doing this job longer than you've been alive, Mr. Forge," the detective drawled. "And I can tell you that cases like this resolve on their own. I'm sure your friend will return in a day or two with a drained Blackberry battery and an explanation for where she's been."

"They don't even make Blackberries anymore," Grace muttered.

The detective smiled indulgently. "Miss Hinton, I'm telling you, there is nothing to worry about."

Ben saw the man's point. If Katie was anywhere near as thoughtless as the company she kept, it was very possible she had left of her own accord. But that didn't mean he wasn't going to take the case seriously. Interviewing suspects was the bare minimum, and it irked him that Detective Hayles hadn't even been willing to do that much.

"Did you speak to the security team at Mistflower Resort?" Grace asked. "Maybe there's some relevant security footage that will confirm Jade's story."

"I'm sure they'll be happy to help you with that, young lady," the man said, hitching up his belt as he got to his feet. "Now, if you don't mind–"

Grace was too polite to press him, but Ben wasn't.

"Look, Detective," he growled, standing to his full height of six foot three. "You don't think there's a crime here. You're overworked and understaffed during spring break. Or maybe you want to go play golf. I get it. But you have a duty to the visitors as well as the residents of this island, and I need to trust that we'll be able to come to you if we have to."

Hayles raised his hands in mock surrender.

"Of course."

"Glad we understand each other," he said, watching out of the corner of his eye as Grace glanced at the case folder he'd left open on his desk. "One last thing before we get out of your hair."

"What's that?"

"I hear there's been potential human trafficking activity going on. Any truth to the rumors?" Ben tried his best to sound friendly, hunching his shoulders a little to remove an inch or two of height. He'd learned over the years that his intimidating physique could be just as harmful as it was helpful, depending on the situation.

Detective Hayles visibly relaxed as he escorted them back into the hall. Good. They would need to stay on local law enforcement's good side if they wanted to figure out what happened to Katie.

"Unfortunately, you heard right. There have been several cases relating to a ring that's active both here and in Mexico. Three girls have disappeared in the past six months, God help them. But so far as I can tell, the Fairman girl doesn't fit the profile. So far, the girls who potentially have been taken were all prostitutes, addicts, or homeless."

Grace visibly flinched at the man's brisk tone, but Ben understood where he was coming from. Even a small-town cop like Hayles had no doubt seen evils that Grace could scarcely imagine. Sometimes, the only way to face such darkness was to pretend it didn't touch you at all.

"We are collaborating with both the FBI and the Mexican authorities to bring those poor women home," the detective continued. "but I do not have any reason to believe Katie Fairman met the same fate. She has a very different profile of risk factors."

"Thank you for your time," Ben said as they reached the reception area, accepting Detective Hayles's business card. "I'll make sure to contact you if we find anything relevant."

As soon as the man retreated into the inner halls of the station, Grace released a loud sigh. "Well, Jade is right about one thing. They're not taking this seriously at all. Half of the stuff he told us Jade said wasn't even written on the notes he was reading."

"Then I guess it's even more important that we interview her ourselves," Ben said. "And take notes. I don't trust her."

"Me neither," Grace said, patting down her hair as they emerged into the mid-morning island breeze. "She doesn't even seem to care that Katie's gone."

"So why did she call the police?" Ben mused aloud.

Jade's attitude and her behavior weren't lining up. She was acting like a reasonable, concerned friend, but her words revealed something much nastier.

Grace bit her lip as she considered this.

"That's exactly what I was wondering. Maybe we're just taking her a little too seriously. Being a jerk doesn't mean she's guilty of any wrongdoing."

"That's true," Ben agreed.

They made their way up the sidewalk toward the SUV they'd rented in silence. Even Grace seemed to be lost in her own thoughts.

As they climbed into the sickeningly hot vehicle and clicked on the air conditioning, Ben turned to face her.

"I don't know how to ask this, but I'll ask anyway," he said.

"Ask what?"

Her blue eyes looked so earnest that he felt even more guilty about what he was going to say, but he had no choice. If they were going to find Katie, he needed to understand more about her, and right now, Grace was the best person to help him do that.

"When's the last time you spent time with Katie?"

"She and her dad came skiing with my family at our cabin in Aspen when Katie was thirteen," Grace said after a long moment. For some reason, she was looking out the window at the passing palm trees instead of facing him, as though something about the memory bothered her. "It was about a year after her mom died. She was having a rough time, and she opened up to me more easily than to her dad."

Ben nodded, feeling terrible for the girl. Losing her mother when she was so young must have been difficult. It had been hard enough for him when his own mother, Mary, had died, and he was twenty-three at the time.

"And have you talked to her much since?"

"Here and there," Grace said.

She didn't elaborate, and for a few moments Ben drove in silence, keeping careful watch of where he was going as more and more college kids filled the sidewalks of the small island town.

He tapped his fingers against the steering wheel. He couldn't let his thoughts go unspoken any longer.

"I guess I just have to wonder what kind of person Katie is today if she's best friends with someone like Jade."

He could see Grace's back stiffening beside him.

"She's nothing like Jade, Ben," she said, crossing her arms over her chest.

"I don't want to speak ill of a potential victim. But there's truth to the idea that we are reflected in the company we keep."

"I know her."

"You said you haven't spent a lot of time with her since she was basically a kid. A lot could have changed since then."

Grace released a sigh. "I'm a good judge of character, and I'm telling you, Katie is still the same person she's always been. There's no way she ran off like the police are saying."

"I'm just saying you could be wrong," he said firmly. "We can't afford to miss something because you've made up your mind that Katie is a saint."

"I just want you to trust me a little," Grace

snapped. "Give me–and Katie–the benefit of the doubt. That's all I'm asking for."

Ben wanted to argue the point further, but he bit his tongue. Grace had never really been upset with him before, so far as he knew, and he didn't like it.

Still, he was skeptical.

Or maybe this job had just made him lose faith in people.

"So you think there's something to the trafficking possibility?" he asked as they pulled onto the beachside road that led to the Mistflower.

To his surprise, Grace shook her head.

"Believe it or not, I actually agree with Detective Hayles. I don't think she fits the profile of a trafficking victim."

"Sure, but what if Jade's right?" Ben pressed, easing the car into the front gate of the Mistflower Resort compound. "She may not have put it in the most delicate way, but it's not totally far-fetched that this criminal ring may have high-end clients looking for someone different from the usual victims."

"I'm not saying it's impossible. But my intuition tells me it's something else we haven't thought of yet."

Before Ben could offer any of his own theories, he was forced to slam the brakes, narrowly avoiding a girl in a visor who had wandered off the sidewalk and into the driveway.

Grace raised a hand to her mouth, gasping in horror as she saw what the girl was staring at.

A plume of acrid black smoke rose above the Mistflower, so huge that it almost blocked out the sun.

Chapter 8

Grace

Her heart was going to burst out of her chest. She was sure of it.

She knew that she should breathe slowly, in and out, but her lungs didn't want to cooperate.

The fire was huge. It was orange and hot, licking at the hollow spaces where windows used to be, incinerating the air that dared to touch it.

The sound of crackling and popping and hissing filled the air for a few seconds and then went quiet again as the windows of the SUV slid closed, sealing them away from the smoke.

Ben said something, but he was very far away, and she couldn't make out his words.

She could feel the pressure of her seatbelt against her chest, holding her down against the seat so she couldn't run away.

She was trapped.

Just like before.

No.

A part of her protested, shouting at her from deep within that she was safe, that the fire wasn't close enough to hurt her, that she could unclip her seatbelt, that she could breathe.

But her body didn't listen.

Her body remembered that terrible day, no matter how much her mind wanted to forget.

Ben's voice faded as she melted away.

Only fear remained. Fear that had followed her like a shadow.

She was there in Indonesia again.

The bricks and mortar were falling all around her, sending dust into the air to mingle with the smoke, silencing more and more of the screams. People ran, tripping and getting up again, pushing their bodies harder as they tried desperately to flee.

She screamed for help from beneath the wooden beam that had fallen onto her torso, but no one stopped running. They couldn't stop.

They were bleeding, crying. Many were injured even worse than she was. Fathers dragged their children toward the doors. Mothers and grandmothers gripped the edges of the heavy wooden pews, trying to remain upright on shattered legs.

"Gracie! Gracie, please, look at me!"

She looked down at her hands instead, shaking uncontrollably in her lap.

Her seatbelt was still pressing into her chest as her lungs burned and her heart pounded. Her throat felt thick, and her stomach roiled.

"Take it off," she moaned, trying to make the muscles in her hands obey. She couldn't breathe, couldn't think, couldn't–

"Take what off?" Ben asked, trying to meet her eyes even as she looked away, wanting to curl into herself, to hide, to do anything to get out.

"Take it off!" she shouted again, her own voice shrill and painful in her ears. "I can't—my chest, my heart, I can't breathe!"

Realization filled his green eyes as he reached down to her seatbelt and clicked it open, freeing her body from the restraint.

Her chest still hurt, but it was better.

"You need to breathe," he was saying, his forehead glistening with sweat as he fumbled in the console for his phone. "I need to call 911."

"Wait," she managed, the words sandpaper in her throat. "No, I'm okay. Just give me a minute."

The panic was already beginning to fade, subsiding almost as quickly as it had arisen.

Thank you, Lord Jesus.

Ben held his phone in his hands as he looked over at her, but he didn't move to make any calls.

Grace pulled the cool, climate-controlled air into

her lungs, breathing as slowly as she could, until her heart's racing slowed.

Already, shame was beginning to replace her fear.

Through the car's windows, she could see that the huge fire was contained in one building, and that it was surrounded by several fire trucks dousing it with water.

On the ground, the people weren't screaming, nor were they covered in blood. Families huddled together, watching the scene. Paramedics were helping a handful of others who looked to have sustained only minor injuries.

Of course, she was not trapped. She was safe, never at the slightest risk.

And she'd just had a full-blown breakdown and probably completely freaked Ben out.

She turned to him, blinking away the tears that had formed in her eyes.

"Grace," he said, reaching up and placing a large hand on her shoulder, "what happened? Are you sure you're okay?"

Despite everything, the weight of his touch sent a shiver through her that she struggled to ignore.

Not that he felt anything in return.

"I had a panic attack," she said, trying to smile even as a few salty tears trickled down onto her lips. There was no point denying it now. "It's no big deal."

Ben lifted a brow.

He already knew that she had post traumatic stress disorder, and that certain things triggered memories of Indonesia, but she still hated saying the words out loud.

"Are you absolutely certain you don't want to get checked out? A resort this size probably has a nurse you could see, at least."

"I'm fine," she said again, ignoring the heat that rose to her cheeks as she forced herself to look into his eyes.

For whatever reason, his steady, concerned gaze only made the tears flow faster.

"You're clearly not fine."

"I'm embarrassed, okay?" she said, hating the shrill tone of her voice. "I feel like an idiot for worrying you over nothing. I'm sorry."

"You have nothing to be embarrassed about," he said firmly. "I just–"

He paused, and she waited for the interrogation that was surely imminent.

No matter what she felt for him, she wasn't about to explain anything else. He and his brothers knew the basics, and that would have to be enough. Wallowing in her fear by talking too much about it had only ever made her feel worse.

"Look, Grace. You watched me sob like a baby on a plane this morning. And even though you had every reason to be terrified yourself, you kept it together and prayed for everyone on that flight. And you were gracious enough not to tease me about it. If there's anyone who's going to be embarrassed here, it's me."

Ben looked out the window at the crowd of onlookers as he spoke, his words fast, as though he had to get them out before he lost his nerve.

She reached out tentatively and brushed her fingertips against his muscled forearm. His jaw softened, and he turned to her, allowing their eyes to meet.

"How about we call it even?" she suggested.

"Deal."

She extended a hand for him to shake, and he did so, the shadow of a smile alighting on his serious face.

Ben

"Thanks, Patrick," Ben said, squinting at the worn name tag on the security guard's uniform to be sure he was getting the man's name right.

"If you need anything else, feel free to contact me," the guard said pleasantly, handing him a simple business card with the Mistflower Resort's logo on it.

Ben thanked him again and headed out of the security office, which was located in one of the smaller buildings that made up the complex. As he strolled back toward the building where he and Grace's rooms were housed, he swung to the right and checked out the remnants of the burnt building once more.

Poor Grace. The fire had clearly brought up some rough memories, and he'd insisted that she spend the rest of the afternoon resting while he continued their preliminary investigation. After the nonexistent sleep they'd had the night before, he wished that he could do the same, but instead he'd spoken to the fire department.

They had assured him that the fire was caused by nothing more nefarious than badly maintained wiring. It was one of the oldest buildings on the property, and the oldest one still used to host guests. Apparently, the adobe exterior was more of a facade, with the rest of the building structured with wood framing. It hadn't taken much for a small fire to grow out of control.

After that, Ben had grabbed a quick lunch at one of the resort's cafeterias, and had spent the last couple of hours going over the details of the case with the head of security, Patrick O'Day.

The man had shown greater concern for Katie than Detective Hayles. However, there was only so much he could do on his own authority, especially since the resort manager was out of state. Ben had initially found this odd, considering how busy spring break must have been for business, but Patrick had only laughed and told him that was precisely why his boss fled the island every spring. Evidently, he trusted his team to handle the place.

Ben hadn't found out anything else of use, but at least Patrick had been able to confirm what the police had told him. He'd set up a meeting with Jade later that evening, and he couldn't help but to hope that they'd catch her in some kind of lie or inconsistency.

If they didn't, he had no idea where the next clue would come from.

With a final glance at the dusty black corpse of the old building, Ben continued toward their hotel. It had been quite a while since lunch, and he was starving. The investigation could wait until later, and in any case, he'd promised Grace he'd wake her up before dinnertime.

He'd never seen her so afraid before, and he hoped he'd handled it okay. He was used to happy, bubbly Grace, the light of Forge Brothers Security. Not the person who had post traumatic stress disorder and dark memories she'd locked away.

Maybe her bright personality was a wall she put up to avoid further hurt.

He tensed his jaw as he walked into the elevator and hit the button for their floor.

He knew what that was like.

When his girlfriend Mikayla broke his heart, he'd hardened his own. It was easier to pretend to be invincible than to admit to his damage.

But Grace had seen him cry.

Sure, he'd been legitimately terrified that they were going to die–it wasn't like he made a habit of letting his fear of flying escalate into hysteria– but still, it was the most vulnerable he'd been in front of another person for a very long time.

She hadn't acted like he was pathetic. Somehow, she'd managed to be strong for him without making him feel like he was weak.

As he took the final few steps that led to her hotel room door, he thought back to earlier in the day, when he'd insulted Katie Fairman's character due to her association with Jade.

He sighed to himself as he rapped his knuckles against the heavy wood.

Grace had asked him to trust in her judgment, and as much as his pride and stubbornness fought against it, he knew he had to try.

The door swung open, and all his thoughts of caution and common sense seemed to rush away like the outgoing tide.

Grace had swapped her sundress for a pair of bermuda shorts and a loose t-shirt that matched her blue eyes, and her tidy waves had been tucked up into a messy bun. She had taken most of her makeup off and left her designer tote bag behind. He noticed that along with her phone and sunglasses, she'd also decided to include a small handgun holstered at her waist.

Ben tried and failed to pick his jaw up off the floor. Something about her more casual look made his stomach do somersaults. Grace was always picture-perfect and put together in a way that made the other women back at FBS jealous.

But here she was with him, heading out for dinner on the beach, looking completely at home in her own skin and ready to take on whatever and whoever came at her.

She was gorgeous.

And no matter how much he tried to deny it, he was in big trouble.

Chapter 9

Grace

Ben was staring at her like she had three heads, and she could tell by the redness of his lightly freckled cheeks that it was a compliment.

It seemed she'd guessed right that he was one of those guys who appreciated the casual look. He'd never admit it out loud, of course, but his stare spoke volumes.

She let him squirm a moment longer, wiping her sunglasses on the hem of her aqua blue t-shirt. After a long nap, she felt a lot better, and she was eager to find out what Ben had learned.

And after such an eventful day, they both deserved to enjoy the scenery a little—even if she'd be looking over her shoulder. She'd resolved to carry her firearm with her for the rest of the trip.

She cleared her throat.

"So, are we going to eat?"

"Er—yes," Ben said, looking down at her feet for a moment before meeting her eyes. "Yes. Let's go. Let's go...eat."

Ben was a man of few words on any given day, but she couldn't help but to enjoy the flustered way he said them now. She offered him her brightest smile. Her day was seriously looking up.

"I had a protein bar from the vending machine around lunchtime," she offered as they walked. "But that's about it. I could really go for a taco. Or five."

"I vote we wander toward the beach until we find a local place," Ben offered.

"Totally. Lead the way."

They headed out into the early evening. A pleasant breeze was rippling over the water, and the sky was blue without a single cloud. Grace felt a flicker of excitement as she imagined just how stunning the sunset was going to be.

"God really did bless Texas, didn't He?" she swooned as they stepped onto the boardwalk behind the resort.

The water was as pristine as the sky, with gentle waves lapping at the pale sand as spring breakers lounged on towels in all directions. It was still fairly quiet. She assumed that the real party would probably start at nightfall.

"He did," Ben agreed. "But the view would be better if it had more nature and fewer bikinis."

Grace pretended to punch his arm. "Are you sure about that?"

"Positive."

He looked over at her with one of his usual stony, unreadable expressions, taking in her own outfit once again, and she smiled down at the worn wood of the boardwalk.

Most guys would be thrilled with the parade of scantily clad, beautiful women that were currently taking up residence on South Padre Island.

But Ben wasn't most guys.

She saw him at church most Sundays, and even though he'd expressed doubts about their faith that she didn't necessarily know how to answer, it was obvious he was still trying to live up to the grace God had given to him.

"That place looks good," she said, breaking the momentary silence as she pointed toward a small taco truck parked nearby. She could smell the fresh tortillas from here.

"It's no Screaming Peach, but it'll work," Ben said.

Grace smiled. The Screaming Peach cafe back in Silver Grove was a favorite with the entire Forge family, and they'd introduced most of their friends to it. Maybe she could convince the owner, Iris, to try putting tacos on the menu.

Several minutes later, they'd found a picnic table, and had eaten through half of the pile of mini tacos they'd ordered.

Ben had covered the check with his own credit card rather than his company one, and she couldn't help but to wonder what the gesture meant. Sure, it had been a cheap dinner, but it wasn't the kind of thing he usually did. They were just friends, and he'd always made it clear that was all that they were going to be. He kept the lines between them stark.

But somehow, with the smell of saltwater and the palm trees swaying in the distance, things felt just a little bit different.

She pulled her phone from her pocket and looked down at the notifications in her lap, not wanting him to see the questions in her eyes. She had a bad habit of obsessing over small situations, and trying to read minds that didn't want to be read.

Ben was her friend and her colleague. And that would have to be good enough.

"So," he said, swallowing the last bite of a taco, "how are things back at the office?"

She smiled and set her phone on the table with her email inbox open, thankful for the change of subject.

Not that he could possibly know the thoughts about him that were always swirling through her mind. Thankfully.

"See for yourself."

Ben picked up the device, and she smiled at the way the glittery blue case looked in his hand. "Good grief. It's worse than I thought."

She laughed, his fingers brushing hers just slightly as she took the phone back. "I know, right? And that's just all the work stuff. I also have about fifteen texts from the Silver Grove Women's Book Club, and several barely-intelligible voice messages from my mother. I'll be up until midnight dealing with everything."

She shoved the phone back into her pocket, and when she looked up, there was an intensity to Ben's eyes that hadn't been there a moment ago.

"What?" she asked warily, picking up taco wrappers and tossing them onto their tray.

"I really don't think Forge Brothers Security would be the same without you," Ben said. "I know we call you the office manager, but you're clearly so much more than that. And I just wanted to say thank you. You know, from all of us."

Once again, Ben looked flustered, and it was the most adorable thing in the world.

Great. Every reminder of how she felt about him–
and how they would never be more than what
they were–was another jab, straight through to
her heart.

"I appreciate that," she said. "I believe in the
work we do. I want to handle the boring stuff so
that you and the rest of the guys have time to
fight for justice. Don't worry, I have no desire to
become a full time field operative."

"That's a relief," Ben said, getting up from the
table and heading toward the trash can with their
wrappers and soda cups. "Who else would dump
bubble tea all over my new mechanical
keyboard?"

Grace stuck out her tongue at him. "That was
one time!"

"Or what about Dolly? None of the other admin
staff play hide and seek with her."

She laughed, giving him another ineffectual
punch on his muscled bicep.

Dolly, their head of security, was a mixture of
kindly grandmother and pitbull. She and Grace
respected one another, but every so often,

Grace's chaotic management style got her into trouble with the older woman.

"Hey, to be fair, I only hid that one time. Usually I just avoid."

Ben chuckled. "You mean the time that you accidentally popped out of Gabe's office closet during a meeting with the San Antonio chief of police?"

Before Grace could smack him again, he started walking back toward the boardwalk, and she had to take several hurried steps in order to catch up.

"Can those stubby legs move any faster?" he teased.

"It's not my fault you have legs like a giraffe. Or maybe an elephant."

They continued to joke around as they continued along the beach, watching as more and more college students began laying out towels on the sand and arranging coolers full of alcohol. The sun was beginning to set in earnest, and Grace knew the party was only just beginning.

She wasn't a fan of drinking, and she doubted she'd appreciate the kind of dancing these kids would be doing, but she couldn't help but to be swept up in the happy energy that surrounded them. Even Ben seemed to be enjoying their walk.

She glanced up at him, once again struck by his mountainous height. His reddish hair gleamed in the light of the setting sun, and he looked even more handsome than the dozens of clean-cut fraternity guys that kept almost bumping into them on the boardwalk.

Just then, he stuck his hands into the pocket of his gray cargo shorts, and Grace caught a glimpse of the Sig he kept holstered at his belt.

The sight of the weapon reminded her that they had more than turbulence and faulty wiring to deal with.

While they were enjoying the beauty of the island, Donald Fairman was worrying about his daughter.

Katie could be anywhere right now, and Grace was determined to find her.

Ben

"What time are we supposed to be meeting Jade tonight?" Grace asked.

"Not until nine," he said, trying to stop himself from frowning at the thought of being forced to interact with Jade again.

The last hour or so had been perfect.

He had enjoyed a leisurely walk, great tacos, and perfect weather. Even the writhing mob of college students and the presence of sand hadn't been enough to sully his good mood.

He glanced over at Grace without really meaning to, taking in the way her tanned skin seemed to glow in the evening light. He didn't see her like this very often. Usually, she had the vibe of a typical career woman, carrying some kind of designer bag that could fit a toddler, making phone calls, and just generally swirling through life like a tornado.

She was different now, with her cheap flip-flops and hair messy from the breeze. She looked so carefree and happy, like some kind of angel who happened to be wearing Ray-Bans.

He stuck his hands in his pockets and looked down at his feet, not wanting her to know he was staring.

He had no reason to be thinking so much about her.

They were here to find a missing girl, not for him to fantasize about what could happen between him and Grace if they were in an alternate universe. He needed to get back to reality.

"How long do you think we have until the dance music starts?" Grace asked, raising a hand to her brow and looking out over the expanse of bodies. "I know you'll love that."

The entire beach looked about three times busier than it had been when they left the hotel, and it was only eight o'clock.

"Yeah, right," Ben said gruffly. "I'd rather listen to Asher's playlists. And that's saying something."

"These kids could benefit from one of your boring lectures on the glorious music of Western civilization–"

Suddenly, Grace stopped short, her near-permanent smile falling away from her face as she glanced out toward the water.

"What's–" he started to say, following her gaze.

Several huge bonfires dotted the shoreline near a jetty that jutted out into the Gulf of Mexico, filling the air with a smoky smell. The orange flames were bright in the twilight, and somewhere farther up the beach, he could hear the sound of a thumping bassline as the night's party began.

Grace's skin looked pale as she stood rooted in place, gripping the hem of her t-shirt with her pale pink fingernails. She hated fire, that much was obvious, but at least she hadn't collapsed into another full-blown panic attack.

"Are you okay?" he asked, walking closer to her and resting a hand on her shoulder. "We can go back to the hotel if you want, or at least walk up the beach. We have a little more time before we have to meet Jade. I can meet her by myself, if you want."

She turned to him, the edges of her soft pink lips turning up in a faint smile.

"Actually," she said, sounding almost apologetic, "can we walk to the jetty?"

Ben's brow furrowed. To reach it, they'd have to pass between two of the bonfires. They'd be close enough to feel the heat. On top of that, the area was packed with college students. If Grace had another episode, she'd be trapped in the middle of a pressing, bumping crowd.

"I'm not sure that's a good idea," he said, realizing that he'd already put his body between her and the fires, as though the flames might come rushing up the beach to attack her.

"Ben, I'm not made of glass," she said, taking a step past him and ducking under his arm. "What happened earlier–I feel so stupid that you even saw that. I really try to keep that part of me under control. I don't want you to see me differently."

"I don't," he said quickly.

She laughed, though it sounded more bitter than amused. "If I hadn't had that panic attack, you'd be making fun of me right now. You'd be daring me to walk out on that jetty and jump into the Gulf."

"Honestly, that sounds more like something Asher would suggest," he said to her retreating back as she stepped off the boardwalk and into the sand, headed toward the thickening crowd. "Swimming in the dark in shark and jellyfish infested waters is dangerous."

"You're missing the point," she called out over her shoulder.

"Am I?"

She stopped where she was and turned to face him for a moment, one hand resting on her hip. Her cheeks were red, and he could see that she was breathing more heavily than usual.

"I want you and Asher and everyone else to treat me the same as you always have," she said firmly. "I don't want what happened this morning to change that."

He watched as she started off again, her flip-flop clad feet sinking into the sand as her legs began to shake.

She was growing more afraid with each step she took in the direction of the bonfires. He could see that much.

But she was still walking. She didn't even hesitate.

"Hey, wait up!"

He stepped off the boardwalk and hurried after her, warm sand filling the bottoms of the sport slides he wore as he attempted to jog. A group of giggling girls passed in front of him, obscuring his view of Grace.

His chest felt tight as he rushed through their ranks, not stopping to apologize properly as his elbow connected with someone's ribs. People were shoving into him on all sides, the smell of fruity mixed drinks and cheap beer filling his nostrils.

At last, he broke through the crowd, emerging at the edge of one of the bonfires where the heat had created a natural clearing.

Finally, he spotted Grace's blonde waves to his left.

"You scared me," he snapped, grabbing her hand and pulling her away as a drunken boy stumbled past her. "I thought–"

"I know what you thought. And I'm telling you, I'm not broken," Grace spat back.

He could see the sparking bonfire reflected in her eyes, and the hardness in her expression to match.

She didn't let go of his hand, and he didn't pull away.

"Okay," she continued a moment later. "I am broken. You're right. I'm scared, and I could freak out right here and make a fool of myself and you in front of everyone."

"You think that's what I'm worried about? That I'll be ashamed to be seen with you if you have another panic attack?"

She bit her lip and looked up at him for several seconds, her hand still resting soft and warm within his own.

"I don't know," she said finally. "But what I do know is that I don't want to live my life in fear. I'm standing here, I can feel the heat of the flames, and I'm okay."

Ben felt his muscles relaxing slightly.

He knew he should let go of her hand, but his body didn't seem to want to obey his brain.

"Do you still want to walk out on the jetty?" he heard himself saying.

Fantasies of holding her hand as they strode out over the Gulf filled his head.

What was he thinking?

They had to meet Jade soon, and in any case, he was playing with fire as it was.

Still, he let her hand rest in his, not wanting to hurt her by letting go, even though he knew that in the long run, he'd have no other choice.

Grace gave him a small smile as she kicked sand out of her flip-flop. "Let's go. I'll feel a lot better once we're away from these bonfires."

The crowd began to thin out dramatically as they got closer to the water. A few seconds later, Ben realized why.

Two lifeguards were standing guard nearby, probably making sure that no drunken college students tried their luck walking on the narrow strip of jumbled rocks that formed the rustic jetty.

"So much for that," Grace said. "Back to the boardwalk it is."

"Let's walk along the shore," Ben suggested, rubbing the back of Grace's hand gently with his thumb. "The ice cream place where we're meeting Jade is up the beach, anyway."

Apparently, his voice didn't obey his brain any better than his fingers did.

Chapter 10

Grace

Grace's heart wasn't racing.

She'd dreamed of a moment like this so many times, when Ben would look at her and see something more than just a friend. She'd imagined the way his hand felt around hers, the way his fingertips would trace across her skin, the way he'd look down so he didn't have to meet her eyes.

She'd expected to be so full of excitement and nerves that her heart would be hammering against her ribcage.

But it wasn't.

She felt calm and warm, like she was basking in her own private sun. Even the anxiety that had been triggered by the sight of the fires had faded away.

Safe.

That's what it was. She felt safe with her hand in his. It was a feeling she'd almost managed to forget.

She glanced up at him and smiled, looking ahead again before his gaze could linger on her face.

There were already plenty of triggers that forced her to remember. Ever since she'd come home seven years ago, just living her life had been like navigating a minefield. No, she wouldn't waste this perfect night worrying about what had happened half a world away.

She felt the wet sand squishing between her toes as the gentle waves rose and fell against her feet.

Neither spoke.

For the first time possibly ever, she could imagine what it was like to be shy or socially anxious, wondering how every word you said might be perceived. This moment was too precious and too fragile to risk.

It had taken her several minutes just to work up the nerve to take her flip-flops off, because it necessitated letting go of his hand. She'd been scared he wouldn't reach for her again, that he'd come to his senses and see that he didn't like her, after all.

Instead, he'd pulled off his own shoes and sunk his pale feet into the sand alongside her. She'd watched as the water found his larger footprints, filling them and then washing them away with each step they took.

And though he still barely met her eyes, he took her hand again, and he hadn't let go.

Ben

Ben focused on putting one foot in front of the other. He wasn't sure his brain was working well enough to do anything else.

Every few minutes, Grace would look up at him, her blue eyes sparkling with happiness, and a mixture of longing and guilt sent his heart racing anew.

He was in great shape, so why was his heart pounding so hard? Why did he feel like he'd just run twenty miles when she readjusted her hand in his?

As far as he could remember, he hadn't walked barefoot on a beach since he was about six years old. Even then, as his brothers playfully fought and tracked sand onto their towels, he hadn't been so sure how he felt about the messiness of the place.

But here, now, with her?

He'd let her dig a hole and bury him up to his neck. He'd let the sand get in his hair and the taste of saltwater kiss his lips.

He felt his cheeks burning at the very thought of what it would be like to lean over and kiss her right now. She'd let him. He was pretty sure she'd like it, and certain he would, but that didn't make it a wise thing to do.

None of this was.

It wasn't fair to a good woman who deserved a whole lot better.

"Hey, check that out," he said. He pointed at a yacht that was anchored out in the water, glad for the excuse to let go of her hand.

There were too many problems to solve when it came to him and Grace Hinton. And so long as his skin was touching hers, there was zero chance of thinking them through logically.

"Whoa," Grace said, her gaze following his gesture.

He expected her to keep walking, but instead she stopped short, squinting as she eyed the large watercraft. He waited, listening as what he assumed was another popular club hit began blaring from across the beach.

He glanced down at the fitness tracking watch he always wore. They didn't have long before they were due to meet Jade.

"It's getting late," he said, raising his watch as though she'd be able to read the tiny screen from where she stood.

"Sorry," Grace said, giving a little laugh as she turned to face him. "It's just not every day that you see a yacht this big. Or this fancy."

"Oh. Right."

Truth was, he knew less than nothing about yachts. Though he and Grace both came from wealthy families, his father wasn't exactly the yacht club type. Or the golf club, for that matter. Gabriel Forge Sr. only felt at home when he could get his hands dirty.

"It's from the Excalibur Platinum line by Santucci," Grace mused, knitting her brows together. "An X-Series superyacht, if I had to guess."

Ben stared at her for several seconds in bafflement before looking down at his watch again.

"I'll, uh, take your word for it," he said. "Seriously, though, I have a feeling Jade isn't the type who will appreciate being kept waiting."

"Don't you think it's weird?"

"What?"

Grace rolled her eyes at him.

"It's like three times the size of everything else on the water, and they have all of their lights off. I guess I just wonder what kind of hotshot owns it."

Ben ran a hand through his hair as he squinted in the direction of the boat.

"It's too far to read the name on the back," he said. "But I'm pretty sure I can make out an 'L'."

Grace nodded. "That's what I thought. Anyway, I guess you're right. It's probably not important. We need to talk to Jade and see what else we can find out about Katie."

As they made their way up the boardwalk toward the ice cream shop, he resisted the urge to reach for Grace's hand. Just because he'd made a mistake once didn't mean that he had to do it again.

Instead, he continued on the safe subject of yachts, which Grace apparently had an encyclopedic knowledge of. She even confessed to her top secret hobby of building and painting miniature boat replicas, though she usually went for historical military models.

As she held a one-sided conversation comparing the relative merit of Supero 5000s and ForceStars, he realized for the first time that Grace Hinton–gorgeous Grace, with her designer clothes and perfectly manicured fingernails–was a nerd.

Maybe as much of a nerd as he was.

Keeping his hands safely in the pockets of his shorts, he stole another look at her.

Her hands were moving as she talked, and the excitement she had while talking about her interest felt contagious. He wouldn't be surprised if he ended up researching nautical miniatures on Youtube later so he could actually contribute to what she was saying.

How was it possible that he'd missed so much about her, even after knowing her for all of these years?

"Anyway," Grace said after a while, shaking her head quickly as though she just realized that she was embarrassed. "Now that I've given you the ultimate ammunition for the rest of the guys to make fun of me, I suppose we may as well get ice cream. Since we're here."

"How practical of you," Ben said with a chuckle. "I'll go get it. You stay here in case Jade shows up. She should be here any minute."

She reached into the pocket of her shorts for a moment and then looked up at him.

"Actually, forget mine," she said, shaking her head. "I forgot my wallet. I usually just use my phone to pay for things, but I wanted to enjoy the view without being tempted to capture it in a photo, you know what I mean?"

Her cheeks flushed pink.

"I do," he said, picking up his own phone and holding it away from him as though it was covered in something filthy. "I always worry I'll need my phone if I leave it at home, but I hate the temptation to pick it up all the time. I spend plenty of time staring at computer screens back at FBS."

"Totally," Grace said. "I hate the way I end up filtering my view of the real world through a camera lens."

He said nothing for a moment, putting his hands on his hips as he stared out at the sea. Now that the sun had fully set, the water looked like deep blue ink. It was beautiful, but there was something ominous about it too–like the island itself, he suspected that danger lurked beneath the surface.

"So," he said, letting his arm brush against hers accidentally-on-purpose as he took hold of his own wallet. "Chocolate? Vanilla? Strawberry? Something else?"

A smile tugged at Grace's lips. "Are you sure?"

"Of course."

"This feels kind of like a date, since you're paying and all," she teased.

"Don't push your luck. I mean, technically I could just charge it to the company," he said, certain that the flustered look on his face had given the truth away, whatever his words said.

It wasn't a date.

But he wished that it could be.

Grace

"Okay, give me that spoon, you're driving me insane," Ben said, reaching out and plucking the ice cream spoon from where she'd been tapping it against the picnic table.

"You can't even hear it over the music," she said, relinquishing the small piece of pink plastic.

"I can still see it," he countered. "It's visual clutter. Like trying to think while staring at Cameron's desk back at the office."

She pretended to shudder. "Okay. That's fair. Even I can't think in there."

She had a tendency to get lost in conversations, and whenever she couldn't pace while talking, her hands had a way of busying themselves. The front desk at Forge Brothers Security was covered with open notebooks and sticky notes, all of them covered in nonsensical doodles she'd taken while on the phone with colleagues or clients.

"Well, I think I'm about ready to call it," Ben said, looking down at his chunky, manly-looking watch.

They'd finished their chocolate ice cream at least a half an hour ago, and still there was no sign of Jade.

Grace knew she should be concerned about the young woman's whereabouts, considering the reason they were on South Padre Island in the first place, but she couldn't help but to feel disappointed that the night was coming to a close.

Though she knew it wasn't a date, coworkers didn't usually hold hands. Neither did friends.

Warmth spread straight through to her fingertips as she remembered. Time had slowed down as they'd walked up the beach, the loud music of the spring break party fading away until all she noticed was the shushing of the sea and the beating of her own heart.

She hated that he'd let go. And she hated that she was too scared to reach out for him again.

"Let's try her phone one more time," Grace said. "Just in case." Ben did as she suggested, letting the phone roll to voicemail once, and then a second time for good measure.

He shook his head, defeated.

"Want me to talk to Detective Hayles?" Grace offered.

"I know we probably should," Ben said, letting out a sigh. "I'll put him on speaker phone, I guess."

The front desk clerk at the North Pier police station picked up in two rings and transferred them to the detective. The older man was quiet as they took turns running over the events of the day, and Grace wasn't sure if he was listening and taking notes or playing Solitaire on his computer in the background.

"Anyway, we've been waiting for well over an hour now, and Jade never showed up. We tried calling her cell phone repeatedly, and even had the front desk at the Mistflower go up and knock on her door. Nothing." Ben finished.

By the several seconds the detective took to react to the words, Grace guessed that the game of Solitaire was more likely.

"Well, I'll make sure to file a report," Hayles said at last. "But just like Ms. Fairhope, I'm sure Jade will turn up sooner rather than–"

"It's Fairman," Grace snapped.

"–Ms. Fairman," the detective amended quickly. "The girls came here to enjoy spring break.

Hooking up with boys, dancing in bikinis on the beach, drinking beer. That's probably what they're both doing right now. I would think you young people would understand that better than I do."

Grace cringed as the man spoke, but he wasn't entirely wrong. Her parents had never permitted her to go on vacation for spring break, precisely to avoid everything he'd just described, and she couldn't imagine Ben voluntarily going even if the Forges would have allowed it.

They'd had plenty of time to observe the behavior of the college kids since arriving on the Island, and she hated to think that both Katie and Jade had probably come here to do the same.

But that didn't mean that they weren't in trouble.

"Thanks for your help, Detective," she heard Ben say calmly. "I guess we'll see where we're at in the morning."

Grace worked up the nerve to give his bicep an approving squeeze. Ben didn't usually suffer fools lightly, but he was wise not to argue with the man. He was a lost cause, and if they pushed too hard, he may not be willing to help them when they truly needed assistance.

"Just give Jade time to sleep off the hangover before you worry me," Hayles quipped. "Good night."

Ben looked down at the phone, his brows furrowed. The man hung up before he could say another word.

"So," he said, stretching out his arms over his head and letting out a loud yawn. "I guess we're on our own."

Grace forced herself to focus on his words rather than his impressive muscles.

She nodded. "First, sleep. Tomorrow, we find out what on earth is going on on this island."

Chapter 11

Craig

The dark water stretched between the boat and the shore, muffling the sound of the loud dance music. Still, the persistent thump of the bass continued to sound in Craig's ears as he leaned against the railing of the yacht.

He wished he'd thought to bring earplugs on board. The only time the college students were relatively quiet was in the early morning, but he'd never been one for sleeping when the sun was out.

Not that he would have been able to sleep even without the noise.

Craig drew his phone out from the back pocket of his khakis for the tenth time that hour. Even though there had been no new beeps or vibrations, he couldn't shake the tensing anxiety spreading across his chest as he waited for the call or the message telling him that his life was over.

He sighed, turning to set the sleek device on a small table that held a bottle of scotch and a half-empty tumbler that had done little to settle his nerves.

He should have stayed in Austin. He could have kept his alibi clean. He had men he could trust who could have handled the situation, but now it was too late.

At least here he could pretend he was in control.

He reached over and took hold of the scotch, careful not to send his phone tumbling onto the deck in the dim light. Fortunately, the moon was bright tonight. He could even see a few faint stars.

He threw back the remainder of the drink, cringing as it burned its way down his throat. More money, right down the drain.

Craig chuckled to himself at the thought. The remaining dollars and cents in his accounts were little more to him now than numbers on a screen. But he had to watch over them more than ever. He owed himself and what was left of his family that much after what he'd done.

He looked down at his simple gold wedding band, swallowing the tears that stung his throat almost as much as the liquor.

He didn't wish he could ask his wife for advice. He knew she'd tell him to call this whole thing off and to turn himself in. But he knew that he couldn't do that.

At last, the alcohol seemed to be doing its job.

His head felt thick now. It was a feeling he usually despised, but at the moment, it took the sharp edges off the questions and worries playing on repeat in his mind.

What if Katie already told someone what she'd figured out before his men grabbed her?

He rubbed his fingers through his hair, wondering how many fresh grays had sprung up in the last couple of days.

He couldn't keep her like this forever. Sooner or later, there would have to be a step two. Eventually, he'd have to let her go–or he'd have to get rid of her.

He took hold of the scotch bottle, not bothering with the tumbler in his other hand, and drank.

He'd heard quite enough of that suggestion. He wasn't a killer.

But as the latest bout of booze-induced fog sloshed around in his skull, he thought of the message that had come up on his phone that morning, and of the man who had sent it.

He leaned over the railing, suddenly woozy, and watched as the black water churned against the sleek white side of the boat.

He laughed again. He'd rather take his chances with the sharks hidden in that water than face the one who would soon be hunting him on land.

Craig wasn't a killer.

But a man whose family was in danger could do desperate things.

Chapter 12

Grace

"Just give me two minutes!" Grace called out from her place in front of the bathroom mirror.

She heard Ben grumbling outside the door about how he'd already been waiting for fifteen, but she ignored him, adding a final coat of waterproof mascara to her lashes.

She'd never been overly anxious about her looks, but realizing she was about to interview a bunch of college students on the beach in the harsh light of day had thrown her confidence off.

Wait. Was that an actual crow's foot?

She leaned closer to the mirror to examine her eye in closer detail, but before she could discern how much money she'd need to spend on new anti-aging skincare, she heard Ben knocking on her door again.

"Okay, okay," she muttered under her breath, giving her hair a final toss before leaving the bathroom and pulling the door open. She was about to tell Ben off for being so impatient, but the sight of him left her momentarily speechless.

"Hi," he said, raising an eyebrow as she stared at him. "Sleep well?"

"Er, yeah, thanks," she said, sliding her feet into a pair of flower-print flip-flops.

"Everything okay?"

"Yes," she said, clearing her throat. "You just look different, that's all."

"Oh, well I figured since we're going to–"

"Did you style your hair?" Grace interrupted him, reaching up to try and touch his gel-slicked auburn strands. Of course, he was tall enough to keep his head away from her without much effort. "Is that product?"

Ben rolled his eyes. "Technically? It's called Dippity-Do and they sell it for two dollars at the grocery store."

Grace made a face. Of course the man would look for hair products in the same place he bought beef jerky and milk.

Like the rest of the Forge brothers, he was effortlessly handsome and had excellent skin, and she would bet that he washed his face with dollar store shampoo or something. It really wasn't fair.

They headed out of the hotel, and despite the morning hour, a small crowd was beginning to trickle toward the beach. Ben had figured that they may as well talk to some of the less wild partiers, seeing as they were more likely to have been at least somewhat sober on the night of Katie's disappearance.

Grace looked over him as he scanned the stretch of beach near the Mistflower Resort. She admired his investigative mind. She really did. But at the moment, all she could think about was how thankful she was that he wasn't the type to take his t-shirt off in public, because her staring would have probably caused her to crash into the side of a building by now. He may have been a total computer nerd, but no one would ever guess as much based on his physique.

All of the guys at FBS had to be in good shape, but Ben took the gym more seriously than anyone else Grace had ever met.

"Okay, you're the college kid whisperer," Ben said, gesturing toward a group of girls in matching neon pink tank tops. "Shall we start with them?"

"Sure," Grace said brightly, hoping she sounded more confident than she felt. She knew that it hardly mattered what these girls thought of her, but she found it difficult not to be intimidated by the group.

Okay, she was a little jealous. Not so much of their perfect hair, tans, and flat abs, per se, but of the fact that Ben might stare.

"Good morning, ladies," she started, walking up to the group like she belonged there. "I love your matching shirts! So cute."

To her relief, no one started throwing tomatoes at her or calling her old. Instead, a skinny blonde who seemed to be the head of the group stepped forward with a friendly smile.

"Thank you so much. We're from Sigma Sigma Chi. It's easier to keep track of all of our sisters when we match."

"I totally get it," Grace said, beaming at her as she rattled off her own sorority credentials, ignoring the eye roll gesture that Ben was almost certainly making.

After they chatted for another minute or so, Ben stepped forward, pulling up his phone and showing the women a picture of Katie Fairman.

"Have you seen her?" he asked bluntly.

Grace watched as one of the girls jabbed another with her elbow, giggling as she whispered something. There was no doubt she was talking about Ben.

To her relief, he hardly seemed to notice.

None of the women had seen Katie Fairman. They didn't have a photo of Jade, but they had described her, and no one remembered running into her, either.

They spent the next two hours or so talking to dozens of people, including bartenders, food truck operators, and beach maintenance staff. Several had seen Katie, and Ben had been taking careful notes, trying to map out her movements the day she'd disappeared. So far, though, they hadn't learned anything new.

Jade was more difficult. Quite a few people had seen a tall black woman with long, straight hair, but since they didn't have a photo, they couldn't be sure it was actually her. Still, Ben took note of the information and took the contact info of anyone who might be able to help them later.

"It's really interesting getting to see how you actually work a case," Grace said as they sat down for a quick lunch break. "I mean, I know the FBS procedures, but I've never really seen them in action."

Ben nodded, swallowing a gulp of his soda. "It's not as exciting as it looks."

"Actually, I'm surprised at how much I'm

enjoying this," she said honestly. "I mean, yeah, there are no gunfights or car chases–"

"Not today, anyway," Ben said, giving her a wink that made her go weak in the knees.

"–Gosh, I hope not. Anyway, I'm learning a lot, and I like the meticulousness of it."

She paused to take a sip of her own drink, making a mental note that she'd have to reapply her sunscreen soon. It was a gorgeous day, but it was already hotter than it had been the day before, and the last thing she needed was to turn bright red and pass out from heatstroke.

"I'm glad," Ben said, crushing the wrappers of their hot dogs into a ball and tossing the clump of paper into a trash can a few feet away. "I was kind of worried I'd bore you to death."

Grace felt her breath catch in her throat. He was so handsome, even with patches of sweat beginning to spread on his dark t-shirt in the stifling humidity. And though she knew how he felt about the beach and the heat, he hadn't complained since they'd left the hotel. He'd been completely laser-focused on trying to find out what happened to her old friend, and she was thankful.

"Anyway," Ben said before she could voice her gratitude aloud, "let's try and talk to a few more kids, and then I think I need to take a break from the heat."

"Good idea," she said, wiping a few beads of perspiration from her forehead. She hoped that she still smelled like the coconut and vanilla body spray she'd doused herself with rather than sweat.

By the time they stepped back onto the boardwalk, Ben had pointed out their next set of targets.

A group of boys stood in the sand nearby, each holding a beer in one hand and taking turns tossing a frisbee with the other.

Even though it was only noon, two of them already looked tipsy, and Grace wouldn't have been surprised if they'd been totally hammered the night that Katie had gone missing. Still, they'd spoken to most of the early risers, and hadn't learned much. They may as well expand their search.

Grace cringed as they stepped onto the beach, the hot sand brushing against her bare, flip-flop clad feet. Ben had the same reaction, lifting his feet up in turn and trying to shake the sand loose. Somehow, the guys in the polo shirts were hanging out barefoot. Maybe they were more drunk than she thought.

"Hey, guys," Grace said, putting on her brightest smile and tossing her hair over her shoulder. "Do you have a sec?"

"Of course, beautiful," one of the guys said, sidling up to her and offering a hand for her to shake. She did so, noticing that the smell of his expensive aftershave was mingled with the unmistakable smell of cheap beer. Clearly, they'd run out of the good stuff.

"Who's the old man?" another guy in blue shorts chimed in, gesturing to Ben.

Rude. Ben was only five years older than her at thirty-two, but she supposed that in the eyes of a college bro, he probably seemed ancient.

"Excuse me?" he growled, standing to his full height and stepping in beside Grace.

"Relax, boys," Grace said, forcing a laugh. "It's just my big brother. He's a little protective sometimes."

"I can see why a stunner like you might need protection from creeps," blue shorts said, running a hand through his spiky blonde hair. He was attractive in a Ken doll sort of way, with icy blue eyes, lean muscles, and a watch that made her prized Louis Vuitton bag look cheap.

Two of the other boys nodded in agreement, ogling her in her tasteful lilac dress. Their attitudes made her want to give them a piece of her mind, but if there was even a small chance one of them knew something about Katie, it would be worth staying on their good side.

Whether Ben would keep quiet was another matter.

"Have you seen this woman?" he asked, holding up his phone again and showing a picture of Katie to the group. Three of the boys shook their heads, but blue shorts and another boy nodded, giving each other a pointed look.

"Oh, we've seen her," blue shorts said, a grin

breaking out on his tanned face. "She was with her friend, who didn't like Tom here very much."

"Shut up," the other boy–Tom, presumably–said, kicking sand in his friend's direction. "Chick was clearly frigid, a real ballbust–"

"Watch it," Ben warned.

The other boys had checked out of the conversation, already focused on chugging their beers and staring at more girls as they paraded across the beach.

For the first time, Grace was thankful for Jade's abrasive personality. These jerks needed to be knocked down several pegs.

"Anyway," blue shorts said, brushing sand off of his chiseled abdomen, "We saw them pretty early, over by the jetty, before the party really got started."

"Do you recall what time it was?" Grace asked sweetly before Ben could start grilling him.

"Actually, yeah, I do," Tom said, taking out his phone and scrolling across the screen for several seconds. "It was around eight-thirty. I'd just gotten off the phone with my..."

"Your mom?" blue shorts prompted, letting out a guffaw.

Tom glared at him. "My girlfriend, but it's cool, okay? We have an arrangement. Whatever happens off-campus doesn't count."

Grace caught Ben's gaze, her own disgust reflected on his face.

"Okay, thank you, that's helpful," Grace said through gritted teeth, even though they hadn't learned anything new. Katie had been seen at a restaurant with multiple witnesses around ten.

"What's this about, anyway?" Tom asked.

"The girl in the picture, Katie Fairman, disappeared on Monday night," Ben said.

"Have you checked the frat houses back in Brownsville?" blue shorts chimed in.

"Can't say we have."

"Might not be a bad idea. Considering."

Ben took two steps closer to the boy, straightening up to every inch of his six-foot-three. "Considering what?"

Blue shorts raised his hands, and Tom cast a glance at his other friends, who had meandered over to the boardwalk. "Hey man, I'm just saying, we weren't the only guys trying to hit up those girls. It was pretty clear what they were after."

Blue shorts nodded in agreement. "I saw the one with the darker skin and black hair on some guy's lap, I guess I figured she looked pretty easy. And the blonde one?"

"My friend, Katie, who is currently missing," Grace prompted. Ben rested a gentle hand against the small of her back. Despite her anger, his touch sent a comforting shiver through her, and she was disappointed when he pulled away a few moments later. Not that he had much of a choice, if he wanted these guys to keep believing they were brother and sister.

"Look, I'm sorry," blue shorts said, making an attempt at a sympathetic expression. "I'm just saying, she'd already gotten a bit of a reputation on the Island, and the way she dressed and the vibes she gave off solidified it."

"We hope you find her, though," Tom added. "I'm sure she's fine. Probably just sleeping off the mother of all hangovers somewhere."

Grace glanced over at the water, lost in her own thoughts as Ben recorded the boys' names and numbers on his phone. Finally, they were alone, and they began meandering slowly up the beach once more.

"Those guys were awful," Grace said at last.

Ben nodded. "Total douchebags, as the kids say."

"I'm not sure the kids say that anymore, actually," she pointed out, smiling a little in spite of herself. This trip was making her feel seriously geriatric, but at least no one had called her a narc yet. "Anyway, they didn't tell us anything new. They saw Katie at least an hour before she disappeared."

Ben let out a sigh, rubbing his hands over his face.

"What?" she asked.

He glanced down at her.

"Grace, I know you don't want to think badly of Katie," he started, biting his lip as though trying to tease out his next words carefully. "But if she was engaging in risky behaviors, I think we need to explore those angles."

"You think she is, and I quote, 'sleeping off the mother of all hangovers' somewhere?"

"Probably not. But I do think that it's possible she went off with a guy who's bad news rather than being grabbed by a kidnapper."

Ben paused.

Grace continued walking, waiting for him to finish.

"Anyway," he said quickly, "I'm not trying to victim blame here, but I do think that if these guys are telling the truth about her, we need to be open to the possibility that she's not this careful, prudent person you once knew her to be."

Grace's heart began to beat more quickly as her cheeks warmed. She hated what he was saying, but she couldn't deny that he might have a point. Katie Fairman was a lot younger than she was. They were friends and kept in touch, but it was a different kind of closeness than she might have had with her had they been closer in age.

"I guess that's fair," she said at last. "I still don't think she'd let her dad worry like this. And I also don't think she would have had much time to develop a reputation here, seeing as she didn't even arrive until Sunday morning."

"That's a very good point," Ben said, giving her an appreciative glance. "But it's still possible. Going to spring break isn't the wisest decision in the first place, and she came here with Jade. Like Dad would say, your heart is reflected in the company you keep, and frankly, I have little trouble believing what those guys said about Jade."

Grace felt a pang of sadness in the pit of her stomach.

She usually tried to see the good in everyone, but so far, it was difficult to find many redeeming features about Jade. Still, if Katie was her best friend, she had to believe there was something about her that they just hadn't had the chance to see.

"Still," Ben continued. "No matter who they might have hooked up with, how they dressed, how much they drank, or anything else, that doesn't mean they deserved to have something bad happen to–"

Suddenly, Ben stopped short and raised a hand to his brow to block the sun.

"What's wrong?"

Ben didn't need to answer.

As she followed his gaze, she realized at once what he was staring at.

Next to the shoreline, Jade rested on a lounge chair in a neon orange bikini, a bottle of beer in her hand.

Chapter 13

Ben

Ben strode across the beach toward Jade, nearly shoving the meandering college kids out of his way. He could hear Grace behind him, asking him to wait for her, and he slowed a little, glad for the excuse to take a few breaths and calm down.

"Where have you been?" he demanded as he reached Jade's lounge chair, surprised by the anger in his own voice. Not that it wasn't justified. The girl had made their job more difficult for no reason, all while they were searching for her alleged best friend.

Jade sat up halfway, nesting her damp beer bottle in a cup holder beside her. She pushed her sunglasses up onto her head and stretched her arms up slowly, basking in the sun in her skimpy bikini. Ben half expected her to pull out a coconut with a little umbrella straw.

"Can you tell him to, like, chill out?" she asked Grace.

He felt Grace stiffen beside him.

"Jade, we were worried about you. Why didn't you show up last night? Katie is still missing, and we never got to finish discussing the last couple of hours before she disappeared."

Ben glanced over at Grace, hating the worry he saw on her pretty face.

As long as he'd known her, she'd always been so cheerful and carefree. Sure, he complained about it back at the office, especially when he himself was in a foul mood and she was trying to cheer him up. But seeing her so anxious about this case made him feel off kilter, as though the earth had tilted slightly on its axis.

"I had a few too many coolers," Jade said, waving a hand at them as she laid back down on her chair and started scrolling through her Instagram feed. "I went to bed early and slept in. I feel a lot better now, thank you both sooo much for asking."

Grace's mouth fell open, and Ben had the sudden urge to pick up the phone and toss it into the Gulf of Mexico.

"Don't you get what's going on here?" he snapped, nearly tripping over her overstuffed beach bag as he took a step closer. "The girl you say is your best friend is missing. She might be hurt. She might be dead."

He flinched as he said the words aloud, not wanting to so much as utter the possibility of Katie's death in Grace's presence. Not that she wouldn't have already considered it.

Jade ignored him, pausing for several seconds on a looping video about something called the curly girl method.

Grace cleared her throat. When she spoke, her voice was much calmer than Ben's own. "This isn't a TikTok storytime video, Jade. This is real life. Katie needs you to remember everything you can about Monday night."

"I already talked to the cops."

"I know. But sometimes talking it through can jog a fresh memory."

Jade set her phone against her lap, not bothering to exit the app she was on. "We spent the day at the beach. Went swimming, talked to people, laid out.

"When it got closer to dinner time we grabbed a few drinks at a place I forget the name of. There were a few frat guys bothering us, so we left. Maybe you should look into them. They were total creeps. A couple of them wouldn't take no for an answer from either of us."

Ben shot Grace a glance. It seemed that Tom and his crew had been mostly telling the truth.

Grace nodded to Jade. "So you went to the restaurant after that? The Salty Spoon?"

"Yeah. I think it was around nine."

"What did you guys talk about? Did Katie seem upset, or worried about anything?"

Ben was impressed with Grace's interview skills, considering she'd never had any formal training.

He would have asked the same questions himself.

He couldn't help but to think about the way it had felt holding her hand the night before. Even now, in front of what could very well be a suspect, he felt the urge to reach out and touch the soft, tanned skin of her arm.

He leaned down, pretending to toss sand out of his slides as he tried to focus on the task at hand.

Even without Jade present, it would be stupid to go near her again. Last night had been a lapse in judgment on his end, and nothing more.

"She was totally normal, Nancy Drew," Jade said, rolling her eyes at Grace. She reached over to take a sip of her beer before continuing. "We talked about how excited she was to start her new classes in the fall. She switched majors last year, and decided to go into business, just like her dad."

"Was there anything else?" Grace asked.

"Nope," Jade said, picking up her phone again and proceeding to scroll through several videos, giving each one less than a second of her interest before she moved on.

"You went back to the Mistflower after that, then?" Grace pressed.

"I told the cops this already," Jade warned. "Katie said she wasn't feeling well. I offered to take her back to the hotel, but she insisted she was fine to take a cab and crash on her own."

"There weren't any men involved?" Ben asked, shooting Grace an apologetic glance.

"No," Jade said firmly, staring back down at the screen in her lap. "She wasn't feeling well, like I told you. I watched her get into a cab outside of The Salty Spoon."

"What about you? What did you do after that?" Grace asked.

Jade put her phone down again, exasperated.

"Nothing. I just hung out for another half hour or so."

"Hung out with who?" Ben pressed.

"The whole football team," Jade snapped, shoving her phone and sunglasses into her beach bag in one fluid motion. "I already told the cops. I was alone. I hung out at the beach, then went back to the hotel. Later, I couldn't sleep, so I went for another walk. That's all I know."

Alarm bells sounded in Ben's head as Jade got off the lounge chair and shoved her feet into her leopard-print slide sandals.

He didn't remember Detective Hayles saying anything about Jade leaving her hotel room later that night.

Then again, considering the way the man conducted his investigation, it was possible he just hadn't written that detail down.

"Thanks for your help, Jade. I know it's difficult–" Grace started to speak.

"What time did you leave your hotel room for your walk? And when did you get back?" Ben asked quickly, cutting Grace off before she could finish her sentence. He couldn't afford to let his question go unanswered, and Grace probably hadn't picked up on the significance of her words.

She gave him a look he couldn't decode, but he turned to Jade, watching for any telltale signs that the woman was lying. It was difficult to read her when every other word out of her mouth was actively hostile.

"I don't remember."

"Give me your best guess."

"I don't know. Sometime between midnight and one in the morning, maybe?"

"Did you see anyone? Did you go to the beach, or stay on Mistflower property? Did you try to call Katie at that time?"

Jade grabbed her bag and tried to walk past him, but he held his ground.

"I already told the police. I crossed the Mistflower grounds, walked up the beach for a while, and came back. That was it. Now leave me alone," she snapped.

Grace had stepped aside, looking shocked by the drama of the situation, but she snapped into action, leaning forward and resting her hand on the girl's wrist.

"I'm sorry you've been dragged into this," she said. "I know it's probably the last thing you want to deal with when you're trying to get a break from school."

Jade yanked her arm away, avoiding Grace's touch, but she didn't attempt to run.

"Anyway," Grace continued, offering a kind smile, "maybe we can continue this conversation later tonight. I could buy you dinner, and we could go over the last few details."

Ben tried to stop his eyes from bulging out of his head. As much as he knew Grace was better at handling Jade, she'd already stood them up once. This might be the last chance they had to talk to her at all.

"Good idea," he said quickly. "But for right now, can you at least tell us what–"

Jade's eyes filled with anger and she shoved her way between them, hard, not even seeming to notice as her heavy bag smacked into Grace's hip.

"Get a warrant!"

Before they could say more, she was already striding off across the beach, her feet sending sand flying as she rushed toward the boardwalk.

Great.

Ben tightened his hands into fists as anger gripped his chest.

"Well, that wasn't how I thought that would go," Grace said after several seconds had passed, watching Jade's retreating back as she stepped onto the boardwalk.

"Not how you thought it would go?" Ben snapped. "There's an understatement. She didn't tell us anything of use, and before I could get any information on the one clue she gave us–in case you missed it, she went out again that night, right around the time Katie probably went missing–you were inviting her to dinner!"

Grace turned to face him, any hint of a smile falling off of her face in an instant.

"I'm sorry," she said. "I was just trying to–"

His gut coiled with guilt, but he couldn't seem to stop the venom from pouring out.

"Gabe assigned me to this case to get practice in the field. Practice. Because I already know what I'm doing."

He let the words hang in the air, their implication clear.

He expected Grace to snap at him. To remind him of what she had to contribute. To tell him he was being a jerk. Which, of course, he was.

Instead, she sat down on the edge of Jade's abandoned lounge chair, looking out at the ocean. Her expression was stoic, and with her blonde hair cascading down her back, she reminded him of a mermaid on a ship's prow.

All at once, the anger and frustration he felt poured away, leaving behind only shame.

Last night, he'd held her hand. He'd let himself feel things that he'd been holding back for years. He hadn't kissed her, but oh, how he'd wanted to.

As he stared at her, she offered him the slightest hint of a smile, turning the dagger in his chest. He'd been mean to her, and she refused to take the bait, even though an immature, spiteful part of him wanted her to.

He swallowed hard. He was certain now. He really, really couldn't let what had happened between them last night ever happen again. It wasn't fair to her.

She deserved a whole lot better.

"I'm sorry for snapping at you," he said at last, glad that the mingling college students surrounding them allowed no opportunity for a truly awkward silence to arise. "It's not your fault. People who behave like Jade just get under my skin."

Grace nodded, gesturing to the space beside her on the chair. He shook his head, not daring to get any closer to her, at least not until he regained his senses. If he ever could.

"I get what you're saying," she said. "She's an immature, bratty airhead. She doesn't even care that her best friend might have been kidnapped, or even killed."

He winced at the mention of Katie's possible death, but Grace went on.

"But have you ever considered that maybe that's exactly what Jade wants us to think?"

She paused, her eyes eagerly searching his own, no doubt waiting for him to experience the same flash of insight she had. Unfortunately, anger had a way of dulling the edges of his brain.

"What do you mean?" he asked.

"You said it yourself," Grace continued excitedly. "She casually let it slip that she doesn't have an alibi. She can see that unlike the police, we're going to keep digging."

"Right. She probably figures it's better to be forthcoming about a half truth than to end up getting caught in a lie."

"Exactly. And if she's scared of getting caught, it's because she knows there's evidence. Evidence that wouldn't look good for her."

Ben paused, trying to work through everything he'd learned about that night. He assumed that the police would have at least checked the security footage, but even if they hadn't, Mistflower Resort security almost certainly would have.

They would have noticed that Jade had left the room for a second time that night, but seeing as neither Detective Hayles nor Patrick had mentioned it, it must not have seemed important to them.

"She clearly knows there's footage of her coming and leaving again that night," he said, thinking aloud. "So why even mention it to us? It's evidence she would assume we already had."

Grace got up from the lounge chair, her face filled with renewed excitement as she paced back and forth in the sand beside him. "Because Jade isn't an airhead with anger problems. She wants everyone to think she is so we take her testimony at face value."

Ben's brow furrowed. "She must know she's drawing us to pay more attention to the details."

Grace grinned at him. "I actually don't think she realized that, at least not at first. She's not stupid, but she has an inflated ego. It's pretty clear she played Detective Hayles very easily."

"So you think she thought she could do the same with us?"

She nodded. "But then you started pushing her, and she got scared. That's why she bolted. In a way, you being a butthead got us exactly what we needed."

Ben chuckled. "If only it had been a strategic move rather than just me losing my temper. I'm sorry. Again."

For a second, she looked up at him, her cheeks lifting as she smiled.

She was so close. He could reach down and kiss her, give her the apology that he knew they both wanted.

Instead, she reached over and rested her fingers against his arm, which was still enough to make his chest warm. He was sure he was blushing, and thanks to his pale complexion, she could probably notice it.

"You know, just because I've had a little crush on you for years doesn't mean I'm desperate for your approval," she said, letting her touch fall away again. "It's taken me years, but I know who I am. I'm a daughter of the King. I'm not going to disintegrate just because you're a grouch sometimes."

Her tone was light, but still, her words left him reeling.

Her crush on him wasn't a secret, but until she'd said it aloud, he'd somehow doubted it was true.

Even more than that, though, he was struck by the rest of her words–and by the look in her eyes that told him there was more she'd left unsaid.

Grace wanted him to know she was strong and capable. She'd more than proven she had far more investigative insight than he'd assumed. But there was something else, something more hidden behind those dancing blue eyes that made him lose his mind.

He glanced over at her again. He didn't mind how dumb he looked as he stared, lost in thought. He didn't mind the way she slipped her fingers into his like it was the most natural thing in the world. He didn't even mind the annoying music that had started up yet again, turning the peaceful beach into another raucous party.

Grace loved God, and she believed He was looking out for her. He knew that, and he wanted that kind of faith that always seemed just out of reach.

But there was a reason that she'd been scared when she'd seen that fire at the resort, and when she'd braved the bonfires at the beach. A darn good reason.

She was a survivor, and like she said, he wasn't going to break her by mistake.

"So, you have a little crush on me, huh?" he said instead.

"Oh, shut up," she said, laughing as she started toward the boardwalk, half dragging him behind her. "We need to get back to the Mistflower. We need to see that security footage."

Chapter 14

Grace

Grace felt Ben's elbow jabbing into her ribcage as they crowded around the monitor.

"Sorry," he whispered as the Mistflower Resort security guard tapped away at the keyboard, as though the man was deep in concentration and couldn't be disturbed.

Compared to the spacious, beautiful rooms surrounding it, the security office was small and dingy, and clearly not meant for more than one occupant at a time. Grace wondered how the resort could possibly keep the sprawling complex safe with what was clearly a very small team, especially during busy seasons like spring break.

"Here we go," Patrick said at last, reaching over to click the mouse. "And don't tell anyone I showed you. This is against protocol."

Ben nodded. "Not a word."

Grace leaned closer to the screen, which incidentally meant letting her body press against Ben's. She didn't mind.

On the screen was a plain hallway, identical to their own floor, but she recognized the number on the door plate. It was Katie and Jade's room, all right, and the timestamp at the bottom of the screen indicated that it was ten in the morning.

A few seconds later, the girls appeared on the screen, both smiling as they said something to one another. Grace made a mental note of the black Eagles t-shirt that Katie Fairman wore, which contrasted with her pale blonde hair.

She swallowed the unexpected tears that threatened to fall as she watched her friend walking across the screen without a care in the world. There was no time to get sentimental or worry. Katie needed her to be on her A-game.

Still, she was comforted by the way that Ben studied the image intently, searching the girls' relaxed body language for some clue they had missed before.

"Now, you'll see there's a big fat nothing for most of the tape," Patrick said, tapping another key. The timestamp on the bottom of the screen began to speed up. Though there was no sign of either of the girls, at least a dozen other people passed through the space, all of them college students save for one housekeeper who showed up around seven o'clock.

A few seconds later, Patrick reached out and pressed another button.

"As I told the police and as you can see here, there's nothing for most of the day. Detective Hayles said that they tracked most of their movements outside of the resort."

Ben nodded, not pulling his eyes away from the footage now playing at normal speed.

"Anyway, we see Jade come back from dinner right around now."

They all watched as the seconds ticked by. It was

around ten-thirty and, so far, Jade's story was holding up just fine.

They watched as Jade walked into the frame, wearing the pink minidress she'd worn when she left the room the first time. She was alone, and from what Grace could tell on the small screen, her expression looked neutral. Jade slid her room key through the door's lock and went inside, closing it behind her, and the hallway was empty once more.

Grace listened as Patrick's fingers clicked across the keyboard, stealing a glance at Ben. He didn't even catch her gaze. He was too busy staring at the screen, deep in his own thoughts.

The time on the screen sped up again. Several more girls wandered through the frame, giggling together as they made their way out of their hotel rooms, probably headed to the party on the beach. At eleven fifty-three, Patrick slowed the footage.

"Here we go," he said, getting up and gesturing toward his open chair. Grace stepped back, letting Ben have the seat. She may have been the one to realize that they needed to see the footage, but this was definitely Ben's domain.

A few seconds later, the hotel room door swung open on screen, and Jade emerged. Her pink dress was gone, replaced with a navy blue long sleeved shirt, black leggings, and sneakers.

"Hmm. Why the outfit change?" Ben mused aloud. "I doubt it was much cooler on Monday night than it is now."

Grace smiled, glad that Ben was noticing the details that Detective Hayles would have almost certainly missed. Unfortunately, after thinking about it for a minute, she wasn't convinced it was a clue.

"She'd already been back at the hotel for over an hour, and that dress looked really tight. She might have just grabbed something comfortable."

Ben pressed his fist against his forehead, watching as Jade walked away, leaving the hallway empty again. "Yeah, you're probably right."

They watched for a few more minutes, this time with Ben fast-forwarding the footage as Patrick leaned against the wall near the door. Jade returned a little after three in the morning, looking the same as she had when she'd left. Ben tapped a key and hit pause, leaving Jade frozen on the screen in front of the door.

"As I said, there's not much to see," Patrick said apologetically. "If there had been, I would have made sure North Pier PD knew about it."

"We know you would have," Grace said kindly, turning to face the man. "Thank you for your diligence and your help."

Grace glanced over at Ben, feeling embarrassed. She'd thought she had a useful hunch, but instead it was a dead end.

"Anyway," she said brightly, "on to the next clue, I guess."

"Wait," Ben said, swiveling in the chair, his eyes lighting up with excitement. "Do you mind?"

Patrick nodded with a sweep of his hand. "Be my guest."

Ben typed away expertly, bringing the timestamp on the screen back to the moment right before Jade left the hotel for her supposed walk.

"Watch."

Grace leaned in, wishing that the Mistflower Resort had spent more money on high quality computer monitors and less money on artisan hand soap.

She looked over the image of Jade again. This time, she noticed that her sneakers were Sperry brand, but she highly doubted that was the detail Ben had lasered in on.

She saw that the young woman grasped her phone in her hand, and had her hotel room card stuck into one of the side pockets of her jeans.

But in her other hand was a red lanyard and a set of keys.

"Those don't look like car keys," Grace said. "And Donald Fairman told me that Katie and Jade flew here, anyway. What would she need keys for while on vacation?"

"Well I'll be darned," Patrick said, leaning in behind Grace and causing her to rest even more closely against Ben's muscled shoulder. She felt herself blushing, and she was glad that the pleasant security guard was oblivious to the constant hum of electricity that was passing between her and Ben.

"There's something written on it," Ben said, leaning in until his freckled nose nearly bumped the screen. "I can't make it out. You try."

Ben got out of the chair and Grace sat down, squinting at the small plastic fob. It was red to match the lanyard, and she could see that there was a small image and some text, all printed in white.

"The bottom line has an '8', but that's all I can see," she said, shaking her head apologetically.

"I need a copy of this footage," Ben said to Patrick. "Highest res you can crank out of your machine. I have better equipment to analyze it."

Grace raised her eyebrows. She hadn't realized Ben had brought along much more than a laptop, but she wasn't surprised. Back at FBS, Ben was known as a bit of an electronics hoarder, but his various devices, tools, and software often came in handy. Right now, they might just be the key to figuring out their next move.

Patrick looked around guiltily, as though his boss might be hiding behind a potted plant. "Not a word of this to anybody, okay? I mean it. I'm not authorized to share footage with anyone other than the police."

Grace nodded. "You have our word, Patrick. Thank you."

Ben

Ben kept his eyes glued to his monitor screen, listening to the satisfying click of his fingers against the bluetooth keyboard he'd brought along for the trip.

He paused the footage of Jade leaving the hotel room and started moving through it frame by frame, trying to isolate the most essential moment.

"Can you make this work? Is the image clear enough?" Grace asked from behind him, her voice filled with excitement.

She was sitting on his bed, leaning against the back of his chair periodically as she tried to get a better view of the screen. Every time she did, the warmth of her breath against his ear sent shivers through his body.

He didn't turn to answer her. Instead, he sent up a silent prayer. This had to work. If it didn't, they'd be back to interviewing frat bros on the beach. He was getting tired of dead ends.

He opened a new program and dropped a dozen screenshots into it, flipping between them quickly so that it almost looked like film footage again. There was no one still shot that revealed the details on the little red key fob, but together, he hoped it would be enough.

"Okay, here's the magic part," he said, tapping a few more keys.

He heard Grace shifting behind him as a progress bar popped up on the screen. Had there been more space between the desk and his bed, she probably would have started pacing.

He smiled to himself.

He was used to working like this. Back in San Antonio, Grace often showed up at his office unannounced, and lingered behind him while he worked, quite literally breathing down his neck.

Sometimes, she tried to tell him how to better use whatever program he was in, which always drove him crazy, considering she had no idea about most of what he was doing in the first place. It was distracting, and he usually told her so.

He had just never told her the full truth as to why.

He looked at the progress bar again. Fifty-two percent. After several seconds, it moved to fifty-four. He could hear the fans on his laptop kicking on. Though it was a powerful machine, it couldn't top what he had back at the office.

Satisfied that he had a few minutes before he'd get his answers, he turned to Grace.

"You know I hate when you lurk back there," he said, feigning a serious tone. "It's the worst kind of backseat driving."

Grace leaned forward, letting her hair fall over her shoulders. He could smell just a hint of her perfume as her face moved closer to his. "No, you don't."

"Yes, I do," he insisted. "It's distracting."

Grace laughed. "Why? I'm not doing anything."

He knew he should look back at the screen. Half a dozen reasons why this was a bad idea hammered against his mind, but he ignored them.

He lifted a hand to her cheek, letting his thumb brush against her skin as his eyes met hers. "You're short-circuiting my brain. It's dangerous."

"Right. Dangerous. You might blow up your computer or something," she teased as he reached behind her neck, his fingers entangling in her blonde waves.

"Shut up, Hinton," he said, his words coming out less playfully than he'd expected them to sound as he drew her closer.

Somewhere in the back of his head, his rational mind was urging him to cool it. They were alone in a hotel room, three hundred miles from anyone who knew them.

Aside from all of the reasons that they would never work, this was dangerous, and stupid, and they'd regret it.

But he wanted her.

He was beyond denying it, or pretending that if he just kept his distance that their feelings would just fade away.

And she wanted him, too. She always had. She'd said it herself.

Before he could raise a defense, she was kissing him, her soft pink lips moving hungrily against his own. Grace let out a soft sound that reminded him of a kitten's mew as she leaned into his chest, and he could feel his heart pounding in his ears as his body responded to every one of her touches.

The computer pinged loudly once, then twice, then three times.

They froze, and then pulled apart, the magic of the moment bursting like a popped soap bubble.

For several seconds, neither spoke.

As his racing heart began to slow, Grace drew herself back onto the bed, smoothing down her hair.

"I'm–I'm so sorry," she said, looking up at him for only a moment before staring down into her lap. Her cheeks were flushed, and she looked almost as ashamed as he felt.

His gut twisted with guilt. Grace loved Jesus, and though he knew he was no match for her spiritually, he never wanted to do anything to wound her relationship with Him.

"No," he said, shaking his head. "No. It's my fault. I know better, and I shouldn't have let us lose control. It won't happen again. I promise."

Grace gave him a weak smile, though her blue eyes were still filled with storms.

"I'm okay with part of it happening again," he clarified, reaching out to give her hand a squeeze. "But not here. Not where the temptation might get the best of us."

She brightened at his words, and he found some of his worry fading away. God had protected them and, so long as they were prudent, he'd continue to do so.

As for the rest of what he'd just said, he'd just have to figure things out. The list of reasons why he should stay away from her hadn't changed, but he couldn't deny that he wanted to find a loophole.

"Anyway," Grace said, disrupting his thought as she gestured toward the monitor. "Let's see what we've got."

He drew a few deep breaths as he settled back in front of the screen, clicking away a couple of warnings about the laptop's waning battery life. He had time to figure out his feelings for Grace. But Katie Fairman needed him to be focused right now. Every passing hour counted.

"The moment of truth," he said, only half joking as he pulled up the reconstructed video, letting it play at half-speed.

"Whoa," Grace said.

The images weren't perfect, but they were good enough.

The key fob was clear now. He could see a little picture of an anchor, followed by two lines of text.

Ocean Rodeo Marina
Slip #118

Chapter 15

Ben

The Ocean Rodeo Marina was even busier than Ben had expected.

Since the place was on the opposite side of the island from their hotel, they'd decided to drive there, but the only parking space he could find was a good fifteen minute walk away.

At least he had a good excuse to hold Grace's hand as they fought their way through the thick crowd of college students that surrounded the marina's signature restaurant.

He could hardly see the rows of sailboats, yachts, and fishing boats through the throngs of people, but he could imagine how gorgeous the view must have been during the off season.

The smell of seafood wafted through the air, and even though dinnertime was still a few hours off, Ben wished they had time to grab something to go.

"Okay, we seriously need to eat here at some point," Grace said, seeming to read his mind. She paused for a moment, resting her weight against the large statue of a dolphin that sat out front. "Also, once we find Katie, I demand we take a dolphin watching tour."

"It's a date," Ben said, surprised at just how natural the words felt.

Ever since that kiss–or maybe even since that first night on the beach–he couldn't seem to get his head right. Things were moving forward, sure, but he couldn't help but to worry about the blowback that would surely come.

What if he screwed this up, and he lost Grace even as a friend?

Not to mention the fact that if things fell apart between them, it might very well be too awkward to continue working together.

He shuddered internally at the thought of Gabe's potential reaction.

Though Ben tried to act tough, the truth was, his oldest brother scared even him. And if he made them lose their office manager, there was no telling how furious Gabe would be.

"Look. I see the sign we want. Numbers 85 thru 125."

"Hmm?" he said, not exactly comprehending Grace's words.

Seriously, he didn't have time for talk of romantic boat rides to see dolphins frolicking in the sunlight–something he probably would have said was lame had anyone but Grace suggested it. For him and his brothers, the op came first. Always.

On the other hand, when they found Katie and left this island, the reality of the hole he was digging for himself would hit. He couldn't win.

"The slip numbers, dummy," Grace said, giving him an affectionate punch on the arm. "Come on. Let's find 118."

He followed her toward the water, where fortunately the crowd had thinned somewhat, probably because there was no beer being served in the immediate vicinity.

The rows of boats crowded the narrow strip of water between the Texas mainland and island, bobbing pleasantly in the light breeze. Though the weather was perfect this afternoon, Ben assumed that the location of the marina served to protect the watercraft from storms out on the open ocean.

"Found it!" Grace said triumphantly, pointing to a compact but luxurious-looking sailboat. There was a small ramp attached to it so that it was easy to climb aboard, but unfortunately, a metal gate blocked the way. Ben leaned around it as best he could, trying to get a better look.

No one was on the deck that he could see, and he doubted that Jade was lurking in the cabin.

"Whoa," Ben said, running his eyes over the slick hull and shining wooden deck. It definitely looked more expensive than any of the other boats bobbing near it.

Grace walked toward the back. "The Lumeneer II," she announced, wrinkling her nose. "Weird spelling. Shouldn't it be Lumineer?"

"How do you figure?"

"I don't know. I thought maybe it was named after the band."

"Then wouldn't it be Lumineers?"

Grace gave him a funny look. "Hold on. How do you even know who they are? You hate folk music.'"

"That's not true! I like authentic folk music just fine. Like, I don't know, 'Down by the Riverside' or something."

She crossed her arms over her chest and raised her eyebrows, waiting.

"Okay, fine," he laughed. "Asher forced me to listen to that one popular one they have and it grew on me. But if you tell him that, I'll kill you."

"That hey-ho one?"

Before he could answer, Grace started to sing the chorus, and though she hit only about half the notes, it was one of the sweetest sounds he'd ever heard. Especially considering the subject matter of the song.

He cleared his throat.

"Anyway," he said, "I'd love to see why Jade came here that night and had a key for this gate."

He rattled the lock against the metal, noticing that it bore the same anchor logo as the keys the young woman had carried.

Grace raised a hand to her brow and looked along the row of watercraft. The place was quiet, with only a couple people visible on the decks of their boats, and none of them nearby.

"We could swim over and see if there's a ladder or something on the other side," Ben suggested.

"You're gonna brave the potential sharks?" Grace said with a shudder.

"I'm kidding," he said with a grin. "But I was more concerned about the witnesses."

Just then, they heard the sound of a metal gate opening.

They turned and watched as a group of college kids climbed on board a medium-sized fishing boat a few slips down, with the two boys in the rear hauling a truly massive cooler onto the sleek wooden deck.

"Hey, guys, can I talk to you for a second before you take off?" Grace called out to them, already rushing down the dock.

Ben hurried to follow her. Without really thinking about what he was doing, he said a silent prayer that these kids would be more helpful than the rest they'd spoken to.

Maybe Grace's faith was starting to rub off on him. In any case, a little Divine intervention would be great right about now. So far, their investigation had resulted in a lot of questions and not very many answers.

"No hurry," one of the girls on the boat called down to them. "Come on up."

Ben waited behind Grace as she climbed carefully up the boat's ladder.

"No rush, guys," the girl repeated once they'd clambered on board, pushing her bright red sunglasses onto the top of her pale blonde head. "It takes us a bit to get this old lady ready to sail. What can we do for you?"

Ben's chest relaxed as the girl and her friends introduced themselves pleasantly. Were it not for the Louisiana State baseball caps they all wore, he would have assumed they were locals.

After Grace had said hello and accepted their offer of a cold soda, Ben asked them about that night.

Unfortunately, their brief streak of good luck ran out just as quickly as it had begun.

"We just got here on Thursday. Last week." One of the boys flicked a few droplets from his iced water at one of the girls, who promptly whipped him with a rolled up towel. "We stayed out late at the party on Monday. I did run back here to get my hotel room key at one point, but I don't recall seeing anything of note."

Ben nodded, trying not to let his frustration show. He asked the boy a few more questions about which one of them owned the boat, and the girl who had first greeted them chimed in that it belonged to her stepmother. No one seemed to be hiding anything.

"You know," one of the girls who had not spoken yet said, pressing a finger to her lips. "There is someone who might know something."

"Oh, of course!" One of the boys smacked his forehead with his open palm. "I mean, good luck talking to her, but–"

"Who? Talking to who?" Grace interrupted him.

"I don't know her name," he said. "Frankly, we've been referring to her as 'cranky marina lady' ever since we got here. She nearly ripped Corinna's head off for messing up her cleat hitch."

"Well, I know how to do a perfect Ashley Bend," Grace said. "I think I can handle her. Where is she?"

Ben waited as Grace got the directions to the woman's boat, wondering briefly if he should pull out his phone and Google what on earth they were talking about.

"Well, good luck to you both," the girl Ben

assumed was probably Corinna said as they climbed back down onto the dock.

"We've got this," Grace said, flashing her perfect smile.

They gave the kids a final wave goodbye as they headed toward another one of the main dock's jutting arms.

"An Ashley Bend is a kind of knot, by the way," Grace said. "So is a cleat hitch, though that one is a lot simpler. You use it to tie off on those little metal things along the edge of the dock."

Ben nodded. "Right. Makes sense."

Neither spoke for several minutes, both lost in their own thoughts as the afternoon breeze washed over them.

Grace walked a little closer to him, letting her hand brush his own.

He reached out and took it without hesitation, letting their clasped fingers swing between them as they walked, not wanting to say a word.

When it came to knowing how to handle the feelings that he had for Grace, he felt as pathetic as a sailor who didn't know how to tie his shoes.

Grace

"She looks like she could be Dolly's cousin. What do we do?" Grace asked in a stage whisper as she and Ben headed toward the woman's sailboat.

Ben chuckled, but she was only half kidding. She found herself wishing that she was still holding his hand.

The older woman was leaning against the railing of the boat, her long white hair whipping against her face as she stared at them. The woman's expression held no shame and made no apologies. It was clear before they said a single word that this woman not only looked like their head of security back in San Antonio, but shared her intimidating demeanor.

"Who's this now?" the woman called out, squinting at them as they drew up alongside the shabby craft. It looked to be a solid three decades older than the Lumeneer II. At least. "I told Wilson I ain't paying til the fifteenth. We agreed. He owes me big time. You tell 'im that!"

Grace's usual cheerful way of greeting strangers felt stuck in her throat. She had no idea what the lady was talking about, and her tone was not the least bit friendly.

Fortunately, Ben was able to turn on the charm once in a very rare while, and he did so now as he introduced them.

"We were told that you know all of the ins and outs of this place, ma'am." Ben said with a smile, gesturing broadly as though she'd been declared the expert on everything happening on South Padre Island. "We just need a minute of your time to answer a few questions for us."

The woman–her name was Connie–took her sun hat off and started using it to fan her face. "Now I'm no gossip," she warned. "Let's get that good and clear."

"We wouldn't dream of expecting you to gossip," Grace ventured. "But we thought maybe you could help. A friend of ours has been missing since Monday night, and we think one of the sailboats moored here might be related in some way to her disappearance."

She had expected the woman's pinched eyes to soften, but instead they filled with fresh steel. "Y'all are cops? Look, I have my gator license, like I says. But I left it at my house on the mainland, and my tenant isn't interested in letting me come hunt it down. I just need a week."

Gator license?

Grace clamped her jaw shut and looked down at her feet, determined not to laugh. If she looked at Ben, she'd lose it.

"Connie, we're not the police," Ben said smoothly, taking a couple steps closer until he could rest his forearms along the side of the railing a few feet from the woman's own. Grace looked up cautiously, unable to help herself from imaging Ben as some sort of roguish pirate. Possibly one that knew how to hunt an alligator with his bare hands.

Briefly, he recounted what they knew about Katie's disappearance.

"You know, I have noticed that boat over in 118," Connie said at last. "Doesn't really fit in 'round here, does it? Too pretty. Looks like it belongs up in Newport or something."

Grace knotted her fingers together, trying to contain her excitement. Katie was out there somewhere right now, wondering if anyone was coming to rescue her. They desperately needed a real lead.

"When did the Lumeneer II show up in the harbor?" Ben prompted.

Connie's brows knit as she thought about this for several long seconds. "Eight months back, I'd say. Maybe a little less. I remember 'cuz Wilson–he runs the rentals–asked my friend Tyrell if he could move his Boston Whaler! Can you believe that? Says it was taking up too much slip for too little money. All so that fancypants Beneteau could get some shoulder space, and so that Wilson could fix up his rottin' old Catalina. Darn that man!"

"It really is hard to believe, ma'am," Grace cut in quickly, noticing the puzzled look on Ben's face as the woman rattled off a who's who of boating brands. "Do you know who Wilson rented the slip to? Did you ever meet the people who own the Beneteau?"

Connie didn't pause to think. "No, never met 'em, I'm sure of that. Even Wilson said he contacted them through some assistant. Had the nerve to complain 'bout it to Tyrell while he was evicting him! The absolute–"

"Does anyone use the boat? Anyone at all?" Ben asked gruffly.

"Lots of folks. Yuppie types, you know. Guys who think they can't step on board without being dressed head to toe in name-brand sailing gear."

Connie paused, pointing toward her purple t-shirt, which had a rip along the right sleeve and a picture of a bunny nestled among a bed of flowers printed on it. "I've been sailing for fifty years, never needed any of that fancy nonsense. Just gon' get sunbleached anyhow! Don't even tell me about these silly college girls, thinking that just cuz it's warm on the shore, they can wear nothing but one of them thong bikinis out in the middle of the Gulf!"

"Right," Grace said, nodding quickly before Ben could lose his patience completely. Connie's shirt was certainly appropriate. The woman seemed to send the conversation down five rabbit holes for every question she actually answered. "So the people you've seen on that boat are poser types. New money with a desire for the right hobbies. I take it they're not locals?"

Ben gave her an approving glance, sending a few butterflies bouncing through her stomach. She forced her eyes back on Connie, who was now chuckling to herself as she flexed the brim of her hat back and forth.

"Takes new money to spot new money, I guess," she said, gesturing toward the designer tote bag Grace had slung over her shoulder. It seemed the woman knew more about the non-sailing-related 'fancy stuff' than she might have guessed. "Definitely not locals. I know most of the salts on the island."

"So how often have you seen someone take that boat out?" Ben prompted. "Once a week? Once a month?"

Connie nodded. "I'd say once a month sounds about right, but they always use the boat for several days off and on. Lots of evening and night trips. I'm just waitin' for the day someone gets too drunk and we gotta mount a rescue."

Grace suppressed a grin. The woman looked positively thrilled at the possibility.

"This is all helpful, thank you, ma'am," Ben said. "Is there anything else you can tell us?"

Connie ignored him and turned to Grace, looking her up and down. "He your boyfriend?"

She was so surprised by the question that it took her a moment to answer.

"Er, no. A friend. Well, a colleague, but–yeah, he's a friend, too," she stammered.

"My husband died a few years back. Married thirty years."

"I'm sorry to hear that," Ben said, rescuing her from the sudden silence.

"Me too. Just take an old sailor's advice–" she leaned in toward Ben until the front of her hat nearly touched his forehead, "–don't be a coward."

Without another word, the woman headed down into her boat's cabin, closing the door firmly behind her.

Grace looked up at Ben, unsure how to follow up that comment.

Instead, she pointed in the general direction of a nearby food stand and started walking.

He walked next to her, but she stayed just out of reach.

She wanted to talk about everything that had happened between the two of them, but every time she opened her mouth to speak, something made her close it again.

Now that they'd kissed, it felt even harder to know what to say.

She could remember everything about that moment. She remembered how badly she wanted him to keep going, and how badly she wanted to run, all at the same time.

She looked up at the blue sky overhead. She knew that she needed to spend some time talking all of this through with Jesus, but lately, prayer hadn't come easy.

She'd wanted this–wanted Ben–for years. She'd tried to pretend to herself and to everyone else that it was just a crush, something she could joke about, but that had always been a lie.

And now that an actual relationship with him seemed to be on the table, she was terrified.

What if all he felt for her was the same kind of little crush she'd deluded herself into thinking she had?

She sucked in a deep breath, the humid air feeling heavy in her lungs.

That wasn't the scariest possibility.

What if he felt something real?

"Well, that was a bust," Ben said, interrupting her racing thoughts as they sidled into a long line of patrons waiting at the food stand. All at once, Grace noticed the hollow feeling in her stomach. Time had passed quickly. It was nearly dinner time. "I doubt the Lumeneer II is related to Katie's disappearance if it's been here for eight months."

Grace fiddled with her dress, stalling for a few seconds as she tried to clear her thoughts.

"Traffickers do use the water to transport victims over to Mexico," she mused.

"But Katie doesn't fit the profile, like you said," Ben reminded her.

"No, she doesn't. But we can't afford blind spots. I'm staying open to all possibilities."

Neither spoke for a moment as Ben dug in his shorts pocket for his wallet and ordered them each a hot dog.

"Not a dolphin tour, but I'll take it," Grace joked, taking the food and heading toward a nearby picnic table. Ben sat across from her, his expression still serious.

"Even if there's nothing weird about the sailboat, we still don't know why Jade had a key for it, or why she visited it on Monday night, assuming she did."

Grace sighed.

"Obviously, we need to talk to Jade again. Lucky us."

Chapter 16

Ben

Don't be a coward.

The old sailor woman's advice seemed to ring in Ben's ears as he steered their rented SUV along the busy road.

He stole a glance at Grace, who was scrolling on her phone in the passenger seat. On the one hand, he hated that her hand wasn't in his own, but on the other, he was thankful to get a few minutes to think without the distraction of her touch.

"So, how are they holding up without you at the office?" Ben asked, returning his eyes to the lane in front of him as a large truck passed them in the far left lane. He liked that Grace never seemed to worry about the road at all when he was driving, as though she trusted him completely to get them from point A to point B.

"I have about fifty questions in my email and another twenty in my texts," Grace said, laughing. "Other than that? Just swell."

"Despite the overflowing inbox, it'll be nice to go home," he said. "It's beautiful here, but it barely feels like Texas."

"Seriously," Grace said with a nod. "And being in the field is a lot different than I expected."

"How so?"

"Honestly? I'm already starting to miss the routine of going into the office every day. There's an order to the chaos, and I kind of like fitting into the machine rather than having to figure out what to do all the time. Is that bad to say?"

Ben considered this, looking out his window as he made a careful left turn onto the smaller, two-lane road that led back to the resort. "I don't think so. I think we make a big deal in our world about the importance of leadership, and that's well and good, but no one can be a good leader if there are no good followers."

As soon as the words escaped his lips, he realized that maybe he was the one who needed to hear them.

Ever since the incident that had driven him out of the San Antonio police force, he'd hated to rely on anyone else but himself. Accepting his eldest brother's leadership within their company was a constant sore spot, no matter how good of a job Gabe did or how trustworthy he was.

"Ben, watch out!"

It took only a second for Grace's words to sink in, but a second was all that it took.

He heard the roar of an engine as a black truck came up behind them, and before he could figure out what to do, he felt himself jolting forward as the two vehicles made contact.

"Hold on!" he shouted, jamming his foot against the gas pedal.

He heard the engine growing louder as they picked up speed, but it wasn't enough to escape the vehicle behind them. He felt his seatbelt going taut as the truck rammed them a second time.

Grace screamed, but there was no time to look over and see if she was okay. His muscles burned as he gripped the wheel, years of training rushing back to him in a heartbeat even as his conscious mind reeled.

He pushed the vehicle to go even faster, ignoring the jarring sensation as they bucked over an uneven patch of asphalt, but a second later, the truck was on them a third time.

Somewhere deep in his mind where the panic hadn't quite reached, he felt himself offering a prayer.

God, please help us. Please help me get her to safety.

He took several deep breaths as he watched the speedometer's needle moving further and further to the right. "Come on, come on," he muttered to himself, daring to take only a brief glance in the rearview mirror as the truck loomed behind them.

On his left, two vehicles passed in quick succession, probably wondering what on earth was going on in the other lane. Hopefully, they'd call the police. Not that he had time to wait for them to show up and save the day.

On his right was a tight row of palm trees that stood in front of a few office buildings.

There was nowhere to go.

He heard the rumble of the truck's engine again, so loud that it seemed to be sounding from somewhere within his own head.

This time, when the crash came, he felt his fingers losing their grip. He heard Grace's scream, followed by what must have been his own as they slid into the other lane.

He fumbled for the heavy plastic steering wheel again as the sound of a horn pierced the air.

A huge brown van was headed straight for them.

"Ben!" Grace shouted from beside him.

The scent of burning rubber filled his nostrils as the other driver tried to brake, but he knew there was no way he'd be able to stop in time.

At last, he managed to get a firm hold on the wheel.

As he yanked it to the right, all he wanted to do was close his eyes.

Instead, he forced them open, watching as the front wheels hit the edge of the dirt shoulder.

The view out the front window changed from sand to sky as the SUV lifted into the air, and he felt his muscles tensing as he waited for the vehicle to roll.

The seconds slowed, and everything was impossibly quiet.

And then, all at once, the view changed again.

The sky rushed away, and he saw the tail end of their attacker's black truck as it roared up the road.

The car fell back to the ground with a crash that made Ben's jaw hurt, but other than that, he felt just fine.

Thank you, God.

He smelled dust and tasted something metallic, and without meaning to, he started to laugh.

"You're supposed to be the serious one," he heard Grace say beside him, coughing as she reached over to unclip her seatbelt. "What's so funny?"

"Nothing," he said, though he couldn't stop chuckling. "I bit my tongue pretty bad, and it tastes disgusting."

Grace made a face. "But you didn't die."

"I didn't die. *We* didn't die."

Chapter 17

Grace

By the time that they dealt with the aftermath of the car accident and made it back to the Mistflower, it was nearly nine o'clock.

"I'm telling you, she's either not here or not willing to talk," Grace said as Ben pounded on Jade's hotel room door for the fifth time. She tried to keep her tone light, but it was of little use.

Since the accident just a few hours before, they were both on edge. Especially Ben.

"She has something to do with it," he muttered as one of the hotel's maids wheeled her cart past them, giving him a disapproving glance. "I'm sure of it now."

Grace reached over and poked him on the forearm with a manicured fingernail. "You don't know that," she reminded him.

"Who else had any reason to run us off the road? We could have been killed. You could have been killed."

She wished she could tell him he was overreacting, and that everything was fine. Instead, she felt a ripple of renewed fear slithering down her back.

Neither of them had been hurt, but the back of the rented SUV had taken a pummeling. Worse, the van driver in the oncoming lane had suffered whiplash from braking so hard. He'd been a sweetheart about the whole thing, but still, Grace felt terrible that an innocent bystander had ended up in danger due to their investigation.

"This is a good thing," she said. "If someone is trying to scare us off the island, it's because they think we're getting closer to finding out the truth.

We're getting somewhere, even if we can't quite figure out how the pieces fit together yet. It's not the time to back off."

Ben looked down at her, and despite the anxiety that lined his forehead, she could see a little of the usual teasing sparkle in his deep green eyes.

"Who said anything about backing off? I thought you knew me better than that."

Something about the intensity of his gaze as he said it made her think his words may have had more than one meaning.

She wasn't doing a very good job at backing away from him, that much was clear. Every step they took toward one another made it more and more difficult for her to pull away.

"You gonna tell Detective Hayles that Jade took off again?" she asked, hoping to change the subject to something less complicated than her confused heart.

The detective had taken their statement at the scene of the ramming attack and had driven them to the hotel, but she doubted he'd be able to do much about finding the unremarkable black truck.

Ben shook his head. "I'll mention it if anything else comes up, but otherwise, I think you're right. We need to just keep pushing forward on the leads we have."

Grace sighed and leaned against the wall, a wave of exhaustion hitting her anew. Their leads didn't feel particularly substantial at the moment, but they were still wasting time standing here.

"I want to talk to Katie's dad again," she suggested. "Give him an update. He might be able to get in touch with Jade's family, and they might know what she's up to."

Ben made a noncommittal grunt that she chose to interpret as approval. At this point, it was worth a shot, though she had a bad feeling that Jade's family was probably just as unpleasant as she was.

"And what about you?" she prompted.

"I want to dig into the Lumeener II. If we can find out who owns it, we may be able to get more information without talking to Jade at all."

"Good idea," she said brightly, hiking her bag up higher on her shoulder.

She expected Ben to start moving down the hall, but instead he remained stubbornly in place, staring at the little red glowing light on the panel of Jade's hotel room door.

She let several seconds pass in an awkward silence, though she wasn't entirely sure that Ben even noticed she was still standing a foot away.

"Ready to get going?" she said. "The faster we go, the sooner we can sleep. Lord knows we both need it after today."

He ignored her joking tone.

"I could get into her room," he said flatly. "These panels aren't very secure. I can get the screws open with my pocket knife, and from there it's just a few wires to adjust the settings and–"

"You are not breaking the law, Ben," Grace cut him off. "No way. It's not worth it."

"The police won't know. Frankly, I doubt they'd care even if they did."

"That's not the point."

"I'm just trying to find Katie. Jade's clearly hiding something."

Grace moved closer and leaned against Ben's ribs, glad to feel his warmth despite their disagreement. "What if you found something? Are you willing to lie to a judge about where you got your evidence?"

To her relief, he stepped back from the door, turning to her and brushing a lock of hair behind her ear. "Okay. Point taken."

Ben wasn't exactly great with following rules, but he wasn't reckless for the sake of it, either. She was glad he'd chosen to see sense.

"So, how about we separate for an hour or so to follow our leads, and meet for a late dinner?"

She hated the thought of being away from him, but she knew it was precisely why she needed to be. It was way too difficult to think clearly with him around, and almost impossible to take a few quiet minutes with the Lord.

"Grace, we almost got run off the road today," Ben reminded her. "You shouldn't be walking around alone. I don't want you getting hurt."

Her eyes searched his own as she looked up at him.

She'd spent so many years lingering like a shadow behind him, determined to draw out his light. Things had shifted so much in just a couple of days.

"I appreciate your concern," she said softly, trailing her fingertips along his chiseled jawline. "I'll be careful. I promise. I'm going to head right back to my room. I just need a few minutes with Jesus. You keep making me—"

Before she could finish her sentence he'd wrapped his arms around her, pulling her closer until his lips met hers.

She was faintly aware of the sound of a group of kids making their way up the hallway behind them, but she had no desire to acknowledge their presence. Even her tiredness had disappeared. His touch filled her with a different kind of energy, and she wished she could feel it forever.

She pressed her body closer to his, her heart fluttering as he rubbed a hand against her back, allowing the kiss to linger for another few blissful seconds.

At last, she pulled away, more certain than ever that some time for prayer was exactly what she needed.

"Gracie?" Ben said after a moment, his cheeks flushing red.

She reached over and gave his hand a squeeze.

"Everything about this is wonderful," he said, a shy smile tugging at the edge of his lips. "I just thought you should know that."

She gave him a final peck on the cheek before turning away and heading back toward the elevator, her own face beginning to ache from smiling so much.

It was wonderful.

It really, really was.

Ben

"Jesus, forgive me," Ben muttered under his breath as the elevator doors slid shut behind Grace.

He waited for the hall to clear of the last few college boys, trying not to let himself get lost in his thoughts. If he did, he'd talk himself out of what he planned to do.

He reached into his pocket and pulled out the small screwdriver and pair of wire cutters he'd thrown in that morning. From the minute he'd met Jade, he knew he didn't trust her, and he'd been waiting for an opportunity to find out exactly what she was hiding.

Just then, another two girls emerged from a door at the far end of the hall, stage-whispering to one another as they passed behind him. He rolled his eyes as he caught something about his muscles.

All through high school, he'd never had any difficulty attracting female attention. Like his brothers and his cousin Reilly, he had been blessed with Forge genes, and his passion for working out had only increased his physical appeal to the opposite sex.

But finding a woman who actually appreciated his personality was another thing entirely. Not many teenage girls were interested in hearing about his latest PC build, it turned out, and he'd spent most of his time in school sitting at the losers' table.

When he'd met his ex, Mikayla, at the police academy, she was different.

She had been placed for adoption by her mother, who had become pregnant with her at the age of fifteen, and Mikayla ended up in a farming family with several siblings. Over time, she became a bit of a tomboy, more at home hunting deer than playing with Barbies.

When she'd befriended Ben, his nerdy interests hadn't phased her, and it wasn't long before he'd fallen in love–or at least, he thought he had, until she betrayed him and shattered his heart beneath her police-issue patrol boots.

The sound of the pinging elevator followed by laughter jolted Ben out of his thoughts. There was no point in looking back on the past.

Instead, as they so often had, his thoughts turned to Grace.

He couldn't stop himself from smiling as he imagined the way she'd kissed him, looking up at him like he was much bigger than six-foot-three.

Guilt twisted in his gut.

He'd lied to her. He wanted them to separate so that he could dig up more evidence on Jade, and she'd suggested it before he had to say a word.

He was worried about her being on her own. That much was true, especially after the bizarre incident with the truck that afternoon. But he figured she'd be safe enough in her hotel room for an hour or two, and finding the information he sought was more important.

As much as he hated lying to Grace, he was doing this for Katie Fairman. And if getting more information on what Jade was up to led to them finding her, he knew that all would be forgiven.

At last, the hall was completely empty.

He used the screwdriver on the door's lock panel, working as quickly as he could without looking up. Though there was a small chance security could see what he was doing on camera, he doubted they were going to bother checking this particular hallway again. It was a risk he just had to take.

Finally, he was able to pull back the metal casing, revealing several thin wires in various colors. He closed his eyes for a moment before taking hold of his wire cutters, recalling the manufacturer diagrams he'd looked at earlier.

A minute or two later, he had finished his task and screwed the metal plate back into place.

He reached into his pocket again and pulled out the plain black swipe card he had programmed the night before. With just two wires cut, it would now function as a master key to any of the rooms at the Mistflower Resort.

With a final glance over his shoulder he slid the card through the reader, a grin breaking on his face as a small green light blinked at him.

Once he was in, his first thought was that sharing a room with Asher and Cameron growing up could have been a whole lot worse.

Jade was unbelievably messy.

Clothing, bathing suits, and mismatched shoes covered the carpeted floor. The desk was stacked with various plastic bottles, makeup brushes, eyeshadow pots, and tubes of lipstick. The bottom edge of the mirror was covered with dark brown face powder, and a smear of some kind of cream makeup sullied the white light switch to a nearby lamp. At his feet, he could see a streak of glittery blue powder that had somehow become pressed into the fibers of the carpet.

He made a silent promise to himself never to complain again about the makeup collection Grace stored behind the reception desk at FBS. At least she had the decency to keep the lids on.

He let out a sigh as he started looking through the space. He tried not to leave anything out of place, but his caution was slowing his search, and he doubted she'd be able to notice anything amiss among such clutter.

Within fifteen minutes, he was digging through her suitcases with little care, tossing clothes out onto the large unmade bed and stuffing them back in when he was done.

He paused to peer out the peephole of the door every few minutes. There was no sign of Jade, but so far, his entire break-in had proven pointless. He couldn't find so much as a sheet of paper, let alone a cell phone or laptop.

Either Jade had nothing to do with Katie's disappearance, or she was a whole lot smarter and more careful than he'd first assumed.

The sudden sound of his phone jangling loudly from within his pocket almost stopped his heart.

He hit the green button to answer without so much as looking at the screen, desperate to silence it.

"Yo, Benny boy," came Asher's voice in his ear. As usual, his twin brother sounded about as serious as an episode of Seinfeld. "How's the tropical island treating you?"

"We still haven't found the missing girl," he said, fresh guilt welling up within him as his adrenaline began to calm once more.

He'd lied to Grace, and for what? So far, his criminal activities had been nothing but a waste of time. And that was assuming Jade didn't become suspicious when she saw the place.

"I figured," Asher said. "Gabe updated us. I just wanted to check in, is all."

Somewhere in the background, Ben could hear one of his brother's favorite obscure 90s grunge albums playing. The spring break party music was about ten times more annoying than his brother's worst playlists, and that was saying something.

As Asher updated him on the latest happenings back in San Antonio, Ben started unpacking and repacking the final suitcase Jade had left on the bed. His stomach was beginning to growl with hunger. A late evening dinner with Grace sounded perfect right about now. Assuming she was still awake.

"So, how's all of the alone time with our missing office manager?" Asher said, seeming to read his thoughts.

"Oh–uh–it's been fun," he said quickly, wishing he'd used a more appropriate adjective to describe a missing person's investigation. "I mean, despite all the sand and drunken college kids, it's beautiful here."

"Ah, so only the island is beautiful, and not the woman you're sharing it with?" Asher teased.

"Whatever, bro. How's it going with that girl you were seeing?"

"Surprise! She cheated on me."

"You don't exactly sound torn up," Ben said carefully. His twin had a way of attracting the worst women possible, and he suspected that Asher set himself up for failure to avoid having to actually commit. Not that he'd say it out loud. Usually, he left the psychoanalyzing and nagging to Gabe.

"I mean, Dad keeps telling me that I won't find the love of my life at a rock concert, and I keep ignoring him. Not that I'm looking for her or anything."

Ben rolled his eyes. He might not exactly have his own love life sorted out perfectly, but he was glad he wasn't spending his Friday nights in a sweaty mob like his brother so often did.

He was about to tell Asher as much when he heard the sound of scuffling shoes in the hall.

He bit back a curse as he headed for the peephole, hoping it was nothing but another passing gaggle of girls.

"Look, bro, I'll call you back," he whispered into the phone, hanging up without giving his brother a chance to say goodbye as he peered through the opening.

It wasn't Jade standing on the other side of the door.

It was Grace.

Chapter 18

Grace

Grace stood with her arms folded over her chest, waiting for Ben to respond to her knock.

Still, she was surprised by the sadness that flooded through her body when he pulled open the door, as though a part of her had been holding on to hope that he wasn't lying to her after all.

"Hey," Ben said, giving her a smile that didn't reach his eyes. "I thought you'd still be a little bit longer. I was going to come ask you if you wanted to get some food."

Ignoring the growing hunger that had replaced her earlier tiredness, she reached into her tote bag and took out her phone, holding it up in front of his face for emphasis. "It's been over an hour. And, yes, despite my reputation, I am capable of finishing my work early now and then."

He looked at her like a deer about to be struck by an 18-wheeler, and despite her annoyance, she found herself softening her tone.

"I knocked at your hotel room door and you weren't there, and then I realized I dropped my sunglasses somewhere. I figured they could be here."

"And you heard me talking to Asher."

She sucked in a breath. "Yup. Pretty much."

She rubbed at the goosebumps that had arisen on her upper arms, feeling suddenly chilly.

He had lied to her face.

As she waited for him to lock up the room with some small tools and a fake key card, she found her thoughts wandering back to the kisses they'd shared.

They'd been perfect, and just enough, even when she could tell that they both wanted more.

"I'm sorry, Grace," Ben said as the door closed with a soft click. "I shouldn't have broken in. You're right. It wasn't worth it. I didn't find anything, anyway."

She could see by the sadness in his eyes that he was sorry.

But for once, she struggled to find the energy to forgive.

She had spent years pining after him, trying to get him to see her as more than a friend.

Things felt so easy when Ben was just a crush, a welcome distraction during a long workday. But now that things had actually changed between them, she was no longer sure about anything.

She knew she wanted to be with a man who brought her closer to Christ. Ben had lied to her.

And he had lied because he couldn't even bother to tell her why he disagreed with her opinion.

It hurt.

It wasn't the first time in her life where someone saw her as nothing more than a pretty blonde with nice clothes.

She just had never expected Ben to be the one to make her feel that way.

"Hey. Can we talk about this?" Ben said, reaching for her hand as she began to make her way back down the hall.

"I'm fine, okay?"

She hoped that the smile plastered on her face would hide the hollowness she was feeling. One mistake didn't prove she'd been wrong about him. She'd just have to give things between them a little more thought, and in any case, they had more important things to worry about right now.

"So," Grace said, "Did you actually get a chance to dig into the Lumeneer II?"

Ben flashed her a guilty look.

"No worries," she added quickly. "I called Katie's dad in China–I had been wanting to check in with him anyway–and I figured maybe he could give us some background info on Jade."

"Good thinking."

She allowed Ben to steer her into the elevator with a gentle hand against her back. Despite her frustration with him at the moment, his touch was just as wonderful as ever. It was infuriating.

"Anyway," she said, trying to refocus on the questions at hand, "turns out Jade's father Craig works for some huge company called Lumen. Apparently, the company owns several boats that they keep in various ports for entertaining clients and so on."

She paused, relishing Ben's approving glance in spite of herself. She wished that she'd called Donald Fairman about Jade earlier.

"Ah, the Lumeneer II. Makes sense."

"He told me that Katie and Jade were borrowing it for spring break, so he was surprised when I told him that Jade lied about taking it out. But you know what was strange?"

"What?"

"Donald Fairman was acting so shifty for the entire phone call. Every time I asked him a question, I got the feeling he just wanted me to shut up. But at the same time, he admitted to me that he and Jade's dad are good friends. Craig

Gorsky has been a longtime mentee of his, in fact."

"Interesting," Ben said as they strode out of the elevator and into the lobby of the hotel. "I think we need to talk to Jade's dad ASAP."

"Way ahead of you. I called Craig right after hanging up with Donald, and he was even more standoffish. He only kept me on the phone for about five minutes. I did find out that Jade's mother is deceased, and he confirmed that the girls had use of the boat."

"Did he know why she might have lied about it?"

Grace shook her head. "He said he had no idea, but that he'd talk to her about it. I tried to tell him that her behavior is actively hurting our search for Katie Fairman, but it seemed to fall on deaf ears. He acted like she was just a typical moody teenager."

Ben let out a snort. "Jade has to be at least twenty. And I don't know any teenagers with her level of bad attitude, anyway."

"Agreed. But it's not like I was going to tell him that."

"Fair enough. So, what's next?"

Ben looked down at her expectantly as they stepped out into the humid island air, his hand still gripping her own. She could see in his face that he was sorry for dismissing her earlier.

Maybe he really did want to hear what she had to say, but she wasn't going to let him off the hook so easily.

She'd just have to wait and see what happened next.

The last time she'd failed to listen to her gut, a church had been blasted to smithereens, and she'd found herself buried beneath the rubble.

She wasn't going back to that again.

Not ever.

Not even for Ben Forge.

Chapter 19

Craig

The phone vibrated against the nightstand, dancing across the smooth surface as a familiar name glowed on the screen.

Craig Gorsky took a few slow breaths.

He stuck a bookmark between the pages of the novel he'd been trying to read for the last hour, too distracted to gather the meaning of the sentences as his eyes ran across the letters.

"Hi, Donald," he said at last as he lifted the phone to his ear. "How are you doing?"

He could hear Fairman's heavy breaths on the other end of the line, making him sound even more stressed than Craig felt. It was morning in China, and Donald should have been at work by now, slinging AveroTech microchips for his latest desperate business deal. If he was calling, something was probably wrong.

He climbed out of his bed and sauntered over to the window of his boat's most luxurious cabin, glancing out at the water. An orange and purple haze lingered along the horizon, slowly following the sun as it bowed out of sight.

Another day had passed, and everyone was still alive.

"I just got a phone call from the private security people investigating Katie's disappearance."

"Oh? Is that surprising?" Craig said, trying to keep his tone neutral as fresh guilt bit at his insides.

"It was when they mentioned Lumen," Donald replied, his voice rising in pitch with each word.

"Calm down, please," Craig said calmly, his words not quite a command. "I know. They already called me."

Donald was silent on the other end of the line.

"Well, that was quick," he muttered after a moment.

"You didn't mention Senera, did you?" Craig asked.

"Do you think I'm an idiot?"

"No, I don't," Craig replied. "We have nothing to worry about. It's common knowledge that you mentored me and that we've remained friends."

"It's hardly the mere fact of our friendship that threatens the future of my company!" Donald snapped again.

Craig could picture him pacing around the lobby of some hotel in Shanghai, dabbing at his brow with a handkerchief like a Xanax-popping businessman in a movie. Despite his guilt about orchestrating Katie's kidnapping, he was quickly losing patience with the older man.

"We made sure that there's nothing to find, Donald. You know that. Even if someone looked at AveroTech's financials, all they'd find is typical intercorporate investment. There's no way to prove you knew anything you shouldn't have. And why would anyone look, anyway? They're worried about finding your daughter, not about your company's finances."

Every mention of Katie made Craig's heart ache.

"I'm sorry," Donald said after a moment, sounding a little more in control of himself. "I'm not sleeping well. I miss Katie. I just want her home."

"Any father would. But you know she'd want you to be focused on nailing this deal. Think of her future."

Craig swallowed, hating the words that were coming out. He wanted to find a way that Katie Fairman got to go home, but he didn't dare promise anything.

He felt like bursting into laughter at the absurdity of it all. He could abduct his friend's daughter, but lying to him seemed to be beyond the pale.

"You're right, of course," Donald sighed into the phone. "I hired the best to find her. Right now, my company needs me to get it together."

"That's the spirit."

Craig let Donald chat for another minute or two before he said his goodbyes, peering out the boat's window again at the now dark sky.

He sighed to himself. For the moment, the chaos was contained, but deep down he felt just as panicked as Donald sounded. There were too many moving pieces, too many gears that had to fit exactly into place. All it would take was a single screw up, and his life would be over.

The door to his cabin swung open behind him without so much as a knock, and his daughter slipped into the room.

"Hi, Jade," he said flatly, knowing that she had probably been listening at his door for the entire phone call. He wasn't in the mood for a fight with her, but he couldn't blame her entirely for butting in.

Her life was on the line, too.

"He needs to chill," she said, gesturing to the phone Craig still gripped in his hand. "He's gonna give himself an ulcer or whatever."

"Had you gotten a rental boat like I told you to instead of using the Lumeneer II to get here, the security team might have never thought to look into Lumen at all," he pointed out.

"I'll be more careful next time."

"It's a little late for that," he said. "The damage has been done. All we can do is hope that they don't start digging too deeply."

"But I thought there was no way anyone could prove anything?" his daughter's voice had taken on the whiny tone he hated.

"Letting Donald freak out will make things worse for everyone," he snapped. "How I feel about your screwup is irrelevant."

Instead of backing away at the harshness of his tone, she took a couple steps closer to him, her dark brown eyes filled with warning.

As he so often did, he marveled that Jade was her mother's daughter.

They looked almost identical–the same smooth brown skin, the same black hair, the same teasing smile–but that was where the similarities ended.

His wife had been gentle. Jade was as dangerous as a midnight storm at sea.

"You know what we have to do about Katie," she said, her face revealing no emotion. "I don't like it either, but we don't have a choice."

"No. I'm not a murderer, and neither are you."

"That huge guy and the blonde chick from San Antonio are not going to back down," she cut him off. "They're going to keep looking for her. And if there's something to find, eventually, they'll find it. You need to man up and do what you have to do to protect us."

Without giving him a chance to protest, she turned heel and marched out of the room, closing the door behind her.

The room was silent and calm once more, as though the human windstorm that had just torn through it had never existed at all.

Ever since his wife had died, he'd messed up raising Jade. One day at a time, he'd let her grow into the spoiled, capricious woman she now was.

The spitting image of her mother, the daughter he still so deeply loved, despite the darkness that seemed to flow from her heart.

And now he was trapped.

Either he lost everything, likely including their lives, or Katie Fairman had to be silenced.

Permanently.

Craig walked over to the bed and laid back on it, staring at the ceiling, falling into his thoughts once again.

If there was another way out of this, he had to think of it.

They were running out of time.

Chapter 20

Ben

The screen of Ben's laptop glowed brightly as several of the overhead lights clicked off one by one.

"I think they're closing up," Grace said, stretching her arms over her head and letting out a yawn.

They were seated in a small cafe attached to the lobby of their hotel, researching online for any information they could find about Jade Gorsky, her father, and the massive tech company, Lumen, that he worked for.

Well, Ben was researching. Grace was seated a couple feet away from him, nursing a cup of green tea and looking over his shoulder whenever the urge struck.

For once, he felt no annoyance at her backseat Google searching.

She had every reason to be upset with him for lying to her.

Grace was usually quick to forgive, eager to make sure everything was okay between her and whoever she was mad at, but tonight, she was different. She didn't quite look angry, but he could tell she wasn't pleased with him.

Still, she'd insisted on staying, no matter how many times he urged her to get some sleep.

He stole a glance in her direction.

Maybe she was just afraid to be alone. But he couldn't help but to hope that despite his screwup, things would be right with them again.

Not that he knew what that really meant, or how he was supposed to feel. Everything in his heart was a tangled mess that he couldn't quite work out.

"So, what's the verdict?" Grace asked, watching as a small man in a polo shirt pushed a large broom across the cafe's floor.

Ben cleared his throat and used the laptop's trackpad to scroll to the top of the document he'd been putting together.

"I'm not sure if I have a verdict," he said carefully. "But there's some interesting stuff here. Apparently, Craig Gorsky found some success at a very young age–basically right out of college–but his wife died before he got hired at Lumen and really made it. Obviously, this was hard on both him and his daughter. I guess she and Katie Fairman have losing their moms in common."

He paused for a moment and glanced at Grace. As he suspected, her face was awash with sympathy. No matter how unpleasant Jade had been toward them, he didn't blame her.

He knew for himself how painful it was to lose a mother, but he had at least been several years into adulthood when Mary Forge had passed away.

"Things fell apart for Jade by the time she hit high school. She was kicked out of four of them, and got arrested for petty offenses several times. Somehow, she graduated and made her way to UT Austin. My guess would be parental help and a lot of networking."

"Definitely."

"Anyway, Craig is now chairman of the board at Lumen, which is where things get interesting."

He paused, raising an eyebrow in expectation until Grace gave him a quick swat on the arm. "Come on, tell me!" she said, sounding almost as playful as she usually did. The simple, teasing gesture filled him with so much hope that it took him several seconds to locate where he was on the page.

"Right. Uh, so, as it turns out, Lumen is expanding into the med-tech space. And you'll never guess which company they've recently acquired."

"Just tell me, Forge," Grace commanded, tilting her paper cup of tea upward as she tried to coax out the final drops.

"Senera."

Grace set the tea down.

"Senera *Pharmaceuticals?*"

He nodded. "The very same. And apparently Craig isn't happy about the acquisition at all. It's caused some drama on their board."

"We should probably call Gabe," Grace said. "That's a pretty striking coincidence. And maybe Asher or Reilly might remember if Lumen was somehow involved in the Senera case. The name didn't ring a bell for me, but I was just filing the paperwork at the time."

"I'll call him," he agreed. "But I don't want to tell him about the thing with the truck."

Grace sat back in her chair and crossed her arms over her chest, waiting as the short man cleaning the cafe passed behind their table with a bucket and mop.

"What?" Ben prompted.

"You know what," Grace said.

"No, I don't," he said. She rolled her eyes at his obvious fib. "Okay, fine, I do. You want me to be honest with him. But you know how he is. You know how he's gonna react."

"Oh, believe me, I know," Grace said, a half smile tugging at her pink lips. "But we're gonna tell him anyway. It's the right thing to do."

For a long moment, she just looked at him, her pretty blue eyes intense and playful at the same time. Her gaze was a challenge, that much was clear.

He could lean toward her, take her hand in his, press his lips against hers.

Instead, he picked his phone up off the table and called Gabe.

Chapter 21

Grace

The seatbelt pressed against Grace's chest, but this time, the sensation brought comfort rather than panic. After being run off the road, she had a new appreciation for the gentle restraint.

"This car is actually pretty ok," she said, glancing over at Ben as he maneuvered the basic black rental sedan onto a busy street near the hotel. "I was half expecting Gabe to tell us to take up cycling."

Ben smiled, but said nothing. She yawned, wiping carefully at her eyes so as not to smudge the mascara she'd quickly applied before leaving her room. He had knocked on her door bright and early, and part of her wished she'd taken him up on his suggestion for her to go to bed while he stayed up late doing research on the Gorskys.

"Is there any particular reason you felt the need to leave so early?" she asked, yawning again mid-sentence. "I thought Asher's flight wasn't landing until ten."

"There's a sunrise to see first," Ben said, his expression unreadable as he made his way through the light morning traffic.

The statement was so out of character that she was briefly rendered speechless.

Ben could appreciate a classical symphony, sure. Maybe even a Renaissance painting or something. But to wake up early, on purpose, to watch the sun?

She was thankful for the opportunity to hide her stunned reaction as she reached into her bag in search of lip gloss. Maybe he was just anxious about going near another airport.

As much as she was sure he'd like to see his twin, she knew he wasn't happy that their big brother had insisted on sending in backup.

Grace hadn't even bothered trying to argue. Gabe usually got extra paranoid whenever anyone was involved in an assignment away from their home base in San Antonio. Though they'd escaped being run off the road largely unscathed, there was no guarantee that the threats wouldn't escalate. And considering how confusing things had gotten between her and Ben, it might not be so bad having Asher around to break up some of the tension.

She glanced out the window, wondering where he was planning to take her. She recognized that they were in the general area of the Ocean Rodeo Marina. Perhaps he had stayed up even later and had discovered some shocking new piece of information?

This assumption was short lived, however, as Ben continued to maneuver the car toward the southern end of the island. They passed several rows of RVs and trailers–no doubt some kind of camping park–until finally Grace could see the water.

"This is the spot," Ben said, pulling the car into a parking space.

"Here?" she asked, pulling a face. The palm trees and the ocean were beautiful, of course, but it was hardly the most idyllic location they'd seen so far.

Ben chuckled. "Sorry, princess. I know this won't meet your standard for viewing a tropical sunrise," he joked.

"You know what I mean!" she said, feigning a stern expression as he gestured in the direction of the gulf and started walking.

It felt good to joke with him again, even a little, but she still didn't feel ready to reach out for his hand. Instead, she followed a few steps behind him, watching the campers.

She could see two older ladies in sun visors jogging up the road, quickly outrun by a pack of six college girls in trendy athleisure, laughing loudly as they discussed their party plans for the night. She imagined how peaceful the island must be during the off season, and wondered if she could convince her parents to choose it for their next family vacation destination.

"So," Ben said, stopping short and turning to face her. "What do you think?"

Finally, she realized why he had dragged her out here.

A statue of Jesus stood near the water, his arms outstretched as though blessing the blue expanse spread out before him as the sun rose.

"It's called *El Cristo de los Pescadores*, or 'Christ of the Fishermen'," he explained, looking suddenly shy.

Grace's heart felt as though it might burst out of her chest as she walked forward, examining the statue more closely. It had gone green with age, and sat atop a base made of square stones with several plaques attached.

"Father! Receive the souls of these brave fishermen who have sailed through this pass and never returned," she read aloud, glancing up at the calm face of Jesus.

It was beautiful. And when so much had already gone wrong on this investigation, it was just the reminder she needed that her Savior was walking with her in every difficulty.

"It's hardly a world-class monument or anything," Ben said, speaking so quickly that he almost stammered. "It's only like ten feet tall, and I mean, it's next to a bunch of parking lots, but I thought you'd want to see it anyway."

She tore her eyes from the statue and turned toward him, her feet bringing her closer before her mind had time to think things through. Her hands found his broad, firm chest, and he smelled so good that she wondered if he'd actually purchased cologne.

"I love it," she said softly. "Thank you."

His hands found her waist, pulling her in. She savored the strength of his hands as they held her. Nothing and no one could hurt her here, not while he was protecting her. Since Indonesia, she'd gotten used to the constant hum of worry that filled her heart. With him, it always faded away like mist.

She tilted her face upward, releasing a murmur of longing as their faces moved closer together.

And then, all at once, he released her and pulled away, his jaw set firm.

She flinched, stepping backward as though she'd been struck.

She could hear nothing but the lapping of the gentle waves against the rocks and the hum of a nearby generator. His face was unreadable, like he'd slipped his mask back on without her noticing, hiding the true person beneath a blank and hollow shell.

"What's wrong?" she asked at last, feeling suddenly exposed and foolish as the group of chattering girls ran past them a second time. Goosebumps prickled along her arms, and she clutched them around her chest, suddenly annoyed by the morning's breeze.

"Nothing," Ben said, his voice devoid of emotion.

"I'm sorry. I thought you wanted me to."

"Gracie, it's not that, okay?" he said, rubbing a hand over his forehead. "Of course I wanted to. It's not you. I mean it. It's not."

"So what is it?" she demanded, growing more frustrated by the second. She stole a glance at the statue. The aged copper Jesus continued to look down on them with his slight, serene smile.

"I just freaked out a bit. I'm sorry," Ben said. "I didn't mean to hurt you."

"Well, you did."

Grace closed her eyes for two impossibly long seconds, inhaling the smell of salt spray.

He'd hurt her already when he lied to her, but she'd been ready to forget all of that. Now, she was even more confused than she'd been when she woke up this morning.

"I've liked you for years, okay?" he said, reaching up and resting his hand gently on her shoulder. "I have, and I was too scared to act on it. Too scared to mess up a good thing, both for us as friends and for the company. But here? Without everyone staring at us and teasing us and wondering? It felt different."

"So why can't you just kiss me and stop playing games?" Grace snapped.

"Because it's not that simple," Ben said. He was pleading now. "It's complicated."

A part of her wanted to act just how she normally would.

She'd tell him everything was okay, she'd be understanding, gentle, sweet. The Grace that everyone knew, who forgave easily and who went through life smiling.

But the truth was, she was so tired of having to be that person all the time. She was exhausted by the all day, every day task of hiding away her fear, doubt, and anxiety deep within her where no one ever even tried to look. And the one person who brought her calm had just rejected her. Again.

"It's not complicated, Ben," she said at last, her voice calm. "You're just a coward."

His face went even paler than usual, and the hurt in his green eyes was like a knife to her own wounded heart, but she wouldn't take the words back.

They were cruel, but they were true.

He needed to hear them.

She turned and started to walk along the coast in the opposite direction of their car, casting a final glance at the statue behind her.

The Bible said that a good husband would love his wife like Christ loved the church.

Christ left the ninety-nine and went after the one lost sheep. He didn't sit around waiting for his bride to chase him. He pursued her, even to death on a cross.

And that was the love she wanted. No matter how broken she was, no matter how little she deserved it, she was done settling for anything less than the standard God had set.

"Come on, stop it," Ben said after a moment, jogging a few paces until he'd caught up with her. "Don't just run off. Let me take you back to the hotel, please."

"You'll be late picking Asher up. Just go. I'll meet you guys later."

She kept walking, picking up her pace. The puppy-dog sadness in his eyes was too much to bear. If she didn't get away from him, she'd lose her resolve, and they'd end up caught in the same place they'd started. Enough was enough.

"Grace, it's dangerous to go wandering around here alone," he called out behind her. "Be reasonable."

"I'll be fine," she said, continuing to look straight ahead as several tears began to fall. She wouldn't let him see her crying over him like this. He may have been acting like a coward, but she was quickly realizing that she was the one who was really pathetic.

She kept walking past row after row of trailers in a generally northern direction. She didn't know exactly where she was going, but it was a small island, and she was confident she could figure it out.

Her flip-flops thwacked against the cement of the sidewalk, the annoying sound warring with the thoughts swirling through her mind.

Somewhere behind her, the eyes of the Christ of the Fishermen statue seemed to burn into her back, condemning her.

She knew she should pray for guidance instead of wallowing in her frustration, but she couldn't bring herself to say even a single word to Jesus. Not yet. Maybe after she'd walked a couple of miles.

Unfortunately, her right flip-flop had already given her a blister.

Just as she decided to sit down on a bench and

give her sore foot a rest, however, she realized that she wasn't alone after all.

Ben was leaning against a nearby lamppost, his arms crossed over his broad chest.

"I don't want to miss Asher's flight, but I will if I have to," he called out loudly, ignoring the stares of two older men walking their dogs.

"Fine. You win."

"Thank you," he said, jogging in her direction. "Just let me get you to the hotel and I'll leave you alone until you're ready to forgive me. I promise."

She got to her feet, removing the offending shoe. On any other day, she would have asked him to carry her to the car. As it was, she was still mad.

She'd let him drive her back to the Mistflower, but that was it.

Chapter 22

Grace

True to his word, Ben had been silent in the car, and had led Grace up to her hotel room without any attempts to grovel.

When he'd finally left for the airport–after making her promise not to leave her room even for five minutes until he got back–she'd collapsed onto the bed, surprised by how suddenly exhaustion had hit.

The flame of anger that had burned so strongly was already beginning to lose its heat, and despite her earlier promises to herself, she knew she had to hear Ben out. Even if it meant that he might disappoint her again.

After staring at the ceiling, debating whether or not she should take a nap, Grace decided that a shower was just what she needed. There were few situations in life that a long, hot shower in a luxurious resort couldn't improve.

When she opened the door to the dark, cavernous bathroom, however, she was struck by a sudden feeling of unease.

Ignoring the shiver that rolled across her shoulders, she stepped across the tile toward the vanity. Her makeup was just as she'd left it, a jumbled mess of lip glosses, powder compacts, and at least four different palettes of eyeshadow in both shimmering and matte finishes.

Chill. There's nothing to worry about.

Just as she reached for the switch that would bathe the room in comforting light, she felt a hand grabbing around her neck from behind, and then another.

She tried to yell as the pressure intensified, but only a gasp escaped her lips.

Her heart was pounding now as panic began to take hold. She tried to steady herself on both feet, but whoever was holding her yanked her body to the side, almost making her fall over on the sleek floor.

She tried to turn to see who was grabbing her, but the man's grip was rock solid, and in any case, he had been well hidden in the shadows. He wasn't quite strangling her. She could still breathe. But she wasn't about to wait around for him to take things up a notch.

She drew as much of a deep breath as she could and lashed out, managing to strike backward with her elbow. She heard the man groan as she felt her bone connecting with his gut, and his grip loosened just slightly.

"Help!" she shouted, the attempt at a scream coming out as little more than a rasp. "Help!"

The man's hands tightened again, cutting off her pleas.

She could feel warm air as his lips pressed against her ear. "If you scream again, I'll have no choice but to do this the hard way," he said in a whisper. "And if I do that, the boss will be furious. So just be quiet. Nod if you understand."

Grace did so, letting her shoulders slouch as though she was admitting defeat and resisting the urge to turn and get a look at her assailant.

"Good. Stay still. I'm not gonna hurt you," the man said, sounding relieved as he loosened his grip on her neck.

Before she could decide how to respond, she felt a jolt of sharp pain in her left shoulder.

It took her only about a second to realize that she'd just been injected with something.

She managed to take only a single step before everything faded into blackness.

Ben

The drive to nearby Brownsville felt like it took forever. With every mile further away from Grace he got, the more anxious he became.

According to his phone app, Asher's flight had been delayed by about twenty minutes. Though he doubted coffee would do much to calm his nerves, it would be better than sitting in the tiny airport's waiting area empty-handed.

"Can I get a large dark roast with two creamers?" he said as he pulled into the drive through of a popular coffee shop chain.

"A venti drip, got it. Okay, sir, will that be Verona, Espresso, or Italian?"

The guy on the speaker sounded nice, and he resisted his immediate urge to make a cutting remark about needless complexity. Seriously, why did coffee shops have to be so pretentious? And why was the most pretentious one located on every street corner in America?

"Whatever one you recommend would be great, thanks," he said instead, pulling out his phone for the tenth time in as many minutes as he waited for the car ahead of him to move. He wanted to give Grace space, but considering everything that was going on, he couldn't help but to worry about her.

Once he paid for his Caffé Verona, he sent her a quick text to ask if everything was okay before pulling out of the parking lot and obeying the commands of his GPS for the next several minutes.

His hatred of flying notwithstanding, Ben generally felt the same way about airports as he did about sand, top forty music, and people who put sweaters on their dogs.

Fortunately, Brownsville International was more tolerable than most of the other places he'd been. The airport was tiny, and at this time of morning on a weekday, he passed only about a dozen passengers as he settled into a seat near a giant map of the United States.

He picked up his phone again as he sipped his coffee. No answer.

After a couple minutes of going back and forth with himself, he finally tried calling her. No answer again. He made one more call and left her a quick voicemail before scrolling over to his inbox and dealing with several mostly unimportant emails from the office he'd been avoiding since arriving on South Padre. Not that they were much of a distraction from his mounting anxiety.

He hoped that Grace was just ignoring him. He could bear her anger, and he had no doubt that he deserved it. What he couldn't handle was the mere thought of something bad happening when he wasn't there to protect her.

For years now, he'd pushed so many people away. Grace had always treated him with such love and gentleness, way more than he deserved, and he'd kept her at arm's length. Even now, after all that had happened between them, he couldn't let his guard down. Not even his brothers fully escaped his distrust. If he was being honest with himself, not even Jesus Christ met his standard for who to open up to.

He was so determined to rely only on himself that he'd become blinded to how foolish he truly was.

He was a coward.

Grace was right.

He had to tell her the full truth about what had happened with Mikayla, or he was never going to be able to move forward. He couldn't let a past heartbreak ruin his future, no matter how painful it was going to be to tell her why he was so terrified of being vulnerable.

Ben pressed his hands together and bowed his head in the middle of the airport, not caring who happened to walk by as he sent up his whispered plea.

"Heavenly Father, I pray that You will grant me the courage to tell Grace the truth about my past. I also pray that she will forgive me for hurting her," he said softly. The words felt strange and awkward on his lips, but he kept going. "Most of all, Lord God, I pray that I will have the courage to lay my heart bare in front of her, and to say those words I have been wanting to say to her for years. In Jesus's name I pray. Amen."

As if on cue, he saw Asher striding toward him at last, carrying a camouflage backpack in lieu of actual luggage. "Hey, bro," his twin said as he approached, his eyebrows raised. "You look freaked. What's going on? Where's Gracie?"

All at once, Ben's attempt at stoicism fell apart.

"We had a fight, and now she's not answering my calls," he said.

"Well, you were probably being a jerk. Let me try."

Asher pulled out his own phone, tapping her name on the screen and putting the call on speaker.

It rang several times before going to voicemail.

"Let's talk on the way," Asher said firmly, running a hand through his blonde hair. "You're not being paranoid. I'm sure she's fine, but still, this isn't like her."

Guilt mingled with his fear as he and his twin rushed toward the parking lot. Maybe he should have let Asher take a shuttle bus to the resort. Not that he could do anything about it now.

"I'll drive," Asher suggested, tossing his backpack into the back seat of the rented sedan. Ben didn't argue.

He filled his brother in quickly on the latest developments in the case, trying to keep his mind from going to terrible places as they sped down the highway.

"I know there's more going on, man," Asher said

when he'd finished. "I can tell. You may as well just spill it."

Ben looked down at his lap, trying to hide the frustration on his face. No matter how hard he tried to put up walls around himself, his twin was the one person in the world who could see right through him.

"I'm falling in love with her," he said at last. There was no point in lying about it now. "I should have told her by now, but I wussed out. And this morning, she figured that fact out for herself. I've ruined everything, and I don't know if I can fix it. Assuming she's not lying in a ditch somewhere."

Asher blew out a breath. "Well, step one, cool it with the self-loathing. You can't go back in time. Step two, calm down. I said it wasn't like her to ignore us, not that she was necessarily in danger. She's almost certainly just sitting in her room at the resort, just like she promised she would be. Or maybe she snuck out to the lobby for a coffee."

Ben said nothing. Despite his twin's light tone, he knew what Asher was going to say next, and he didn't have the energy nor the conviction to argue.

"Mikayla and Josiah betraying you wasn't your fault," he continued after a long pause. "I don't know why you can't stop blaming yourself."

Ben recoiled at the mention of his former partner on the San Antonio police force and his ex-girlfriend. He tried to think about Josiah as little as possible, but he found Mikayla invading his thoughts more often than he'd like to admit.

He was no longer in love with her, so why did her betrayal continue to hurt? Why did he spend so much time digging through his past actions, wondering what he could have done to make her stay?

"I don't blame myself."

"You know," Asher started, ignoring his obvious lie, "in a healthy relationship, you don't have to be perfect to be loved. You get to screw up and you still get to be forgiven."

Ben considered his words for several more minutes until they pulled up to the Mistflower's front entrance.

It was similar to what their father often said about the mercy of Christ and his special love for those who carried a heavy burden of serious sin. He met them where they were, but He didn't leave them there. Jesus knew all of their brokenness and chose to love them anyway.

Was it possible Grace could reflect some of that love toward him, even though he didn't deserve it?

"You go park the car and check in," Ben ordered. "I'll head upstairs and make sure Grace is okay."

Chapter 23

Grace

Grace opened her eyes, but saw nothing.

She felt her heart beginning to race as she blinked, trying to make something–anything– come into focus, but the effort was futile. She was in the dark, and so far as she could tell, she was alone.

She reached down and felt for her phone. It was gone.

Worse, so was her gun.

"Okay, breathe," she told herself in a whisper as

she climbed up from the bed she'd woken up on. "Think. Just think."

She stretched out her tired limbs, and as she did so, several details began to solidify in her memory. She'd visited the Christ of the Fisherman statue. She'd been angry with Ben and stormed off.

He'd followed her, and convinced her to let him take her back to the Mistflower.

All at once, she reached up to her shoulder, a shiver running across her back as she felt a small piece of tape holding what seemed to be a piece of cotton.

Someone had waited in the hotel room's bathroom, injected her with something, and had brought her somewhere else once she passed out. Clearly, whoever had taken Katie Fairman had more power and resources than she had anticipated having to deal with.

She stretched out her hands in front of her in the dark, trying to feel around until the room made sense. Just as she found one of the walls, she heard the sound of nearby voices.

She froze, sitting back down slowly on the bed as she tried to listen.

It sounded like a man and a woman, and they were arguing about something. As they moved closer, Grace caught something the man said about a 'third option'.

When the female voice responded, she couldn't pick out the exact words.

But it took her only a few seconds to realize that without a doubt, the voice belonged to Jade Gorsky.

"–and this is the only way we avoid Katie Fairman getting hurt," the man said.

Grace stood again and inched closer to the sound, making it only about a foot before her shoulder smacked into what might have been another wall. Wherever she was, it didn't seem very big.

"Dad, you're not thinking clearly," Jade said.

Grace stood up straight.

It was all she could do not to gasp in shock.

Craig Gorsky wasn't the innocent, bumbling single dad that he had presented himself to be.

By the sounds of it, Donald Fairman's friend and mentee was the man responsible for kidnapping his daughter.

The very thought of it made her feel sick. Even after all of the digging they'd done, they hadn't come close to catching on to his plan. Now, she found herself ensnared in it.

But at least it sounded like Katie was still alive. For now.

"If you commit new crimes, you'll be exposing us to new risks," Jade continued. "We should have just killed her to begin with."

Grace tightened her fist in the fabric of her dress. Jade's tone was flat, as though the terrible words she was saying meant no more to her than musing aloud over which new Amex card to open.

"Everyone would have blamed the traffickers anyway," she added.

"I'm not a killer," Craig said after a moment, sounding defeated. "This is the best option, honey. We'll be in Mexico when we get the money, and from there, we'll be able to run."

"We can't do this. We'll lose everything!" Jade snapped. "We took Katie to prevent this exact scenario, remember? And now you're willing to just give up?"

"Things have changed."

"And what if they still come after us? Have you thought of that?"

Grace wondered what she meant. She doubted that Jade was referring to the Forge Brothers Security team. Who was it that had them both so terrified?

When Craig finally spoke again, he sounded positively broken.

"They won't come for us, okay? I'll pay them once we have the money. It's not like loan sharks care about how their debt repayment is funded."

The voices out in the hall went quiet again.

Grace forced air into her lungs as she tried to figure out what could possibly be going on, glad for the distraction from her own present predicament. However angry she was with Ben, she wished she had listened to him instead of demanding to stay at the hotel on her own. It had been a needless, stupid risk. She had put herself in danger, but worse, she had no doubt that Ben would risk his own safety to find her.

"I already lost mom," Jade said at last, breaking the quiet. "You can't ask me to give up on everyone I know, and everything we have."

"How dare you bring up your mother," Craig said, his voice rising. "The whole reason I made the choices I did is because of how important her memory is to me."

"You don't understand what it's like. It's not fair."

"Fair? It's not fair?" Craig shouted. "What's not fair is the thought of my friend losing a child like I lost a wife."

"You made your choices, dad," Jade pleaded. "We both did."

Grace listened.

For a moment, everything was silent again, the shadows of the darkness wrapping around her, drowning out everything but the rushing sound of blood in her ears. At last Craig spoke, more calmly this time.

"Whatever I should or shouldn't have done about Senera, it's too late now. Getting ransom money in exchange for Grace Hinton is the only way we get out of this without spilling blood."

Ben

The elevator ride felt like it took forever.

When the doors finally opened, Ben nearly sprinted toward Grace's hotel room door. He knocked, but there was no answer, and he noticed that the 'no housekeeping' sign was still in place. She'd left it that way earlier that morning, claiming that she wanted to organize her makeup in the bathroom before subjecting one of the maids to her chaos.

He took out his phone and tried to call her again, but this time, instead of ringing, the computerized voice on the other end of the line informed him that her phone was no longer in service.

He knocked on the door several more times, with increasing intensity. Still nothing.

He felt the panic he'd tried to push down growing once again. Asher's optimism was misplaced. Clearly, something had gone wrong.

Ben dialed Asher's phone as he rushed down the hall, skipping the elevator and heading for the stairs instead. "Meet me in the security office in building C. She's not answering my knocks and her phone is off."

By the time he got downstairs, went outside, and reached the smaller building, Patrick and Asher were already standing outside waiting for him.

"You need to unlock Grace Hinton's room," he said, not bothering to say hello. To his credit, the head of security did not look offended by Ben's brusque tone.

"Look, I know you're worried, but with management gone–" Patrick started.

"Grace is like a sister to me," Asher said, cutting the man off before he could say more. "I swear on my life that she would be absolutely fine with an invasion of her privacy under these circumstances."

Ben shot him a grateful glance, glad he didn't say like a sister to 'us'. His feelings for Grace definitely ruled out referring to her as his sister, except maybe inside a church.

"If anyone ever asks, I'll tell them we broke in," Ben added, hoping he'd never have to tell the promised lie. "I'll take full responsibility."

Patrick looked between the two brothers before finally relenting with a long sigh, reaching into his pocket and retrieving a ring of keys. "I'll stay here and check out the camera footage of her hallway from this morning. You two go and see if anything is amiss upstairs."

"Thank you, man," Asher said, shoving the keys into his pocket and heading out of the office with Ben at his heels.

As he'd suspected, Grace's room was empty, with clothes half-folded on the bed and several piles of cosmetic products littering the bathroom counter.

"Okay. She didn't vaporize into thin air," Asher said. "So there must be some indication of where she went. Probably somewhere in this room. We can't freak out and miss something important, so stay cool, okay?"

Ben nodded wordlessly and started rifling through the clothes in the closet, trying to see if maybe she'd changed into another outfit and left the room voluntarily.

He may as well keep his hands busy.

It was the only way he'd be able to stop himself from spiraling completely out of control.

Chapter 24

Ben

"Just eat, all right?"

Ben gripped the fork more tightly as he stared down at his bowl of pasta. He wasn't hungry in the least, but Asher was right. They'd been looking for Grace for most of the day, and so far, they hadn't turned up anything useful. Starving his already frazzled brain of nutrients wouldn't do her any good.

He stabbed at a few pieces of garlic-butter-soaked rotini and shoved them into his mouth, hardly tasting the Mistflower's delicious dish.

"So, we've searched the resort buildings from top to bottom. Nothing," Asher said.

Ben nodded, swallowing a bite of food.

He peered at Ben as though waiting for confirmation to continue. Ben's glare delivered a sufficient hint for him to get on with it.

"I ended up on the Gulf-side beach, and talked to people from end to end. A handful of people claim to have seen Grace, but it's hardly a certainty that it was her, and in any case, they didn't see her go anywhere with anyone or anything else suspicious."

"So, nothing," Ben said.

"Nothing. But at least Detective Hayles has become a little more helpful now that three women seem to have disappeared off of South Padre."

"They passed the cases to the FBI," Ben reminded him, not feeling particularly impressed with the North Pier police. But at least he could trust that the FBI would actually investigate if they suspected the disappearances were linked to human trafficking activity.

"Well, maybe they'll turn something up," Asher said, stuffing a large bite of steak into his mouth. "But we need to figure out what we're going to do in the meantime. I'm lost."

Ben felt his throat going tight as helplessness and rising panic began to take hold.

He skewered another few pieces of pasta and shoved them into his mouth, chewing furiously.

He wasn't going to cry. Not even in front of Asher.

No matter what it took, he was going to find the woman he loved.

Grace

The voices were quiet again.

Grace stood still, hearing nothing aside from the rushing of her own breath. It sounded loud in the small space, and as desperately as she wanted to move, she knew that it would be better if Jade and Craig and whoever else might be nearby thought she was still knocked out.

After several painfully slow minutes had passed,

she stuck out her hands again, trying to feel for something that made sense of the dark room.

She could tell at once that the area was as small as she'd assumed, perhaps eight feet across. She knew there had to be a light switch somewhere, but it was difficult to find in such complete blackness.

At last, her fingers landed upon something that felt like fabric.

With a silent prayer of thanks, she yanked the curtain back, revealing a round porthole.

As far as she could see, there was nothing but ocean, the gentle current lapping against the side of the boat as they raced through the water.

The sudden glow of the sun made her eyes burn, but the tears that followed were her own as she realized what she was seeing. It was sunset in what looked to be the middle of the Gulf.

She was trapped on a ship somewhere, a large one, if the lack of rocking motion was to be believed.

And she'd been passed out for almost an entire day.

Ben

As Ben swiped his company-issued credit card through the restaurant's machine, the insistent chiming of Asher's phone almost made him jump.

"Gabe," Asher said as he answered it, giving the waitress a quick nod before getting up from the table. "What's happening?"

Ben's fingers shook as he entered the tip amount and his PIN number. Before the machine had finished printing a receipt, he was on his feet, rushing after Asher through the back exit.

As they emerged into the warm evening and slipped past a few wandering Mistflower guests, Asher put the phone on speaker.

"Ben, you hear me okay? You guys alone?"

"Yes, what's going on?" Ben asked impatiently. The look on Asher's face was enough to make it clear that their oldest brother wasn't calling to chat about the weather forecast.

"The Hintons got a ransom note," Gabe said calmly.

"Asking for one million, eight hundred thousand dollars," Asher added.

Ben's mouth felt dry, and he said nothing, unsure what it was that he could say. The demand for cash was a good reason to hope that Grace was alive and well, but it was hardly enough to put his mind at ease.

"It's pretty strange for a kidnapper to seek such a specific amount," Gabe said.

"Super weird," Asher agreed.

"Whatever," Ben said gruffly. "Who cares what the amount is. We need to get it. I'll sell everything I own if I have to. It doesn't matter."

"Mr. Hinton is working on getting the necessary assets liquidated," Gabe said, his typical fatherlike tone returning. "And I'm sorting out travel arrangements. I'll be coming down with the Hintons myself."

"Whoa," Asher said, sounding shocked. "Won't the place fall apart if you leave?"

Ben could understand his reaction. Gabe was an excellent field operative, but he preferred staying in San Antonio where he could supervise the rest of their team. It was the ideal setting for his favorite activity of bossing people around.

"Cameron will hold down the fort," Gabe said firmly. "And I already talked to Reilly. He's agreed to come off paternity leave if it comes to that."

"If Lauren doesn't kill him in a fit of postpartum rage before he can reach the office," Asher added.

"Do you want us to tell the police about the ransom demand?" Ben asked, lowering his voice as a group of college boys sauntered past them, followed by two girls who looked barely old enough to drive, let alone be attending college.

They were in a secluded area of the resort, behind two buildings, but with the spring break crowds it felt like nowhere was truly private. The last thing Ben wanted was for someone to overhear and start asking questions.

"I told them to," Gabe said. Asher clicked the volume button on the side of the phone several times, and he and Ben leaned in closer as Gabe continued. "But the Hintons refused. The ransom message they got was clear–come alone by car, no cops, no weapons, or Grace dies. They're supposed to show up at noon tomorrow at a certain dock on a Mexican beach near the town of La Pesca, ready to transfer the money digitally."

"Will they let you talk to Allie, at least?" Asher asked in a hushed voice as more college kids sauntered by. Ben nodded in agreement. Officer Allie Parker was their liaison at San Antonio PD, and everyone on the team trusted her implicitly. It seemed wise to Ben to at least inform her of what was about to go down, especially if they needed help from the Mexican authorities after the fact.

"Nope," Gabe said. "Believe me, I pushed for it, but the Hintons weren't willing to take any risk at all. I don't like it, but I can see where they're coming from. And I'm not going to go against their wishes. They need our help; I can't jeopardize their trust."

"So where does that leave us?" Ben asked, eager to hang up the phone and get moving on whatever came next. Standing around here while Grace was in trouble felt like torture.

"Well, the Hintons agreed to let me go with them part way," Gabe said. "If I take every precaution not to be spotted, of course. I'll drive them as close as I can to the coordinates the kidnappers gave us, and from there I plan on planting one-way surveillance on the Hintons and keeping a close watch unless I absolutely need to engage."

Asher shot Ben a glance. As usual, Ben felt as though he could read his twin's mind even before he spoke. "You be careful. For Grace's sake, and your own."

"I'm supposed to be the one worrying about you guys, not the other way around," Gabe said, releasing a loud sigh over the speaker. "I can't exactly let Mr. and Mrs. Hinton deal with this on their own."

"Especially Grace's mom," Asher said, a smile breaking his solemn expression. "Maybe have Bristol or Lauren help her pack. Somehow I doubt she owns anything appropriate to wear to a potentially deadly meeting in middle-of-nowhere Mexico."

"I'll make sure she leaves the family diamonds at home," Gabe said flatly, clearly in no mood for Asher's commentary.

Asher opened his mouth to speak, but Ben cut him off before he could set off a round of time-wasting bickering.

"Where did the ransom note come in?" he asked.

"That's the silver lining," Gabe said. "It was an email, and if anyone can trace the source, it's you."

Ben closed his eyes for a moment in a silent prayer of thanksgiving. If it had been an actual letter, there would have been no way to figure out anything useful in time.

"And get this," Gabe continued. "It was delivered via a spoofed Hinton Logistics internal email address. I already sent you everything the guys at the office have. They'll keep digging, but, well, they're not you."

"Okay," Ben said. "I'll get started."

"Keep me posted," Gabe said before hanging up.

Ben followed Asher without a word as he made his way toward the back of the building that housed their rooms and started heading up the back stairwell.

As his legs climbed up several flights of concrete, the rest of his muscles itched for real, tangible action.

"All I want to do right now is tear the island apart inch by inch until we find Grace," he admitted as they reached their floor.

Asher reached over and placed a hand on his shoulder. "I plan on changing my clothes, grabbing a coffee and a couple extra guns, and doing just that," he promised. "But God gave you the nerd magic. And right now, figuring out who sent that email is our best chance at getting ahead of the kidnapper."

Ben cleared his throat. "Thanks, man. I guess you're right."

"Always am," Asher said, giving him a final friendly slap on the arm before brushing past him toward his own room.

Ben paused for a long moment as several older guys in business suits sauntered past, deep in a quiet conversation he couldn't make out.

As soon as he was alone, he took a few steps, crossing the distance to the window that looked out at the Mistflower Resort complex stretching out before him.

Despite his confidence in Patrick's loyalty, even the hotel no longer felt safe. It was likely that Grace had been taken from her room somehow, and whoever had done it had pulled off the feat without being detected. Whoever they were up against clearly had even more power and resources than he'd first assumed.

Fortunately, he knew that FBS didn't have to take on their enemies alone.

"Jesus, Grace loves You," he started, clasping his hands together as he looked out at the darkening sky, thankful for the beauty of the place, despite everything. "And I know You love her even more. I beg You, watch over her tonight. Make sure she knows that we–that I–love her, and that we won't give up on her, no matter what it takes. Grant me the wisdom to find the information I need to ensure her safety. Thank You, Lord Jesus. Amen."

Chapter 25

Ben

A knock sounded at the door of the hotel room as Ben stared at the computer, his eyes roaming over the rows of text until the words all seemed to bleed together. It was after two in the morning, and he was already eager to procure a morning coffee.

He pushed himself to his feet and looked through the peephole before pulling the door open.

"Find anything?" he asked the waiting Asher, who had kicked off a sandal and was examining a nasty looking blister on his toe.

"No. I'm sorry. I must have talked to at least a hundred people," he answered. "No one knows anything. I checked out the statue again, just in case, and then I went back to every place you've eaten since you guys landed here. And then a few more."

"Thank you."

Ben forced the words from his lips despite his rising frustration. South Padre was a small island, but not that small, and his brother was clearly doing all he could to find her. The truth was, there was no one to blame.

Not yet, anyway. He feared what he might do to whoever had taken Grace when he figured it out.

"What about you?" Asher asked, pointing at the laptop and the separate monitor that sat on the plain hotel desk.

Ben shook his head. "I think Gabe's confidence in me might be misplaced. I've been at it for hours, and so far, there's no concrete answer. Whoever sent the email is very technically skilled."

"Like someone from Craig Gorsky's company,"

Asher said. "Someone who works at Lumen would know how to spoof an email."

"Or who to pay to do it," Ben added. "Then again, so could someone from AveroTech, though I'm not sure what motive Donald Fairman would have, unless Katie's in on the whole kidnapping thing and it was a ruse to kidnap Grace for ransom. But he couldn't have known she was going to be part of the investigation, so that doesn't make sense, either."

His head hurt. There were so many people that could be involved, and yet so few concrete clues to go on.

The time was passing far too quickly. He hadn't even gotten a chance to dig deeply into Lumen's recent acquisition of Senera Pharmaceuticals, and for the time being, he wasn't going to get the chance.

"We need about ten more people on this case," Asher observed. "Seriously, we need to convince Jacob to join the team. We need more people at FBS that we can trust."

"Right."

Ben didn't want to say more about the possibility of their brother coming home and joining the family business. It was a long shot, and he wasn't in the mood for making wishes right now.

"So what's next?" Asher said, reaching over for Ben's half-empty bottle of water and draining it in a few sips. Ben pulled a face but said nothing.

"I think we need to go to the exchange point with Gabe," Asher declared without waiting for Ben's opinion. "We can stay hidden, of course, but at least we could act as backup. Why do the kidnappers want to meet the Hintons near La Pesca, anyway? I Googled it earlier. It really is in the middle of nowhere, along the coast. It's basically a fishing village with a few cheap hotels."

"Is there an airport nearby?" Ben asked.

Asher shook his head, his bright blue eyes flashing what almost looked like excitement. "That's the weird part. There is a small local airstrip, but it's been crawling with federales for the past three weeks. You'll never guess why."

Ben narrowed his eyes at him, saying nothing.

Asher cleared his throat. "Turns out this airfield was tied to a certain human trafficking ring that has also been known to operate up in Texas."

"Whoa," Ben said. "That's quite a coincidence."

"Yup. But I think that's all it is," Asher said. "The kidnappers would have to be insane to try bringing a full-sized bottle of sunscreen into that airport right now, let alone anything else. I guess the kidnappers are planning to take off by speedboat or something. Who knows."

Asher went quiet, and Ben tried not to think about any of the darker possibilities. They'd get Grace back in just a few hours. There was no other option.

Still, something seemed to be prodding at the back of Ben's consciousness as he considered Asher's words.

"I still feel like there's some detail I'm not seeing," Ben said aloud. "It's right there, but I can't figure it out."

"Love has a way of confusing us," Asher said.

Ben turned to him, expecting to see a grin, but his brother looked completely serious.

"For the record, I think you're holding up better than anyone else would be," Asher continued. "And I'm proud of you. Grace will be, too, when we find her. Which I promise you we will."

Ben felt warmth pooling in his chest despite his anxieties. He was thankful that he had his family by his side, no matter how dark things became. And he knew that God was there too, even when He chose to stay quiet.

"The last couple of days with her have given me some of the greatest moments of my life," Ben admitted, not bothering to try and hide the blush that was surely rising on his pale face. "I just wish I'd let her in instead of always being so afraid. On our first night here, we went to the beach, and–"

He stopped short, his mouth pressing into a firm line.

"What?" Asher asked.

Ben hardly heard him.

That night on the beach came back to him in stark detail. The grit of the sand between his toes. The lapping of the water along the shore. The huge bonfires that had frightened Grace.

The feeling of her fingers intertwining with his own.

The huge yacht off of the coast.

"Grace was right," Ben said to a bewildered Asher. "Her intuition was right from the start. We need to get to the beach."

"In case you missed it, I've been combing the beach up and down for half the night," Asher protested as Ben headed for the door of the hotel room. "I told you, I didn't find anything."

Ben reached down and picked up Asher's sandals, tossing them in his twin's direction.

"That's because you didn't know what you were looking for," Ben said, a smile tugging at the corner of his mouth. "I think I do. Let's go."

Chapter 26

Grace

Grace stepped back from the porthole and drew the curtain away as far as it would go, bathing the room in the last of the evening's warm light. She took a moment just to breathe, thankful for the chance to get her bearings, and then began to examine her surroundings.

It was a small cabin, with a bed, a cupboard for clothes, and a desk. There was no light switch– she supposed it must be on the outside wall. The furnishings were simple, but she could tell by the gleaming white walls and the immaculate cream carpet that whatever boat she was on had to be expensive.

"Okay, there isn't a bunk bed, and it has its own separate head, so it's probably not a basic crew cabin, but I doubt it's the captain's quarters, either," she muttered to herself, the words sounding loud to her own ears.

She swallowed a fresh wave of panic as she wondered who the captain was. She seemed to be on some sort of private craft, not a large vessel filled with people who would be able to help her.

She walked over to the desk and sat down, resting her head on her hands as she considered the information she had.

If Craig and Jade were looking for her parents' money, that would require them to know she'd been taken. And if her parents knew, that meant Ben would too. And Asher, who had surely made it to South Padre by now.

Better yet, a ransom demand meant that her captors needed her alive. Her odds of survival were good, even if they were on their way to Mexico by now.

Grace got up and walked over to the small round window again, squinting into the distance in an attempt to see if they were on the inside of the barrier island or out in the Gulf. At the moment, all she could see was the endless ocean, but perhaps they were facing the other direction, leaving the island on the other side of the boat, hidden from view.

"I forgot, there's more good news," she said out loud to herself, refusing to allow her voice to shake. "Katie is alive. Maybe she's even onboard."

Despite her efforts to look on the bright side, she couldn't shake the fear of the unknown that gripped her. More than anything, she wished that she could go back to that morning and choose to control her emotions. However legitimate her reasons had been, her anger toward Ben felt utterly foolish in hindsight.

She looked out at the water as it rushed gently against the side of the boat, carrying her toward an unseen destination.

She'd give anything to have him beside her right now.

She wouldn't care if he kissed her, or even if he held her hand. Just his presence had always been enough to make her feel like everything was going to be okay. When had that changed?

When had she begun to feel this urgent need for more?

She walked back over to the bed and lay down, tucking a pillow under her neck in an attempt to get comfortable. Despite her long blackout, she felt utterly exhausted.

She didn't remember falling asleep, but she must have.

Some time later, she awoke, her eyes opening to find only darkness.

The terror clutched at her chest instantly, and she struggled to take deep breaths. In her mind, she knew where she was, and why it was so dark, but the panic attack she was experiencing was impervious to reason.

She tried to get to her feet, hoping that there would be moonlight if she could reach the porthole, but before she could make it even a few steps, she felt her head beginning to swim.

She sank to the floor, barely noticing how close she came to smacking her head off the edge of the desk. The tightening in her chest was stronger now, demanding all of her, dragging her down within herself where her deepest fears lived.

She felt her breaths coming faster, and she could hear their desperate sound.

Curling her knees against her chest, she pushed herself back against the wall, grounded by the pressure of the firm wood against her spine.

Not now, not now, not now.

Please, God, I need to be able to think straight.

No matter how hard she tried to remain focused on the reality of the present, she found herself back in Indonesia, back beneath the rubble, the taste of dust clinging to her tongue.

Her parents hadn't wanted her to go.

Grace swallowed hard, remembering their warnings about being an outspoken Christian in a Muslim-majority country. She'd heard them out, but in the end, she'd been committed to teaching English, and the agency had assured them all that Jakarta was a safe place for tourists.

For three months, everything had been perfect.

She loved the warm, bustling city, and the feeling of being on a grand adventure thousands of miles from home. She'd even begun to make progress in carefully sharing Christ's love with her Muslim students, despite the country's disapproval of evangelism and their blasphemy laws.

Grace closed her eyes tight against the shadows. She was breathing a little slower now, turning over the past events in her mind. She would give anything to go back in time, to make different choices.

She was crying now, tears spilling onto her cheeks as she sat there in the uncaring darkness. She didn't bother to wipe them off.

Only God was there to see her, and He felt very far away.

She couldn't go back, not ever, and the guilt ate her alive.

Grace knew how the story ended. And that ending would always be the same.

Ben

The moon shone down on the black water, casting a blue glow across the rippling surface. Even at nearly three in the morning, the beach was still busy, with easily a thousand bodies crowding around a DJ as he blared loud dance music from his raised platform.

"It's Friday, I guess," Asher observed with a shrug as he hurried along next to Ben. "There are probably a ton of locals joining the party."

Ben barely heard him as he continued to rush toward the jetty. He crossed his broad arms over his chest, resisting the urge to start shoving the drunken revelers out of his way. The bonfires were burning again, bright and fierce, competing with the gleam of the moonlight as the spring breakers danced.

He stopped before he reached the jetty and turned, taking off along the shoreline as quickly as he could without breaking into a run. Asher glanced back over his shoulder at the party they were leaving behind before catching up to him.

"It's gone," Ben said, coming to a stop and pointing out at the Gulf as he caught his breath. "It's gone. I knew it would be."

Asher pulled a face. "Bro, you seriously need to tell me what you're even talking about."

He turned to his twin, trying to calm his racing heart long enough to explain himself.

"Grace and I noticed a yacht anchored out here when we first arrived."

"So? I've seen a bunch of them here. Probably manned by rich kids who want a more private party."

"It was huge. At least three times the size of any of the others. And it had almost all of its lights off."

"Look, man, I still don't–"

"It had a name on the back. I didn't see the whole thing, but it started with an 'L'," Ben said in a rush. "It started with an 'L', and now it's gone."

Asher only looked more puzzled.

"We know there's a Lumeneer II," Ben added.

"The sailboat Jade visited? Wasn't that a dead end? I thought you talked with her father and he confirmed that she and Katie were free to borrow it while they were here."

Ben shook his head in frustration. "He did. But what if there's another ship here that Lumen owns? What if that's where Katie and Grace are being held? It was huge, man. Way big enough to be a floating prison. You've never met Jade, but believe me, I wouldn't find it hard to believe that she'd kidnap someone, with or without her father's help."

"That's reaching, man," Asher said, sounding almost apologetic. "I know you're worried about Gracie, we all are, but it's not like you to take a shot in the dark like this. Jade sounds like a world-class turd, but that doesn't mean she'd kidnap someone."

"Look, it's worth looking into," Ben pressed. "We have exactly zero other leads right now, and I'm not about to just sit around here and hope that the kidnappers hold to their word when the ransom money is paid."

"Are we at least gonna call Craig Gorsky and rattle his cage?"

"We can't," Ben said firmly, stepping out of the way as a couple holding hands sauntered up the beach beside them. "We can't risk tipping him off if there's even a one percent chance I'm right. We can't risk him moving Katie or Grace if they're on that boat."

"I've looked into Gorsky myself," Asher protested, rubbing at his temples as he followed Ben away from the water. "He's no slouch in the tech biz. There's no way he'd be dumb enough to use a corporate-owned vessel for a kidnapping."

Ben paused for a moment as he considered this, reaching down to shake sand out of one of his sandals. "Grace thought that the huge yacht was kind of strange at the time, but had Jade not lied to us and snuck out onto the Lumeneer II, we probably would have never given it any further thought. And like I said, Craig may not be in on it at all. Jade doesn't seem dumb, but she is nothing if not arrogant. If she's involved, she's probably making a lot of her plans as she goes along, just assuming we won't figure her out."

Asher shrugged. "Admittedly, meeting near La Pesca makes a lot more sense if the kidnappers are traveling by water."

"Exactly what I've been thinking. Let's go," he said, turning to cut across to the nearest road. "I know just the lady we need to talk to."

Chapter 27

Ben

The Ocean Rodeo Marina was barely a mile away from the beach, but the fifteen minute walk still felt like an eternity. Asher was walking painfully slow as he attempted to text Gabe an update on their plans.

"Can't you just call him?" Ben asked in annoyance after having to stop and wait for him for the tenth time.

"You could," Asher challenged, holding out the phone in his direction. Ben held up his hands, warding him off.

"Point taken."

Gabe was probably not going to be pleased about the plan that was beginning to take shape in Ben's mind, and in any case, it was likely he was on a flight to Mexico with the Hintons by now. If he was, he'd be fast asleep in his seat. It would be safer to text him now and check in again after he'd had his morning coffee. And preferably after the sun had time to rise.

"She's right down here," Ben said, gesturing to their right as they approached the marina at last. Asher followed him past a row of sailboats until they reached Connie's ramshackle watercraft.

"Wait. Never mind Gabe. How likely is it that she will kill us for waking her up in the middle of the night?"

Ben couldn't stop his grin from escaping as he recalled his last interaction with Connie. "I'd say there's a solid fifty percent chance. May as well get this over with."

Asher walked up alongside the boat, examining the rope ladder that hung from the side. "You first."

Ben pulled himself up onto the narrow sailboat and headed over to the door leading belowdecks, giving the solid wood several firm knocks. Asher followed, shivering as a rush of wind whipped across the water.

"Connie?" Ben called out, knocking again when she didn't answer.

He flipped up the hood of the sweater he'd wisely grabbed on his way out of the hotel as another gust of wind blew salt spray into their faces. She had to be here. They didn't have very much time to put his plan into motion. Their noon deadline would arrive before they knew it.

"Allow me," Asher said, leaning over and pounding on the door with both fists. Ben flinched. He didn't want to scare her half to death, but–

The door swung inward, revealing the sun-worn woman standing there in a neon pink robe, her arms wrapped tightly around her chest. "I can't sleep as it is thanks to this dang music blastin' the island," she snapped. "Do you mind?"

"We're really sorry to disturb you like this,

Connie," Ben said, offering the woman his most charming smile. "But we really need your help."

She stepped out onto the deck, her hair flying in all directions as the wind caught the dry strands. "Again?"

"Yes, ma'am," Asher said, stepping forward and extending a hand. "Hello. I'm Asher Forge. I'm Ben's twin."

Connie didn't take his hand. "Son, I been meanin' to get a new robe. This one's got no tie left on it, and I don't think y'all want to get a look underneath."

Ben looked down at his feet, hoping that Asher wouldn't make any attempt to be funny, but fortunately Connie continued talking before he could get a word in.

"You're his twin? You sure they didn't mix y'all up at the hospital?"

Connie looked Asher up and down, taking in his pale blonde hair and compact frame.

"Yes, ma'am, we're sure," Ben said. "Look, last time we met, I was here with—"

"You think I'd forget that pretty girlfriend of yours so fast?" Connie interrupted, lifting her finger to scold him, allowing the pink fabric of the robe to shift just enough to make Ben nervous. "I ain't that old yet."

Ben could see Asher's smirk out of the corner of his eye, but he didn't correct her. Even if he had actually had the courage to open up and ask Grace to be his girlfriend before now, the word didn't seem to be quite enough to describe how deeply he felt for her.

If they ever got out of this, he wanted Grace to be his wife.

No matter how terrifying the thought was of having to tell her as much.

"Grace is missing," Asher said, his expression becoming serious once again.

Ben nodded, listening as his brother gave Connie a brief rundown of everything they'd learned about the Lumeneer II, Craig and Jade Gorsky, and Lumen.

"Does any of this sound familiar to you?"

Connie shook her head. "Can't say it does. But it explains the sorts of folks I always seen on that sailboat."

Ben drew a breath. "Okay, this is very important. Do you ever remember seeing a large yacht on the other side of the island, anchored out in the Gulf?"

To his surprise, Connie needed scarcely a moment to think. "That ridiculous Santucci, you mean?"

He nodded.

"Course I seen it. Kinda hard to miss."

Ben and Asher exchanged a glance.

"I've always wondered who owns that thing," she continued. "It's the nicest boat here, and that's sayin' something. It's strange, though. I've never seen anyone on the deck enjoying the sunshine, but someone has to be in there drivin' it. Autopilot aint quite that good."

Ben's heart began beating faster in his chest.

On her very first field op, Grace had already figured out the most important part of investigative work. She knew how to listen to her intuition, and it was becoming more and more clear just how right it was proving to be.

"What makes you say that, ma'am?" Asher prompted.

"Now, I am usually over here on the lagoon side, so I can't promise I haven't missed some goings-on," Connie cautioned, "But I know I seen them lights belowdecks on at night before."

"Has the yacht been here since the Lumeneer II arrived?" Ben asked.

Connie shook her head. "No, not at all. It got here right before the beginning of spring break."

Ben's heart sank.

Maybe Asher was right. Maybe he was seeing connections where there was only coincidence after all.

"Did you see anyone actually take it out?" Asher pressed.

"I did. Was the first time I'd ever seen it in motion, and they weren't wastin' no time."

"When?" Ben asked, a hair away from losing his patience entirely. If this whole lead wasn't going anywhere, they couldn't waste any more time chasing it.

"Yesterday morning," Connie said. "Not long after sunrise. I remember. I was out for my morning pilates class on the beach."

Sunrise. Right around the time Grace had been taken.

That was all Ben needed to hear.

Grace was on that yacht. He could feel it in his gut.

And he was going to bring her home.

Chapter 28

Donald

The phone began to ring, filling the calm hotel room with noise.

Donald glanced down at the screen, yanking his eyes away from the bustling streets of Shanghai that he had been watching through the window.

It was Craig.

Why was he calling now? It had to be the middle of the night in Texas.

He let the blaring sound continue, not wanting to answer, and not quite wanting to hang up, either.

He needed to think before he talked to his friend again.

He padded over the plush carpet until he reached the bed and fell back onto it, staring up at the smooth cream-colored paint on the ceiling.

His daughter was gone, and now Grace Hinton had disappeared as well. His life felt like such a mess on so many levels, and yet, he couldn't quite figure out why that should be so.

Sure, AveroTech was having financial problems, but few within the company realized how dire things had become. The internet news outlets and struggling business magazines had not caught wind of it yet. He was sure of that.

His friends and colleagues and even the police had tried to convince him that Katie's disappearance was probably random, that it had nothing to do with his work at all. There was no real reason to think otherwise, and yet...

He lifted up his phone and looked at it again. Craig Gorsky's handsome face waited on the screen, which reminded him that he now had two missed calls.

A thought rose in his mind, as sudden and attention-grabbing as a red notification bell.

Could Craig be connected to all of this somehow?

He closed his eyes, as though shutting out the serene decor of his luxury hotel room would help him to concentrate on the puzzle set before him.

He had mentored Craig from the very beginning of his career. He'd watched as he founded Lumen as a new college graduate, bringing the company up to a billion-dollar valuation in record time. He had no motive to kidnap Grace Hinton for ransom, and in any case, no ransom had been demanded for Katie at all. He was far more successful than Donald himself was, especially now.

He released a breath and sat up in bed, rubbing at his temples.

Craig Gorsky had nothing to do with any of this.

Still, he knew that he should have told the team from Forge Brothers Security the truth about their dealings from the start. He supposed he still could, but for what?

It wouldn't do anything to bring his daughter or Grace home, and it would probably end in him losing the company he loved forever.

There had to be some piece he was missing, something that brought everything together, but he felt no closer to figuring out what it was.

He glanced over at the suitcase that he'd left near the closet door. He desperately wanted to shove all of his clothes into it and catch the next flight back to Texas. He could pound the sidewalks of South Padre Island until his daughter turned up. At least it would feel like he was doing something to help.

Instead, he moved for the door, scooping up his sleek leather Hermès wallet as he passed by the desk. If he left China now, if this microchip deal didn't go through before he was able to dump his Lumen stock, AveroTech was finished. He'd be selling the wallet on Facebook marketplace to rustle up some cash, and he'd be getting off easy compared to the hundreds of employees who would lose their jobs.

Katie would understand why he had to stay. He'd hired the best to find her.

His life was a mess, but everything would work out in the end. There was simply no other option.

Chapter 29

Grace

Grace's eyes shot open.

Somewhere outside of the confines of her cabin, she could hear footsteps.

She hadn't expected to be able to fall asleep, but apparently, her exhaustion had outweighed her anxiety. As she sat up on the narrow mattress, she realized she could see a little. The porthole revealed a slight hint of light. The sun would rise soon. She'd been gone for almost twenty-four hours.

She swallowed the fresh tears that threatened to escape. Her parents would be so worried about her.

And so would Ben.

He'd blame himself for letting her walk away, but how could he have known that someone was stalking her movements while wielding a syringe full of sedatives?

They both could have made better decisions, but it was too late now to take anything back. She hoped that God would lead him and Asher in the right direction, but it wasn't like she'd had a chance to leave behind a clue.

Before she could ponder the issue further, she heard a knock at the door. The overhead light flicked on.

A well-dressed man in his early forties strode in, carrying a large plate with an omelet, three slices of bacon, and some toast. All at once, she realized she was ravenous, but she stayed where she sat, eyeing the food warily as he set it down on the small desk.

"You can eat," the man said. "If we–if I was

going to poison you, I would have made sure the poison was in the syringe already."

He had a point.

As she sat down at the desk and took several bites of the hot meal, he watched her, the light of the rising sun gleaming on his deep copper skin. She knew she should be afraid of him, but there was something in his demeanor that allowed her to let her guard down just a little.

"Thank you," Grace said after nibbling through her final piece of toast.

"You're welcome," the man said, flashing a set of impossibly white teeth. "I wanted to reassure you. You're going home today. I've been in contact with your parents, and they're paying the ransom money I've asked for. You'll be back to your normal life soon."

Grace looked at him, a false smile frozen on her face. It was a lot to take in.

She wanted so desperately to go home, but she hated that her parents would be putting themselves in harm's way in order to pay off a kidnapper. What would stop him from snatching some other innocent person the next time he needed money? The thought made her sick.

Maybe Ben and the others had a plan that the man wasn't aware of. At the moment, though, she had no choice but to go along with whatever was proposed.

"Are you all right?" the man asked, his mouth tilting into a frown as he settled down onto the bed. "You don't look very happy to be heading home."

"Oh, no, I'm very excited to see my family," Grace said, injecting a false lightness into her voice. At least she had no temptation to lie.

Unfortunately, her captor didn't look convinced.

"I'm sorry for putting you through this," he said.

He paused, and Grace nodded. She had no idea what he expected her to say. It wasn't like she was going to tell him everything was fine.

"I hate that innocent people have gotten caught up in this whole mess. But I have no choice now but to keep going. It's complicated. I think if you were in my shoes, you'd understand a little more, but I don't blame you for hating me."

After listening to the man's voice for a few minutes, she realized that she knew exactly who he was. Considering the man's good looks, it made perfect sense.

"You're Craig Gorsky, right?" she asked.

The man's eyes widened, and he glanced over at the door.

"I mean, I heard you talking to Jade yesterday," Grace added quickly, not wanting the man to bolt. "I already knew you were on board. I just figured you'd send in a henchman with my breakfast. Did you drug me yourself, too?"

As soon as the final words slipped out, she wished she could take them back. She needed to keep him talking if she wanted answers.

"I apologize for that," he said. He paused for several seconds. "Yes, I'm Craig. No point in denying anything now. It's not like you're going to have the chance to use the dirt you have on me."

Coldness spread through Grace's spine. She hoped that he meant what he'd said about her getting to go home. It seemed like it would have been a whole lot simpler just to kill her if he wanted to ensure she never uncovered his secrets. It was an option that he still could take advantage of at any point if he changed his mind.

"Anyway," he continued, "I didn't sedate you myself, no. I had an associate handle bringing you in. Before that, I had him try to scare you off, but clearly that didn't work."

Grace flinched as she remembered the black truck that tried to run her and Ben off the road. Craig looked genuinely apologetic. Nothing about him made her think he was a hardened criminal. Even after all that had happened, perhaps he could be reasoned with.

"You didn't want us to find Katie Fairman."

It was Craig's turn to flinch.

"Where is she, Craig?" Grace demanded. "Just please tell me she's still alive. Please."

The door to the cabin opened just then. Grace jolted upright, her knee banging against the desk and making the breakfast plate clank against the wood.

Jade Gorsky sauntered into the small space, her face ugly with rage.

Ben

"Connie, do you know anything about a place called Playa La Pesca?" Ben asked, not bothering to hide the urgency in his voice. Noon was racing toward them with every passing minute. If his plan was going to work, they had to get moving.

The woman nodded. "I sail down that way now and again. It's a nice beach, but more of a local spot. Why?"

"Could your boat get us there by noon?"

Connie's brows raised as she looked him up and down. "Not a chance. Even with the engine runnin'. I usually make it a weekend trip when I go down that way. Besides, I'm no tour guide. Why the sudden interest in random Mexican villages anyhow?"

"Because we think that Grace and Katie might be there," Asher cut in. Ben shot him an appreciative glance. He hadn't had a chance to discuss his sailing plans with his twin beforehand, but he caught on fast.

"Them cops have a boat that can get down there easy," she said, waving a hand in the vague direction of the North Pier police station. "Go ask that Detective Hayles. Clearly he needs the help. Can't find two missin' girls but has time to be after me for nabbing a gator. Jus' one! One gator!"

Ben stuck his hands in the pockets of his shorts, staring down at the worn wooden deck beneath his feet. They didn't have time for one of her rants. "The police aren't going to go storming Normandy on Federales turf."

"Stormin' what now?"

"1944. D-Day. The beach in–" Ben gritted his teeth. "It's not important. I just want to get these innocent women home safe. Please."

Connie pushed her hair behind her ears as the wind whipped over them again, her wrinkled face tight like an apple left out in the sun.

"Ben won't say it, so I will," Asher said. "He's madly in love with Grace and desperate to protect her. Surely a lady like yourself can appreciate how far a man will go for romance. "

Ben's eyebrows shot up. What was he going on about? There was no way that was going to work on Connie. Not in a million years.

To his surprise, he noticed the glistening of tears in the woman's pale blue eyes.

"One time, my late husband sailed out into a hurricane for me," she said, her voice suddenly gentle. "I got lost, 'n even the Coast Guard was wary of the wind, but he didn't give up on me. We coulda both died out there instead of just me, but we didn't."

Asher looked over at Ben, who could only shrug.

Truth was, he was amazed.

He remembered Connie mentioning her husband had died, but he hadn't told Asher as much. Yet, somehow, his twin had known just the right words to say to tug at the woman's heart.

Maybe, despite how badly he'd screwed everything up, God was still looking out for them after all.

"That's beautiful, Connie," Ben said, reaching over to rest a hand on the woman's robe-clad shoulder. "I think–I mean, we're not married, so I know it's not the same, but I–I feel–"

"You feel the same way about that girl that my husband did about me," she finished matter-of-factly.

"I do," Ben admitted. "And you were right. I was a coward. I should have told her that a long time ago."

"It's not too late," Connie said, standing to her full height. "I know a boat you might be able to borrow to make it to La Pesca in time. Let me give my son a call."

Chapter 30

Grace

"You can't be serious, Dad," Jade spat, closing the door to the cabin behind her. "Are you really this stupid?"

Grace shrank back closer to the desk. The room felt even smaller now with three people in it. The memories of being trapped beneath the rubble of the fallen church pressed at her consciousness, threatening to pull her under once more. She said a silent prayer to God for His protection, drawing in several gulps of air. She wouldn't lose control. She had to stay right here in the moment. Katie needed her. And she needed herself.

"Was I supposed to let her starve, Jade?" Craig said, sounding even more meek than he had a few moments before. "Is that what you would have preferred?"

"You could have left the food outside. Why are you in here giving her more evidence? Why are you letting her see your face?"

"You're showing your own right now."

"She's already seen me, and she knows you're my dad," Jade said, enunciating each word as though she was trying to ensure a young child's understanding. "Not exactly difficult to puzzle out why I'm not bothering to hide. Honestly, it's amazing you've held onto Lumen this long. I'm surprised the rest of the board hasn't ousted you for someone smarter."

Grace gripped the edge of the desk with her fingers, sure that if she wasn't careful, she'd end up giving Jade a well-deserved slap across the face. Despite the circumstances, she actually felt a little bit bad for Craig.

"It doesn't matter," he said, shaking his head. "Whatever Grace sees or doesn't see, it doesn't matter. We're all walking away from this regardless."

"What about Katie?" Grace asked, ignoring Jade's hateful glare. "Does she get to walk away?"

"She's none of your concern," Jade snapped before Craig could answer. Despite the harshness of her words, Grace could see the sadness in her eyes. There were so many dynamics at play that she didn't understand. Had Jade's relationship with Katie been nothing but a very long con? Or had she truly seen her as a friend despite everything?

Craig turned to Grace, brushing a hand over his coily black hair. "Katie is here," he said. "She's probably still asleep. She's okay."

"For now," Jade muttered under her breath.

Katie was alive. That was something.

Grace sent up a silent prayer of thanks and leaned back in her chair, trying to figure out what her next move was going to be.

Ben

Ben pushed his sunglasses up on his nose as they raced along the coast, the spray of water salty against his lips.

"Can we go any faster?" Asher called out, his voice barely audible over the rushing water and the roar of the speedboat's engine.

Patrick glanced over his shoulder, shaking his head. "Not if we want our fuel to last."

Ben sat back in his seat next to his twin, picking at the scratched cream leather with a fingernail. The boat wasn't much to look at, but he wasn't exactly going to complain. As it turned out, Connie's son was not only a solid security guard, but an excellent captain. He'd assured them that they were going to make it to Playa La Pesca with time to spare.

Ben felt a vibration in the pocket of his shorts. Gabe was calling, probably looking for an update.

"Ha," Asher called out, grinning. "This one's all you, bro."

Ben rolled his eyes and answered the phone, turning up the volume as loud as it would go.

"You might wanna text," he said before Gabe could say hello. "It's a little loud here."

"Why? What are you doing?" Gabe asked, shouting to be heard.

He glanced over at Asher, who mimed locking his lips and throwing the key over the side of the boat. Ben shook his head.

"I know where Grace is right now," he said. "She's on a yacht, and we're going after her before they make it to the drop point."

"Are you two out of your minds?" Gabe snapped. "You didn't think to, I don't know, talk to me before just taking off?"

"We had to act," Ben said. "Grace gave us a major clue."

The engine's growl grew louder as Partrick coaxed it over a patch of choppy water.

"I'll explain when I can hear myself think," Ben yelled into the phone.

"This isn't the plan! Let me handle this!"

Ben gripped the phone more tightly as droplets

of water peppered his skin. "Did you get any new info about the swap since we talked?"

For a moment, the other end of the line was silent.

"No," Gabe admitted.

"So all we know is that the kidnappers are expecting the Hintons to come by land," Ben said, needing to shout a little less as Patrick eased the boat through less turbulent water. To his right, along the horizon, he could see the coast rushing past. Surely they had to at least be in Mexican waters by now.

"Correct," Gabe said.

"So they won't be expecting us by boat," Asher chimed in. "We'll be able to see what's going on. Best case scenario, we can extract Grace and apprehend her captors. Daddy Hinton saves some money. Everyone is happy."

"Worst case–" Gabe started.

"Worst case," Asher continued, "You have the two of us nearby as backup. And besides, what if Katie is with them? We can't just bring Grace home and abandon her."

"So much could go wrong," Gabe said at last. "I don't like it, Asher. Can't you ever just stick to the plan?"

Asher shrugged, saying nothing. Ben knew he would hardly argue that point. Gabe liked to play by the rules, and Asher took a more spur of the moment approach, and they frequently butted heads over it.

"He can't," Ben admitted. "But I usually do. That should tell you something."

He waited for Gabe to concede, but his older brother said nothing.

"You need to trust me, Gabe," he said. "This is what we need to do. I'll see you in Mexico."

He hung up without another word, and rested back in his seat again, closing his eyes and letting the warmth of the mid-morning sun bathe his face.

There were risks to what they were about to do, but he was confident all the same that it was the right thing. Things had fallen into place this way for a reason. He had to see it through to the end.

Grace

"What's going to happen to Katie?" Grace pressed, meeting Jade's angry eyes for a long moment before turning to Craig. "I'd like some answers."

The man looked down at the floor, but Jade's face broke out in a humorless grin.

"What are you going to do to her, Jade?" Grace demanded again through gritted teeth.

"Come on, Dad," Jade said, ignoring her question. "There isn't much time left before we need to make the swap."

She turned to Grace. "Don't worry, Grace. You'll be back to your normal life soon. You have shopping to do and nail appointments to go to. You won't need to worry about Katie Fairman any more."

Grace started to get to her feet, but managed to suppress her anger long enough to force herself to sit back down. She was used to the jabs made about how she chose to present herself to the world. She hoped Jade still thought she was an airhead and that Ben was both the brawn and the brains. Maybe it would lead her to do something careless and give her a chance to escape.

"Let's go," Jade said to Craig.

Craig shot Grace an apologetic look and followed her out. A moment later, she heard the click of the lock as they shut the door behind them.

Grace looked down in disgust. Craig was pathetic, but she figured that, too, might work to her advantage.

She wasn't sure how much time she'd have before the supposed swap. Even if they were telling the truth about returning her to her family, Katie Fairman was on this boat. She had to find her.

She scanned the room, trying to find anything that could be used as a weapon. It was quite sparse, but she doubted it was thanks to any intentional effort on the part of the Gorskys. It wasn't like anyone would keep a glass vase or a heavy statue sitting around in a ship's cabin, even if it wasn't being used as a makeshift prison cell.

She glanced up at the porthole window, watching

the rippling of the bright blue water that stretched as far as she could see.

A small smile spread over her face.

Could they really have been so careless?

She reached up for the rod that held the curtain and pulled on it. With only a little pressure, it came free of the hooks that secured it to the wall. It was light in her hands, but it might be strong enough to work as a weapon.

She had worked behind the scenes on enough cases at Forge Brothers Security to know how a hardened criminal behaved. Neither Craig nor Jade seemed to be the type, though Jade's nasty demeanor was far more worrisome.

They were expecting her to be what she was–an office manager with big blonde hair and a French manicure. She was sure they'd left her here expecting her to patiently await rescue, not to try and escape and rescue Katie herself.

She stood up near her bed, grasping the curtain rod firmly in both hands. Whenever they opened that door, she was going to be ready.

Chapter 31

Ben

"We're cutting it close," Ben said, looking down at his watch. It was already eleven in the morning, and the sun was high.

Asher pulled out his phone.

"Uh-oh," he said, holding up the screen so Ben could see. He'd expected a paragraph-long, bossy message from Gabe, but what he actually saw was much worse.

"No service," Ben said, pressing the heel of his palm against his forehead as he let a few swear words escape his lips. He could have acquired a satellite phone, but he hadn't even considered the possibility that they'd need one. Worrying about Grace was clouding his judgment.

"Well, hopefully we won't need to talk to Gabe," Asher said. His tone was jovial, but Ben knew him well enough to sense the anxiety that lingered beneath his unflappable demeanor.

They were going in blind, and if they weren't careful, things could get dangerous fast.

"Look straight ahead," Patrick called from the cockpit area of the speedboat, gesturing with one hand.

Ben gazed out across the impossibly blue water. In the distance, he could see several colorful mid-sized fishing boats dotting the Gulf.

"La Pesca beach is close now," Patrick continued loudly. "Lots of commercial fishermen work here."

Ben got up from his seat next to Asher and walked closer to where Patrick sat at the controls, gripping the safety bars that lined the edge of the boat. He waited in silence as they continued to draw closer, the sound of the growling motor filling his ears.

They were close, but were they close enough? What if they didn't make it before Grace got off the boat?

"Ben, yo!" Asher shouted out from behind him. "Check your three o'clock. Is that it?"

Ben squinted at the horizon, trying to figure out what Asher was talking about without having to raise his voice over the noise to ask him.

And then he saw what his brother meant.

"It's the yacht!" he cried. "Can you go any faster?"

Patrick didn't say anything, but he felt the grumbling beneath the deck deepening.

For a few minutes, he waited as they motored toward the much larger craft.

"Here's good!" Asher called out, getting up from his own seat as Patrick eased off of the throttle and stood up.

"Once you get in that water, I'm out of here,"

Patrick warned, stretching his arms high over his head. "I'm a security guard, not a cop."

"Neither are we."

"I carry a baton."

Asher paused for a moment, halfway through stuffing their pistols into two small waterproof bags. "You know, that's fair. Thanks for everything, man."

"Thank you, Patrick," Ben added quickly, his mind already focused on the task ahead.

"Best of luck," Patrick said, clapping them both on the shoulder.

Ben forced himself to breathe slowly as he and his twin climbed onto the edge of the boat. Suddenly, the reality of what he was about to do started to sink in. Gabe had been right from the beginning. He was rusty in the field, and now that the moment of truth had come, he was terrified of failure.

If it had been just some client, it would have been easier to fake confidence, but it wasn't. It was Grace, and failing her wasn't an option.

"You ready for this, bro?" Asher asked, a grin spreading across his face as he eyed the crystal water spread out before them.

Not even close.

Ben nodded, said a final desperate prayer, and jumped into the blue.

Grace

The water shushed gently against the boat as Grace waited, the sound only just loud enough to be heard through the thick glass of the porthole. The sun's reflection was her only clock, and time was passing with impossible slowness.

She no longer bothered to grip the curtain rod in her fist. She had set it against the edge of the desk where she could easily reach it, but as minutes drew into hours, she began to second guess whether she would even try to use it after all.

When the door opened–whenever that would be, if Craig and Jade's promise of freedom was even real–she wouldn't have a chance to stop and think. She'd have to act right away, and she wasn't sure if she could bring herself to do it.

She had been furious at both of them, but her anger had settled slowly into a combination of pity and terror. Craig was in over his head. She could see that. The thought of harming him felt wrong, even though she could argue with herself that he deserved it. Jade was much more dangerous, but if Grace attacked her, Craig might suddenly become a protective father.

She sighed, taking the three steps required to reach the bed and sinking onto it, letting her arm rest in a pool of sunlight streaming in through the porthole. She took several belly breaths, trying to calm the racing thoughts crowding her mind. They would do her no good. She was here in this room until something changed. She wasn't in control.

But she knew exactly who was.

She opened her mouth to pray aloud, not caring who might hear.

"Father in Heaven," she began, "please watch over me. Please help me to be patient as I await whatever comes next. Help me to take this time to relax my body, and most of all, to rest in You. Please grant me wisdom."

She paused, swallowing hard as unexpected tears began to blur her vision.

"Please, Jesus," she added, "just tell me what I need to do. I'm scared."

She waited there for several minutes, eyes pressed shut, trying to think and not to think at the same time.

There was no voice calling out in her mind, no words written in the seamless blue sky outside the boat. But she knew.

All He was asking of her right now was to wait.

She sat up on the bed and shuffled toward the desk, reaching out her fingers until she could wrap them around the curtain rod.

Renewed anger swelled up within her with sudden force.

She didn't want to let go of the weapon. She wanted that door to open, and she wanted to start swinging.

The last time she'd waited instead of acting, her life had changed forever.

Maybe it wouldn't have mattered what she did. Maybe she and everyone else in that church would have ended up beneath the rubble just the same.

She always told herself that, and maybe it was true.

Then again, maybe it wasn't.

Had she continued to report her student's suspicious comments about jihad, she might have been able to prevent him from blowing himself up that Sunday morning.

She could have been persistent. She could have had the courage to keep trying. They could have kept calling her a liar, paranoid, prejudiced. Why did it matter? Why had she cared what they thought, so long as she knew that she was doing all she could to protect the innocent?

But she had cared.

She'd gone against her instincts. She'd let herself be convinced that everything was fine.

In the end, thirty people had died.

"Jesus, please," she begged, her knuckles white against the curtain rod, every nerve in her body tensing in wait. "Please, don't make me sit here and wait for the roof to cave in on me again. Let me do something. Let me try and save her."

She hated the answer, but she could feel it deep within her, and she knew she could not disobey His gentle command.

Wait.

Grace walked over to the porthole again and threaded the curtain onto the rod before hefting it back into place.

Chapter 32

Ben

The side of the yacht loomed before them, growing taller as they swam toward it. The sun was high now, reflecting off the sleek white fiberglass.

"There's no one on deck, just like Connie said," Ben said to Asher beside him as they paused to catch their breaths.

"Are you sure?" Asher asked, rubbing saltwater from his eyes with pruny fingertips.

Ben nodded. "Let's just check one more thing."

He started swimming toward the back of the boat, and Asher followed.

"Boom."

Ben pointed upward. There it was, written in a neat black font across the stern of the boat.

Lumeneer

Asher stared for a long moment. "Okay, you better enjoy this, because it won't be happening again any time soon, but I can admit it. You were right. Now let's get Grace back."

His twin turned and started swimming toward the other side of the boat. He followed, lost in the depth of his thoughts as the surprisingly cool water turned his skin to gooseflesh.

What if it was too late? What if they lost her?

He couldn't bear the thought.

For years now, he'd seen her nearly every day. She'd been there for every important moment in all of their lives, already family to him and his brothers. He had denied it for so long, but his life would never be what it was without Grace Isabella Hinton in it.

It was selfish to think of himself and how he would feel. He knew. He knew that if they got out of this, she'd have every reason to walk away and find a man who valued her like she deserved. He wouldn't hold it against her if she did. But right now, all that mattered was that she had the chance to choose. He'd deal with whatever pain he had to, just as long as she was okay.

"There's a way up!" Asher called out to him, yanking him back into the present moment. After a few more breaststrokes along the yacht's far side, he saw the ladder. His brother was treading water at the base of it, looking down at his phone screen.

"It's quarter past eleven. I hope they're still here."

Ben nodded. No matter how they looked at it, climbing up there would be risky.

If everyone had gone to shore to make the ransom swap with Grace's parents, there would be nothing they could do to help without a boat. All of this would have been for nothing, and Gabe would have to work a miracle on his own, especially if he planned to help Katie Fairman.

On the other hand, even though no one seemed to have heard Asher shouting or noticed them in the water, the enemy could be hiding just out of sight overhead.

As usual, Asher seemed to know exactly what his fears were.

"God has brought us this far," he reminded him. "If you still feel in your heart that she's here, I believe you."

Ben paused, looking up at the perfect sky for a long moment. Asher struggled with maintaining his childhood faith in God even more than he himself did, and yet, here his brother was, finding ways to trust Him more and more each day.

"I do," Ben said at last. "I know she's close."

As he said the words, he felt a strange peace washing over him, warming him even as the shadow of the boat chilled his damp skin.

Maybe if he wanted to learn to open his heart and to trust others, he had to ask God to break down his walls. Maybe that was step one. Not that he had time to get too vulnerable at the moment.

"God, please be with us," he said as he started up the ladder, Asher close at his heels.

Before he stuck his head above the edge of the deck, he reached over with one hand and unzipped his waterproof bag.

He gripped the pistol in his hand, and let out a calm, controlled breath.

He may have been out of practice in the field, but he still spent a lot of time at the range.

No matter what was coming, he'd be ready.

Gabe

Gabe rested his arm against the windowsill as the inconspicuous Ford Bronco sped along the narrow country highway. The sun was shining bright, and he was sure he'd end up with a weird single-arm tan, but the fresh air was worth it. He could almost smell the sea.

Every few minutes, the vehicle bucked over a pothole or two, but for the most part, he'd been pleasantly surprised by the level of road maintenance in middle-of-nowhere Tamaulipas.

"Looks like we've almost hit the actual town of La Pesca," he said, gesturing toward the windshield. Up ahead, he could see more traffic, and a few taller buildings sticking out over the tops of the palm trees. "It'll still be a couple of miles until we reach the beach, though."

Isla Hinton leaned forward, sticking her hairspray-scented head in between the driver and passenger seats.

"You're sure that Gracie wasn't taken by the cartel?" she asked in a stage whisper, as though the rental car they had taken from the airport might somehow be bugged.

Gabe pressed his hands more tightly around the steering wheel. "I'm not sure of much, Mrs. Hinton," he reminded her. "But there's no evidence of that, no."

"They're dangerous," Mrs. Hinton continued, undeterred. "Not the sort of men we should be taking on alone. They might poison our tequila. Or shoot us in cold blood, leaving our lifeless bodies floating in a pool at their fancy estate!"

Gabe furrowed his brow. "Why would we be drinking tequila? What estate?"

Mrs. Hinton pointed in the direction of the road ahead with one long pink fingernail. "You never know, Gabriel. Best to prepare ourselves. Do you know how to create a bomb out of an Etch-a-Sketch board? Just in case?"

"What–"

"I don't care if we have to take on every criminal in the state," Mr. Hinton snapped from the back seat. "We're getting our girl home. I'll do it myself if I have to!"

Gabe pressed his foot gently on the brake, slowing the SUV as they entered the town.

"Let's just focus," he said, giving Mrs. Hinton a pointed look. She sank back into her seat and clicked her seatbelt back into place. "I need you both to keep your eyes open, all right?"

He didn't, of course–their help would probably prove more dangerous than handling everything by himself–but hopefully it would give them something to do aside from arguing.

The car was quiet as he rolled through the main strip of La Pesca. As always, he was struck by just how colorful Mexico tended to be compared to San Antonio. It was a simple but pleasant looking place, with at least a dozen family-owned restaurants and food stalls lining the streets.

Within a couple of minutes, they'd passed through the entire town and returned to an even wider highway. The back seat remained quiet as they passed a mile or so of farmers' fields until finally they passed beneath a blue archway that informed them Playa La Pesca was just ahead.

"Ooh, that lighthouse is so cute," Mrs. Hinton exclaimed as they drew nearer, rolling down her window. Gabe heard the click of her digital camera behind him, and watched as several unfriendly-looking guys stared at the car from where they were standing on the side of the road.

He tipped an imaginary hat brim in their direction and offered a friendly smile, which was fortunately returned by the locals. There weren't cartel drug lords hiding under every rock, to be sure, but they were still traveling in a state under a current travel advisory by the American government, and he wasn't going to let his guard down.

"There's the beach. We're coming, Gracie girl," Mr. Hinton said quietly.

Gabe slowed the SUV as they reached what was apparently the end of the paved road and continued onto the dusty, bumpy streets that led closer to the coast. It was quieter here, but he could still see several obvious tourists milling around the ramshackle buildings that housed local eateries and other small businesses.

He glanced out at the beach and the blue water beyond, as well as the long stone jetty that reached out into the Gulf. He could imagine the location of the nearby dock where the kidnappers were supposed to arrive, but he didn't dare get any closer.

He turned off of the road that served as a main street and continued until he reached a secluded area behind a few buildings that was little more than a driveway. He turned off the Bronco and closed his eyes, taking a couple deep breaths. He could almost hear his father's voice in his head, reminding him to pray, but he ignored it. The clock on the dashboard indicated just how little time they had left.

He turned to the back seat. "How are you both feeling?"

"I'm ready to get my daughter back," Mr. Hinton said without a moment's hesitation.

"Me, too," Mrs. Hinton chimed in.

Gabe looked over the older couple. The two of them were supposed to be dressed as ordinary tourists, but their outfits looked just a little too expensive to be fully convincing. Especially Mrs. Hinton, who had probably assumed the Forge Brothers Security staff members were joking when they suggested she pick up something at Walmart.

Worse still, her immaculate makeup and perfectly styled blonde bob screamed money.

Once again, Gabe was reminded of just how many things Grace handled as office manager at FBS. Despite having a similar flashy style to her mother, she excelled at putting together disguises for undercover work.

"I think you would look better with a hat," Gabe said, thinking quickly. He reached over and plucked his own baseball cap from where it had been sitting on the dashboard.

Isla Hinton looked at it like it was a rotten fish before reluctantly balancing it on top of her head. "Yes, much more authentic," her husband said, planting a kiss on her artificially smooth cheek. "We need to blend in."

Gabe nodded. "It's very possible that the kidnappers have people around. I don't want you two doing anything that might make you stand out. Just follow the plan, and everything will be okay."

He wished he felt as confident as he sounded. Truth was, he didn't know what to expect, and the plan he'd put together was only as good as the limited information he had.

He had tried to get ahold of Ben and Asher again, hoping they'd dug up something new, but neither of them were answering their phones. He wasn't worried about them–they'd probably just lost service–but he hated how blind and isolated he felt.

"Now we just go to the dock and wait?" Mrs. Hinton asked, breaking the tense silence.

Gabe nodded. "You remember where you're going?"

Mr. Hinton placed a protective arm around his

wife's shoulders. "I studied the map about fifty times on the flight here. I'll find the dock."

"Good. Okay. Go to the dock and wait. When the kidnapper or kidnappers arrive, follow their instructions. Do not argue. Do not talk back to them. And do not give them a single dime until Grace is within your sight," he said, pausing for emphasis. "You got that? You have to see Grace before you transfer the funds, no matter what."

The couple bobbed their heads up and down in agreement.

"We can do this," Mrs. Hinton said, sticking a few stray strands of blonde hair back under the baseball cap.

"I'll be close by," he assured them. "Everything is going to be fine."

Chapter 33

Ben

Ben stuck the gun into the waistband of his shorts as he climbed the last foot or so up the ladder, squinting in the sun. Just as they suspected, the deck of the yacht appeared to be empty.

Just in case they weren't alone, however, he ducked behind a row of comfortable-looking lounge seats before beckoning for Asher to follow him the rest of the way.

"This feels a little too much like a ghost ship," Asher said as he settled in beside Ben and did a visual sweep of the area. "But I have to admit, it's nice. Maybe I should tell Gabe we should work toward buying a company yacht. Man, that would be awesome, right? Like a supervillain lair, but for the good guys."

Ben stood to his full height, trying to get a better look at their surroundings. 'Nice' was an understatement. Everything on the yacht looked unbelievably expensive and well-maintained, which was strange, considering he could see no crew members anywhere.

There were couches, lounge chairs, and side tables dotting the space, all upholstered in blue fabric. A round bar sat in the center of the main deck, and toward the bow, he could see what appeared to be a dining area with several tables. It would be the perfect setting for an upscale company party.

"That's what I don't get. I looked into Lumen's financials, and they're just as solid as this yacht suggests. So why would the company be linked to two kidnappings?"

Asher shrugged and gestured toward the dining space. "Beats me. I think I see a door over there. Let's move."

Ben patted the gun at his waist, reassured by the firmness of the metal beneath his fingertips. If he was right, Grace was close. Maybe only a few feet away. But that didn't mean actually finding her would be easy.

Asher took the lead as the two men made their way around a curving white wall. As they drew closer, Ben noticed that there was a staircase leading up toward a smaller deck above as well as the door that led to the main floor's interior space.

"I wish we had a map," Asher said, raising a hand to his forehead and trying to get a view of the upper deck after taking a couple steps up the stairs.

Once again, the pain of Grace's absence seemed to leech the air from Ben's lungs. She had told Ben the exact model of the yacht, which he'd long since forgotten. With her help, they would have been able to find a floor plan.

"If Grace is here, she'll be inside," Ben said firmly, moving toward the door. "Let's go."

The interior of the yacht was just as luxurious as the deck. The two men made their way through a second dining space and a small indoor bar until finally they reached a staff door.

The hall on the other side of it was empty, just like the rest of the ship, but Ben knew it wasn't possible that they were truly alone. He could feel the soft hum of the engine below as they made their way along the carpeted passage.

"Look," Asher whispered, their voices sounding suddenly loud in the tighter quarters. "Kitchen."

Ben nodded, letting Asher take the lead once more as he pushed his way through the door. If there were any dishes or leftovers left laying around, they might be able to get an idea of how many people were on board.

The room was large, though unlike the public-facing areas of the ship, the aesthetic was purely functional. The sink was completely empty and wiped clean. "Well, that's no help," Ben said. "Check the fridge."

Before Asher could do so, however, Ben heard the sound of footsteps in the hall. They were close. "In here!" he called out, yanking open a door that led to a walk-in pantry. Asher ducked in beside him just in time for them to hear the metal door to the kitchen swinging open.

"Let's hope they don't need any flour," Asher muttered.

Ben shushed him and pressed his eye against the small crack he'd left between the door and its frame, waiting for whoever had entered the room to step into view. Despite his lack of recent practice in the field, his body was tense with anticipation, as though muscle memory had kicked in.

He forced himself to take a few quiet breaths. There would be no use in taking the kidnappers by surprise if he dove in without a plan.

"It's just about time," said a male voice.

Ben squinted as he peered through the narrow space. Jade Gorsky stood several feet away, leaning against a countertop. In front of her was a handsome man that he recognized from his research into Lumen to be her father, Craig.

"Whatever."

"I told you, Jade," Craig snapped. "It's all arranged. I have a local guy on shore to make sure the Hintons send the money to an untraceable, offshore account. Once we have confirmation, we send Grace over in the dinghy, and we'll be on our way."

Asher made a low scoffing sound next to him, and Ben jabbed him sideways in the ribs. His brother didn't have to make a sound for him to know what he was thinking.

Gabe was no amateur. He'd never give the Hintons the go-ahead to transfer the 1.8 million without seeing that Grace was alive and well. But the less Craig and Jade knew about who they were dealing with, the better.

"Great," Jade said, tossing her dark curls back as she rolled her eyes at her father. "And what if Grace tells everyone who we are, Dad? Ever think of that?"

Craig's jaw tightened. "I keep trying to tell you. It doesn't matter. We'll be gone."

"What if we aren't? What if we don't make it out of here fast enough?"

"Everything is going to be fine."

Jade laughed without mirth. "You're grasping at straws. We both know it. Even if those new-money bumpkins actually give us the funds, which I doubt, the whole reason we kidnapped Hinton was to stop her from getting any closer to the truth."

"She doesn't–"

"She knows everything now, thanks to you!" Jade snapped, not allowing her father to so much as finish his sentence.

"Jade."

Craig stepped forward, resting a dark hand gently against her shoulder. "I know how people like Robert and Isla Hinton act," he continued. "They don't care about money. They just want their daughter back. We can all walk away from this with at least some of what we want."

Ben waited for Jade to argue, but instead she pouted like a toddler, crossing her arms over her chest. His mouth twisted in disgust at her behavior. He had been right to trust his instincts about her from the beginning. She was a snake.

"Once we get Grace out of here, we'll dump Katie Fairman off on the streets of Tampico, and then we'll keep running. I have it all figured out. Who cares who finds out about us after that? We'll be free! It's not perfect, but it's going to work. You need to trust me."

Jade's expression only hardened, but Craig pressed on, pacing back and forth between the countertop and a serving cart.

"It's the only option we have left. I'm not going to follow along as Lumen spits on your mother's grave. I won't do it."

Jade hesitated.

Ben watched her face, trying to read what lay behind the pained expression that he found there. He had looked into Amira Gorsky's untimely death, but his research had mostly been focused elsewhere. What was it he had missed?

At last, Jade spoke again. Any hint of possible gentleness disappeared in an instant.

"This is insane," she said firmly. "I should have handled all of this from the start, right when Katie figured out what was going on."

Craig said nothing, but Ben could see tears shining in his rich brown eyes as he looked over at his daughter. He was a broken man if he'd ever seen one.

"The plan was perfect," Jade continued. "Donald would have kept paying. We would have escaped all of this in less than a year. But no. You had to ruin everything with your cowardice."

"This is not who I raised you to be," Craig said, his voice caught in his throat. "Your mother, she wouldn't want this, she–"

Ben watched as Jade reached somewhere out of his line of sight.

"Stop," Craig whimpered, raising both hands in the air.

Jade let out another barking laugh. In her hands, Ben recognized the metallic gleam of a pistol.

He started forward, ready to burst through the door with his own gun raised, but Asher had taken hold of his t-shirt, yanking him back. He had no choice but to oblige if he wanted their position to remain hidden. He allowed Asher to move in front of him.

Their eyes met in the dimness of the pantry. Neither could speak, but they didn't need to.

Asher must have some sort of plan in mind. Before he could decide whether or not he was going to trust his twin's judgment, Jade spoke again.

"I'm not going to shoot you," she said, her voice laced with disgust. "Be serious."

Ben released the breath he'd caught in his lungs. So she wasn't going to shoot her own father. Good, but hardly reassuring, considering who else was on board the Lumeneer.

"Just hold on," Asher whispered, just loud enough for Ben to hear. "I have a plan."

Ben almost nodded before he remembered his face was pressed against the crack of the door.

"What are you doing, Jade?" Craig asked, his voice unsteady. Ben tightened his fists. Craig Gorsky seriously needed to grow a pair, but he supposed that ship had long since sailed. Especially now that his daughter was holding a firearm.

"Nothing yet–" Jade said, sticking the gun into the pocket of her jeans. Craig pressed his fingers hard against his temples, as though massaging away a terrible headache. "–but I am going to act."

"Jade–"

"I'm going to do what you should have done in the first place. When the money hits the account, we dump Grace Hinton and Katie Fairman right here in the Gulf. No more messing around."

Chapter 34

Ben

The floor seemed to fall out from beneath Ben's feet.

Jade wanted to kill Katie. She wanted to kill Grace.

"Wait, Ben," Asher was whispering beside him, his fingertips biting into his forearm. Every muscle in his body was burning, eager for action. All he wanted to do was to fight, and were it not for his brother's insistence, he would already be out that door.

"Wait until the moment is right, and then go after the girls."

Ben backed up a couple of steps, allowing his twin to slip past him, toward the door.

Please, God, keep my brother safe.

Asher waited for several seconds for Craig and Jade to begin arguing once again, and then he burst out of the pantry, weapon drawn.

The door swung shut behind him, leaving Ben alone, trying to calm his too-loud breaths. He pressed his eyes shut and took a couple steps closer to the door, trying to listen to what was going on. The pantry door was heavier than he'd realized, muffling the sounds in the kitchen now that it was completely closed.

"Drop the gun, Jade," he heard Asher say, his voice calm.

Ben could imagine him standing there, his own pistol raised, every word exuding authority. His twin could be a goofball, but his military expertise and private security training always resurfaced when it counted.

"Drop it!" Asher shouted. "Now!"

The silence extended for what felt like a very long time, until at last Ben heard Craig Gorsky's meek plea.

"Do what he says, honey. Drop the gun."

Ben heard the sound of metal clattering to the floor, but it was scarcely audible over the sound of his heartbeat hammering in his ears. He was relieved that Jade was no longer armed, but the danger wasn't over. Especially since he couldn't see what else was going on.

"You're coming with me," Asher ordered. "You too, Craig."

Ben waited until the sound of footsteps faded, and then forced himself to count out another agonizing minute, just to be sure.

He yanked the door of the pantry open and escaped into the kitchen, his eyes adjusting to the brightness of the overhead lights. He had no idea how much time he had, or if Craig and Jade had any accomplices on board. He imagined that such a big yacht would ordinarily require a crew, but so far, there was nothing to indicate the presence of anyone else.

He made his way out into the hallway, scanning the area for any hint at which direction to take.

He had to find her.

Grace

Grace's eyes shot open.

Somewhere overhead, she heard the faint sound of a male voice. It was deeper than Craig's, but aside from that, she couldn't make out any more detail.

She leaned back against the wall, closing her eyes for several long seconds. She'd been trying to pray, but it was difficult to focus.

Her mind raced as she wondered where her parents might be. She could only hope that if they were going to pay the ransom the kidnappers demanded, they would do so safely from the shore.

Her stomach twisted. Her mother and father might be willing to meet their demands, but her friends from FBS wouldn't. Ben wouldn't. No matter how they'd left things, he'd never abandon her. And that meant he'd put himself in danger to make sure she was safe.

The sound of footsteps began again.

She looked up at the porthole, considering the curtain rod she'd replaced once again, but it was too late.

The door swung open.

It was Ben.

For a second, she said nothing, placing her hand over her mouth as relief swelled within her chest along with all of her unspoken questions. How had he found her? Were her parents okay? Had he found Katie? Was Asher here, too? What had happened to Craig? Jade?

Without a word, Ben closed the short distance between them, taking her by both hands and pulling her from the bed.

She made no attempt to shy away as he pulled her into his muscled chest, holding her tight enough to still the air in her lungs. She felt his face pressing against her hair, and then he drew back just a little, reaching down to hold her jaw carefully, tilting her face up toward his own.

"I'm so sorry, Gracie," he said, his green eyes piercing through her as he began to speak, the words tumbling over one another as he tried to let them all out. "Thank God. Thank God you're okay. You were right about the yacht from the start. Were it not for your instincts, Asher and I never would have–You were right about a lot more than that, but I–"

Grace lifted herself up onto her toes and kissed him.

She allowed herself to enjoy the taste of his lips for several precious seconds as he knotted his fingers in her hair, pulling her closer, speaking a thousand unspoken promises without a word.

Warmth rushed through her heart, burning away the last remnants of her frustration and hurt. None of that mattered now. She had three words to offer him, her own promise to make. Before she could blurt them out, however, Ben drew back.

"We need to move," he said, the lingering smile falling away from his face in an instant, replacing it with the professional, calm mask he wore so often.

Grace gave his hand a squeeze. Ben Forge had finally let her see into the depths of his heart, but at the moment, she was thankful for the presence of a man who knew how to put up walls in order to protect those he loved.

"Do you have any idea where Katie is?" Ben asked as he ducked into the hall, looking up and down the passage before ushering Grace to follow.

"They said she's here on the boat," she said quietly, staying only a few steps behind him as he made his way forward, gun drawn. She swallowed. "But I haven't heard her."

Ben turned to face her.

He reached over and tucked a lock of blonde curls behind her ear, giving her a slight smile that still reached his fierce green eyes.

"Hey. Have faith. She's okay."

Grace smiled up at him, wishing that she had time to run her fingers through his auburn hair and kiss him all over again.

"Asher needs my help. We need to find her and head above deck," Ben commanded, his serious expression returning in an instant. "Stay behind me. If anything happens, run."

Chapter 35

Gabe

Gabriel peered through the binoculars as the Hintons strode toward the dock at a slow, natural pace, just as he'd instructed them to do. So far, so good.

They were wired with mics, but he couldn't risk giving them earpieces and having the kidnapper's lackeys spot them. Their communication was solely one-way, and it made him nervous. The beach was fairly busy, but so far, he had been able to maintain his line of sight.

Still, there were enough people that keeping an eye out for suspicious activity on his own was difficult. The milling beachgoers weaved across the thick sand, laughing with one another and sipping beers as the ocean lapped at the shore. There were several docks with small fishing boats to watch, and near where he stood there were at least a dozen small buildings.

Trouble could be hiding anywhere, and he had no idea what he would do if he had to deal with a threat. He needed backup, but with Ben and Asher otherwise occupied, Reilly on paternity leave, and Cameron holding down the fort back in San Antonio, there was no one else to pull.

He could have sought the help of one of their hired operatives, but this job was particularly sensitive, and he was stubborn.

He thought of his brother Jacob. Maybe someday, he'd come home and join the team. But for now, he seemed content to trek across the world, evangelizing and trying to aid persecuted Christians. Or perhaps he wasn't content at all. Perhaps he stayed away because he still hadn't forgiven himself for the sins of his past.

Gabe's thoughts shifted abruptly as he noticed a man emerging from the crowd and heading straight for the Hintons. He followed with his binoculars, taking note of his appearance. He was Latino, and fit in perfectly with the rest of the crowd in his casual cargo shorts, flip-flop sandals, and bright orange t-shirt. Probably a local hired hand.

The man extended a hand and took hold of Isla Hinton's forearm. Gabe saw the woman flinch, but she didn't try and pull away.

For several long seconds he could hear nothing but the crowd surrounding them as the couple and the strange man walked onto the narrow dock where they'd been instructed to meet the kidnappers. Gabe held his binoculars steady as they headed down the worn wood, now far enough away from the rest of the beachgoers that they wouldn't be overheard.

At last, the man spoke.

Gabe fiddled with the controls on his radio as it crackled, struggling to deliver a clear sound with the voice in close range of the microphones the Hintons wore. He'd enlisted the help of some of the other FBS technical staff in rigging up the surveillance equipment, but none of their skills matched Ben's.

"I'm going to give you a sheet of paper, Mr. Hinton," the man said over the slight static in accented English. So far as Gabe could hear, he sounded calm, almost robotic, like he was following a script. Which he probably was.

"On it, there is an account number and the security information you'll need. You will borrow my mobile phone, and you will call whoever you need to in order to get this money safely deposited into the account. I assume your people are already waiting to be contacted?"

Gabe watched as Robert Hinton opened his mouth to speak.

"No," the man said firmly, cutting him off. "Just nod."

Both of the Hintons complied.

"Good. I'll talk, you listen."

The man shifted his weight, and Gabe saw the silvery flash of a pistol holstered at his side. He was only inches from Isla, and considering the wide-eyed look on her face, she had probably spotted the gun as well.

"As soon as the money hits, I'll know about it. Don't bother trying to have the cops or your pals at that little security company your daughter works for run a trace. My associates on the other end will have the funds split and routed within minutes."

"W—we don't care about the money," Mrs. Hinton stammered. The man glared at her as she spoke, but she continued. "We just want Grace to come home. That's all that matters."

"Good," he said, nodding his head. "Now get to it."

Gabe stared through the binoculars, searching Mr. Hinton's face.

Uh oh.

He watched in horror as the man produced a simple black flip phone and handed it to Robert.

Gabe swore under his breath, glancing around him to be sure no locals or tourists had wandered over to his secluded lookout. "No, no, no, not without seeing Grace," he said aloud. "Don't give them the money. Don't do it."

Mr. Hinton was typing a number into the phone, and then he raised it to his ear. He had to be calling Cameron, who was handling the deposit back at Forge Brothers Security.

"I need the transfer now. I will text message you the details," Mr. Hinton said, keeping his request simple, just as Gabe and the others had instructed him to do after they had Grace.

Gabe fumbled in his pocket for his own smartphone, debating whether he should call Cameron himself and tell him not to send the funds. But if they didn't get the money...

He swallowed hard and paced a few steps, trying to think.

This whole thing was going south, and fast.

"He's sending the money," Mrs. Hinton said. "Where is my daughter?"

"I told you to stop talking," the man snapped, following up his admonition with a string of Spanish words Gabe only somewhat understood. None of them were pleasant.

Gabe lowered the binoculars, wiping sweat from his brow. This was a disaster. In a matter of seconds, they had lost all of their bargaining power.

He glanced around the beach, the buildings, and the boats bobbing out on the waves. Where was Grace? Where was Katie?

For the first time, he noticed a large yacht resting in the blue water. It looked out of place, exactly as his brothers had described. Maybe they were right. Maybe the two missing women were on board right now.

He quickly navigated to his recent calls list and dialed Ben. No answer. He tried the same for Asher, with the same result. Just as before, it seemed neither of them had phone service.

He raised his binoculars to his face again, his gaze settling on the Hintons as they took a few steps back down the dock, toward the beach. What were they–

Just then, the sound of a gunshot pierced the sky.

Chapter 36

Ben

A gunshot rang out somewhere on the deck above before they could reach the next room they planned to check.

In a heartbeat, Ben had drawn his own weapon, scanning the narrow hallway.

"You need to get Katie and try to find a way to call for help," he said firmly, turning to face her. "I need to get to Asher."

Grace stared up at him, her bright blue eyes steeled with determination. "I'm not leaving you again, Ben. I can't do it."

He wanted to demand that she do what he asked. He could be persuasive when he needed to be, especially if he was willing to hurt her for her own good. But she was right. He couldn't stand to separate from her any more than she could walk away from him. It was her clue that had brought him this far. They had to do this together, whatever the risk.

He sighed. "I assume they took your gun?"

She nodded.

"Stay behind me."

The hall was quiet again. They stepped forward until they reached the door.

To Ben's deep relief, they heard the sound of a woman sobbing on the other side.

Grace rapped her knuckles on the wood.

"Katie? It's Grace. Grace Hinton. Open the door."

They could hear a muffled female voice attempting to respond, but the door was apparently locked from the outside. Grace glanced over at Ben expectantly, her eyes lingering on his shoulders. Turns out, the time in the gym was even more worth it than he'd previously thought.

"Stand back!" he ordered.

After giving Katie a couple of seconds to get out of the way, he lunged forward, heaving all his weight into the pale wood of the door. He heard splintering, and his shoulder ached, but it didn't give.

He bit back a curse. Had he been wearing sturdier shoes, he would have kicked it in, but it was too late for that. He rushed forward again, ignoring the pain that jolted through his arm and torso.

This time, the door crunched inward.

Grace rushed past him. A girl who looked a little too young to drink sat on the bed inside, dressed in the same black Eagles shirt she'd been wearing on the security footage. She was blonde and pretty like Grace, though Ben noticed that her eyes were brown instead of blue.

They were also filled with tears as Grace climbed up onto the bed and hugged her younger friend, pulling her close and assuring her that everything was going to be okay.

Guilt clutched at his heart. He'd questioned Katie Fairman's character due to her association with Jade and her choice to spend spring break partying. His assumptions may have had some truth to them, but the poor girl had been betrayed by someone who was supposedly her best friend and had spent days in captivity. She needed empathy, not rash judgment.

He allowed the two women a moment to connect, but unfortunately, a minute or two was all they could afford.

Gabe

The crowds on the beach rushed off in all directions at the sound of the gunshot, pouring out onto the narrow streets and ducking into buildings. Gabe didn't bother to hide his binoculars as a group of teenage girls nearly bowled him over, shrieking with fear as they ran in the direction of the main road.

He managed to get the Hintons in sight, but for a moment he struggled to hear what was being said over the panicked shouts of the crowd. He looked out at the yacht. Had the shot come from that direction? There had been too much chaos for him to place the sound.

"The money!"

The speakers cracked and protested in Gabe's ear as the Latino man barked at Mr. Hinton, grabbing him by the front of his shirt. "You sent it, yes?"

Gabe watched Robert nod. "Yes! Yes, I sent it!"

The man let go.

"I'm not getting paid to join a gunfight. Good luck to you both."

He started taking off across the dock at a run. Gabe dropped his binoculars, trying to follow his movement into the crowd. He could hear the Hintons shouting at the man's retreating back. Fortunately, they didn't attempt to give chase.

"Wait! Please, I know you're not the mastermind here. Just tell me where my baby is!"

Gabe's heart ached at the sound of Mrs. Hinton's plea. This operation had fallen apart almost as quickly as it began. If there was any hope of making things right, he had to choose carefully what he was going to do next.

Gabe paused, watching as the man slowed down near a stack of crates. He pulled out his phone and punched a few buttons before raising it to his ear. A few seconds later, he pocketed it and took off again.

Every muscle in his legs longed to race after him. Gabe had little doubt he could take him down, especially since the man was scarcely taller than Mrs. Hinton. But he doubted there would be any point. He was probably a local like he'd assumed, someone who was given a task to do and little other information. Otherwise, he would have properly confirmed the money was deposited before taking off.

Meanwhile, someone else out there not only had a gun, but had used it. Katie and Grace were in danger. And so were his brothers.

He shook his head in frustration as he watched the man blend into the crowd, disappearing from view. No time to change his mind now. It was time to fetch the Hintons and figure out how on earth he was going to get everyone out of this nightmare.

Chapter 37

Grace

The ship was bigger than Grace had assumed. A lot bigger.

As Ben led her and Katie through the twisted maze of corridors, she worried he'd gotten lost, but she kept her thoughts to herself.

Instead, she kept glancing back at Katie, wishing she had time to ask some of the questions that plagued her about her disappearance. She hoped that Ben and Asher had found some answers, because as far as she could tell, nothing Craig and Jade had done made much sense.

"This is it. Wait until I say you're clear," Ben ordered, raising his pistol as he came to a stop at one of the doors. Grace didn't argue. She hung back with Katie as he pushed his way forward, letting a ray of harsh sunlight filter in.

She watched as he surveyed the area in practiced motions, moving his pistol in a wide arc. It was obvious to her that he was just as good an operative as Gabe, Cam, Asher, or Reilly, and she couldn't help but wonder why exactly he tended to lock himself away with his computers rather than picking up a gun and heading into the action.

She knew he'd lost his job with the San Antonio Police, but she didn't know exactly what had happened. She resolved to work up the nerve to ask him about it again. Just as soon as their lives were no longer in danger.

"Keep quiet," Ben said, his voice rising just above a whisper as he ducked his head back into the hall and ushered them forward. "I hear voices. Katie, I need you to head left and make for the bridge. Radio for help. Tell them we're near La Pesca, Mexico, and that we're close to shore. It's not like they can miss a yacht of this size."

Grace turned to meet Ben's eyes, giving him a questioning look. He nodded once.

Clearly, he had good reason to believe they were alone on the ship aside from Jade and Craig. They'd just have to trust that Katie wouldn't run into any more accomplices, and hope that she could figure out how to work a marine radio.

"You can do this," Grace said to her friend, giving her shoulder a squeeze.

"You got it," Katie said firmly. She moved past Ben and started walking along the wall slowly, following the signs overhead that indicated the direction of the bridge. She stood tall, and she didn't look back.

"You're not going to tell me to go with her?" Grace asked, turning back toward Ben.

"Would you listen?"

"Not a chance."

Their eyes met, and unspoken words filled the space between them. Grace's heart began to beat a little faster as his intense gaze held her own. She could hear the whispering of the gleaming blue ocean as it touched the side of the yacht. The sunshine warmed her skin.

Despite her fear, she felt peace.

Ben had walked away. He'd hurt her. But when it counted, he showed up, just as he always did.

"Let's finish this," he said.

He started off toward the right, and Grace followed a couple steps behind.

Nothing could have prepared her for what she saw when they rounded the corner.

Craig Gorsky was lying on the ground in a pool of blood.

It was so much more blood than she would have expected a gunshot wound to produce. In the movies, it looked so sterile, all tidy pools of red, stretching slowly over the ground.

The reality was so much worse.

It was smeared against the lacquered wood of the deck, decorating it with streaks and unintelligible patterns. It stank of metal, so strong that Grace could taste it on her tongue. She swallowed hard and closed her eyes for a long second, determined not to throw up.

Asher was on his knees in the red liquid, using his balled-up t-shirt to apply pressure to the wound in the center of Craig's chest.

Jade stood a few feet away, her smooth, pedicured feet speckled with tiny dots of red.

She was holding a gun, and it was pointed straight at Asher's back.

Ben

Ben stood perfectly still against the wall.

His mind was reeling. Whatever had happened prior to their arrival, Jade now held Asher's black Glock. Her hands were perfectly still, and her face revealed no emotion. Her coldness terrified him even more than her rage. He had no doubt in his mind that she'd shoot his brother without a second thought if it would benefit her.

He could feel Grace pressed in behind him, and could hear a slight whisper as she sucked air in and out of her lungs, trying to quiet her breathing. He wanted time to think, but there was none.

The element of surprise was their biggest advantage. It would put Grace in danger, but so would anything else he did.

Lord, please keep her safe.

He jumped forward, his own gun raised.

"Jade, drop your weapon!" he shouted in his best police officer voice, hoping to startle her into compliance.

Instead, the young woman laughed.

"Yeah, right," she scoffed, examining her immaculate fingernails as she continued to grip the pistol. "You won't shoot me."

Ben felt his palms beginning to dampen as he held the gun even more tightly.

The smug witch was right. He couldn't do it. Not with his brother at the other end of his target's weapon. All it would take was a split second for her to pull the trigger.

Before he could argue with Jade, Grace stepped forward, walking toward her without so much as a glance at the deadly firearm she held. "What happened here?" she demanded.

Her voice shook a little, but Ben's heart warmed with approval. He hated that she was here and putting herself at risk, but until they figured out their next move, the only option was to try and keep Jade talking.

Katie had hopefully called for help by now, and when Grace failed to show up for the ransom swap they'd planned with the Hintons, Gabe would eventually come to their aid. He knew that they had been going for the yacht. Biding their time might be enough for all of them to survive this. Unless he could think of another way out of this that didn't involve jumping Jade for her weapon or shooting her himself.

He glanced down at Craig. He was breathing, but it was clear he was in very bad shape. Without medical care, Ben doubted the man could go on much longer.

Asher looked over his shoulder.

There was none of the usual laughter in his blue eyes, only hollowness and sorrow.

"He got hold of a liquor bottle and swung it at my face," he said, turning back to Craig and continuing to keep a firm hold on his gunshot wound. "I was keeping Jade close," he added quickly. "I thought she was the threat."

The side of Jade's mouth quirked up into a half smile as she listened without comment.

She was the threat, all right.

Ben felt the gun wavering ever so slightly in his fingers.

When he'd been a cop, he'd never been forced to kill.

But his partner had, and it almost ruined Ben's life along with his own.

He steadied his hand.

Jade was still holding the gun, but she didn't look like she was fully prepared to pull the trigger.

It would be so easy to move his finger and fire his own. She wouldn't have time to react.

But could he bring himself to do it if there was any chance of de-escalating the situation some other way?

"He had to have known he had no chance attacking me with a bottle while I had a gun in my hand," Asher was saying, his words mingling together as he tried to explain himself. "He had to have known that, but he did it anyway. Protecting his daughter, I guess. He actually got a partial hit in before I moved."

Asher looked down and tensed his jaw, resettling the makeshift bandage on the man's chest. Ben could read his twin's emotions, no matter how he tried to keep them buried.

"Asher, it's going to be okay," Grace said gently. "It was self-defense–"

Ben shot her a hard glance. To his relief, her mouth snapped shut at once. He couldn't focus on helping Asher if she was going to draw Jade's ire. He wished that he'd insisted she go with Katie. He could have dragged her to the bridge using brute force if he had to. But it was too late now.

Instead, he turned to his twin once more.

"And then what?"

"Obviously, I pulled the trigger!" Asher snapped, a rare burst of anger flashing in his eyes. "I made a choice. I didn't want to. As soon as he went down, I started trying to help him."

Ben felt his stomach twisting before his twin spoke again. It wasn't difficult to predict what had happened.

"She grabbed my gun when I bent down to help her father. I screwed up. I know I did, all right, so don't start."

Ben swallowed hard, determined not to let his brother's defensiveness affect his own emotions. It had been a foolish rookie mistake. Asher knew better than to let his guard down for even a moment. But right now, he had to maintain control. Nothing else mattered.

"Asher, you need to focus on helping him," he ordered.

His brother gave him a brisk nod, adding pressure to the t-shirt he was holding against Craig's heaving, blood-soaked chest.

Ben's mind raced as he tried to think of how to get this situation under control, starting with making sure that his twin held it together.

It was already too late for anything he did to matter.

All at once, he felt his head beginning to swim.

Jade's gun was no longer pointed at Asher.

Her attention–and the barrel of the Glock–was now focused on Grace.

Grace

Grace felt the air rushing out of her lungs in a single, panicked breath.

Like the needle that had pierced her shoulder, the barrel of the gun pressed against her head without warning, as cold and unfeeling as the sick young woman who held it.

"I'm telling you one more time," Ben said, his tone so authoritative that Grace could almost believe he'd be obeyed. "Put the gun down, or I am going to shoot you."

Grace dared to glance in his direction, but he didn't look at her. His eyes were trained on Jade, and he aimed his pistol without the slightest quiver in his hands.

No one said a word.

The gun was still jabbing into Grace's skull, threatening to shatter all of the coherent thoughts in her head even before Jade pulled the trigger.

She had to think of something. Anything, anything at all to turn this around.

Just when Grace was about to blurt out the first thing that popped into her head in an attempt to create a diversion, she heard Asher clearing his throat.

He lifted his head. His jaw was clenched tight, and most of his shaking had passed.

"Put the gun down, or I'm going to let your father bleed out," Asher said. "If I stop applying pressure, he's finished."

Jade considered this, and for the flash of a moment, Grace wondered if it was really possible that this might all end without any more violence.

Her hope was dashed an instant later as Jade looked down at Craig, her brows knitting together.

"Do what you need to do. I don't need him. I never did. Sorry, Grace," Jade cocked the gun. "I'm not sure I see a reason I should let you live."

Chapter 38

Ben

Sheer willpower kept the gun clasped in Ben's hand.

What was the point?

If he shot Jade, she'd shoot Grace. If he tried to jump her, she'd shoot Grace. If he tried to shove her out of the way of Jade's weapon, they'd probably both get shot. Ben's pulse pounded in his ears as he tried to think.

This had all been a terrible mistake. Grace should never have been here. She should have stayed home at FBS, behind the scenes, where she was safe.

Where on earth was the Coast Guard? Katie had to have called for help by now.

Should he try to call Gabe? Maybe the ship had wifi that he could tap into. Maybe he could–

"Whoa, whoa, whoa," Asher said, looking over his shoulder at Jade without moving his hands from Craig's chest. "Killing Grace doesn't fix this, okay? Think about it."

Despite the severity of the situation, his twin's voice had taken on its usual lighter tone. Ben swallowed his fear and anger, trying to calm his own words before he spoke.

"He's right. Had your father let you kill Katie Fairman from the start, you might have gotten away with all of this," Ben added. "But it's too late for that now. Don't do something you're going to regret."

It took every ounce of mental strength he had not to scream at her, but he knew that Asher's approach was more likely to work. If they could keep her talking, help would come eventually. He had to believe that.

Before Jade could respond, her phone rang, the bright screen glowing through the pocket of her jeans.

"Gonna try and shoot me if I answer?" she asked Ben, rolling her eyes.

He said nothing, and she pressed the phone against her ear and listened for several seconds. He looked over at Grace. Even with a weapon touching her head, she looked more calm than he felt.

Was it possible her faith in God was sustaining her in this very moment? Did she trust in His mercy even more than she feared death?

Before he could consider the matter further, Jade jabbed at the phone screen and ended the silent call.

"Change of plans. It's your lucky day, Hinton. Guess you get to live after all."

Asher shot Ben a confused look, and he suppressed a shrug.

"And you-" Jade pointed in Asher's direction "- you don't seem like the kind of guy who is going to let a helpless man bleed out. Stay with him, and out of my way."

Without allowing the gun to waver even an inch, Jade gestured in the vague direction of the bridge.

"You two, come with me. But first, I want you to throw that gun overboard."

Ben didn't bother to argue. He had no leverage here, and they both knew it.

Taking a few steps closer to the side of the vessel, he hefted his pistol and threw it into the glimmering turquoise water.

Chapter 39

Grace

As soon as Grace saw the dash panel of the ship, she knew that Katie Fairman hadn't managed to call for help.

Various screens, buttons, and switches seemed to cover half of the bridge, and there were three leather chairs. Clearly, the Lumeneer was designed to be manned by an entire crew, but they saw no one save her terrified friend.

"Leave it alone, Katie," Jade said from her position behind Grace, holding the gun aloft to ensure that the young woman saw it.

She raised her hands in the air immediately, sinking down onto the center captain's chair and staring helplessly at the array of controls. Grace examined the equipment from where she stood, watching as Ben did the same. Perhaps there would be a chance for one of them to try and figure it out, but at the moment, keeping Jade from shooting anybody was their first priority.

Fortunately, Katie seemed to realize the importance of keeping their captor talking.

"I want an explanation," she said to Jade, who had now lowered the gun a little. "You were my friend. I cared about you. Why would you let your father do this?"

Grace cringed at the blank look on Jade's face. She wondered if Jade had lured Katie to South Padre Island to have her taken, or if the trip was merely a useful coincidence. It would have been a lot more suspicious if Katie had been snatched from her dorm room at UT Austin, let alone from her family's mansion.

"Let him? It was my idea," Jade said, scoffing at Katie's open-mouthed expression. "Well, kind of. You should be thanking my bozo of a dad for keeping you alive all this time."

Grace's gaze flicked over to Ben again. He was watching the exchange with clenched fists, his pale face reddening in anger. He cut an intimidating figure, but Jade barely seemed to notice him. Then again, she was now the only one who had a gun, unless the one that she had taken from Asher was still laying around somewhere.

"What could I have done that made you want to kill me?" Katie said. Her forehead was wrinkled in puzzlement, but Grace could tell there was more hiding beneath the surface of her expression. Her mind raced. Could Katie be involved in something shady that had gotten her into trouble, or was she truly nothing more than an innocent victim?

Not for the first time, she wished she could talk things through with Ben. He was standing only about a foot away from her, but the distance felt like miles. All she wanted to do was to be in his arms again, safe and warm, but the glint of Jade's gun in the Mexican sunshine stopped her from daring to step even an inch closer to him.

"You really don't know?" Jade asked.

Katie's mouth opened in surprise, but she quickly snapped it shut again, looking defeated. "I came to you about what I overheard at your house that day because I didn't want both of our dads to go to jail. Don't you get that? I was just trying to help. I didn't think you'd try to hurt me to keep me quiet."

Jade chuckled to herself. "Yeah, right. I'm sure Saint Katie was just trying to make sure everybody did the right thing. You should have minded your business."

Grace's teeth grated as she listened to Jade's mocking imitation of Katie's voice. She tried to catch Ben's eye, but he didn't look up from the patch of wood on the floor he was staring at, no doubt trying to put together the information into a story that made sense.

"Believe whatever you want about me," Katie said bitterly. "But remember that not everyone would treat their father the way you treat yours. I wanted to give mine a chance to make things right."

"They *were* making things right," Jade snapped. "Until you got in the way."

"Messing with Senera Pharmaceuticals and breaking the law isn't making things right, Jade," Katie said gently. "She's gone. Believe me, I understand how much you're hurting, but none of this is going to bring her back."

"It's not about bringing her back. It's not about my hurt," Jade scoffed. "She had a long life ahead of her, and those monsters destroyed her. We can't get true revenge, but at least we can take care of ourselves by balancing the scales."

Once again, Grace could see the hint of humanity in Jade's eyes, and she felt for her and for Katie.

Her own mother was alive and well, but the Forge family matriarch, Mary, had died almost a decade ago. It had been devastating to their entire family, and even as a family friend, losing her had hit Grace hard, too. Even someone as seemingly heartless as Jade had to have been badly wounded by losing the one person who should have been there.

"I get why your dad doesn't want to be part of Lumen once they acquire Senera, but there has to be another way he can leave the company, even with a non-compete in place," Katie said, trying to keep her voice even despite the gun that Jade was still casually brandishing in her direction. "He has connections. He can do something else."

Ben caught Grace's eye, and she gave him a small nod of unspoken understanding. Both she and Ben had grown up with their parents running large companies, and they knew how the behind-the-scenes politics worked.

She remembered that Ben had told her Lumen was buying the shady pharmaceutical company as part of their expansion into the med-tech space, against Craig Gorsky's wishes. Even though he was the founder of the company and had been instrumental in forming it into the powerhouse it was today, he ultimately had to answer to the board and to the investors. And they wanted Senera.

What surprised Grace the most was just how much Jade knew about her father's work, and how involved she seemed to be in his decisions, including illegal ones. Ben hadn't been the only one to underestimate her.

"Nothing that would give him the money he needed," Jade spat. "Not even close."

"So? That's when you ask for help," Katie argued. "I mean, clearly he did. He went to my dad and roped him into this whole scheme! He could have just asked him for money. They've been friends for decades. He would have helped you guys with whatever you needed."

Jade shook her head, another one of her cruel smiles twisting her beautiful face into ugliness.

"You really don't know how deep in the pit your own father's company is, do you?" Jade asked. "Your dad isn't just helping mine out of the goodness of his heart. He's not giving my dad charity any time soon, not that he'd want to take it, anyway. AveroTech is going under. They're totally done."

This time, Katie's look of shock seemed entirely genuine, and Grace was right there with her. Donald had failed to mention any of this when he'd solicited the help of Forge Brothers Security. Ben looked equally stunned.

"That's not true. No. There's just no way. He would have told me. He's in China for a big deal as we speak. He—"

"He's desperate? He's slinging microchips because AveroTech has nothing new to offer, and it's killing them?" Jade finished for her. "His China deal might be enough to get the company through the next eight months, but after that, he's going to need more cash. A lot more."

Katie's brows furrowed.

"So what's the play here?" Ben asked. "Embezzlement? Fraud?"

Apparently, the fear of ticking off the crazy woman with a gun was overridden by his need to understand the truth of what was going on. Grace couldn't blame him. Everything that Jade admitted to only raised more questions.

"Insider trading," Jade said matter-of-factly. She didn't reprimand him for speaking, probably because she enjoyed any opportunity to hear the sound of her own voice. Fortunately, they could use this fact to their advantage.

"My father knew that an acquisition was coming, and he wasn't about to climb into bed with the big pharma company that killed my mom. But he knew he'd need to find a clever way to distance himself from Lumen. Like Katie said, he had a non-compete. A strict one. And he's too young to retire."

Grace noticed Katie nodding in agreement with the story thus far, though no one else seemed to be looking at her. Unfortunately, Jade still had a good grip on the gun, and she didn't really expect that her old friend would try for the radio again.

"Anyway," Jade continued, picking an invisible piece of lint off her slender forearm, "when Katie's dad came to him with his company's own problems, he realized that he'd found a perfect opportunity. Both he and his old mentor would get the money they needed."

"By breaking the law, of course," Ben growled. "How original."

Jade shrugged her shoulders, a smile appearing on her full lips. "It's a shame I'll have to kill you. You've got a certain charm, even if those muscles make you look a little too much like Donkey Kong for my taste."

Grace felt prickles of anxiety tracing up her back as she stared at Jade. The young woman's cold indifference to human life went far beyond anything that could have been caused solely by grief. They had to stop her from doing whatever she was planning, but right now, she was armed and unpredictable. The worst combination.

Grace glanced out toward the open waters of the Gulf. Help was on the way. The only question was how long it would take.

"Insider trading is illegal, sure," Jade continued, "But so what? No one will be able to prove it. My father and Donald Fairman have been friends for years. There's nothing suspicious about them talking, even before a big acquisition."

Grace picked at a fingernail, trying to think. She was starting to understand some of what was going on, at least in regard to why the Gorskys had wanted to keep Katie quiet, but there were still too many unanswered questions.

"So Craig told Donald to buy up Lumen stocks before the Senera acquisition caused them to skyrocket?" Ben asked.

"Pretty much," Jade said with a nod.

"It wasn't for free," Katie cut in, sounding less meek and more angry now that Jade was giving her side of the story. "On the phone, I heard your dad demanding money from mine. He said he was late and that he needed it immediately."

"Obviously the information wasn't *free*," Jade said, waving her gun-hand dismissively. "No wonder AveroTech is in the toilet. You probably get your business sense from your father."

Katie opened her mouth with a retort, but Grace cut her off before she could speak.

"So Donald agreed to pay Craig some kind of fee in exchange, right?" she asked, shooting Katie a warning look. Now was not the time to defend her father's honor.

"Yep," Jade said flatly. Already, she was starting to look bored. She touched the phone in the pocket of her jeans again, and Grace half expected her to pull it out and start scrolling on TikTok. "Donald is paying up front, but after a year or so, he'll be able to dump his shares and make a killing. He'll have the money for R&D that his company so desperately needs to get out of the stone age."

"So why go to such lengths to keep me quiet?" Katie asked, looking up at Jade. "It seems like my dad has a lot more to lose."

For a terrible second, Grace wondered if Donald had neglected to tell FBS about more than just his financial crimes.

Had he been involved in his own daughter's disappearance?

She dismissed the idea as soon as it came. Her old family friend was clearly not the man she thought he was, but she couldn't imagine him doing anything to hurt his only child.

But Katie had a point.

Did Craig hate Senera Pharmaceuticals enough to take such a huge risk? And would his daughter really be willing to kill three people just to keep their secret?

Chapter 40

Grace

Jade's phone began to jingle within her pocket.

"Well, it's noon. Looks like I'm done answering stupid questions," she announced as she took out the phone, her dark eyes seeming to glow as they reflected the bright screen.

Grace caught Ben's eye for a moment as they waited for her to say more.

Katie looked equally nervous, fiddling with the armrests of the captain's chair she was sitting in. Through the front window, Grace noticed for the first time that she could see the shore in the distance.

They were close to land. Could they get off the ship and swim to shore somehow?

Grace looked over at Ben's thick arms.

Maybe he and Asher could propel their bodies that far, but she and Katie wouldn't make it. Not to mention the fact that Craig would be left alone to bleed out.

The sound of the phone ringing again yanked Grace from her reverie.

This time, the tone it emitted was brief, like a notification for a text.

Whatever it was, the smile that spread across Jade's face as she read it made Grace feel instantly sick. The woman looked between her three captives, clicking against the side of her gun with her perfectly buffed artificial nails.

"What? What is it?" Katie snapped, meeting Jade's amused expression with a rage-filled one of her own.

"I got the money," she said with a shrug of her slender shoulders. "Not as much as I want, but enough to get out of this mess and start over somewhere else."

"No," Ben said, shaking his head. "You're lying. There's no way the Hintons paid the ransom money. Not possible."

She held up the phone. Sure enough, Grace could read a one, an eight, and just enough zeroes that she didn't have time to count them before Jade stuck the device back into her pocket.

Grace felt goosebumps tickling at the back of her neck. That ransom money had been their final bargaining chip. And now it was gone.

She glanced over at Ben. She expected him to yell at Jade, but instead, he took a few steps toward her, taking her hand before she could pull away. His touch felt warm and safe, and all she wanted was for him to be there beside her. But she couldn't let him get that close, not with the lethal weapon Jade still had pointed in her direction.

"Ben, don't touch me," Grace said firmly.

She watched as Katie shifted in her chair, looking around the room, probably looking for some sort of weapon she could use if Jade turned on her. There was little in the room save for some wired keyboards, a few thin binders, and a plastic cup of ballpoint pens.

After a couple of seconds, Ben let go of Grace's hand, and raised both of his palms to shoulder height.

"Listen," he started, trying to sound meek but unable to completely hide his gruff timbre. "You got the money, like you said. You can start over. You can let Grace–and Katie–go."

Grace pressed her eyes shut for a moment, not wanting to see the disturbing, blank look that washed over Jade's face.

Ben must realize that this was not the sort of criminal who surrendered. But she supposed he had to try.

"No, I can't," Jade said flippantly, giving the gun another tap with her fingernails. "Anyway, I think I've done enough explaining. Time to go. We're going to take the first leg of our trip together, just in case you guys brought along some followers that I need to shake. Though it doesn't look like my friend here figured out how to work the radio."

"I'm starting to think you were never my friend in the first place," Katie spat. "I cared about you. But you clearly don't have a heart."

Jade ignored her.

"Now, Grace, I figure you're a little more familiar with how to operate this sort of watercraft? Or do you just stick to your little toys?"

Grace's cheeks burned with anger. Not that she cared what this awful girl thought of her hobbies, but she hated that Jade had been digging deeper into her background than she'd realized.

"Even I can see that this ship is not meant to be manned by a single person," Ben interrupted before she could answer. "You might have been able to make it just puttering down the coast, but if you want to get out into the open ocean, you'll want a crew."

"Did I ask for your opinion?" Jade snapped, aiming the gun toward him. Grace's heart hammered in her chest, guilty for the slight sensation of relief she felt now that the gun was pointed at someone else. Even though that someone else happened to be the man she loved.

"No crew," Jade said firmly. "Modern autonav is a beautiful thing. My dad didn't have to do too much to keep this thing floating."

She pointed the gun back toward Grace, stepping closer so that she had a nice view down the barrel. "Do you know how to drive this boat?"

Out of the corner of her eye, she could see Ben's face. It wasn't very difficult for her to read the thoughts hidden behind his stormy eyes. She doubted they differed much from her own.

If they could stay near shore, they might have a fighting chance. Her parents were close by. Surely, they'd realize before long that the ransom swap had gone south, and they'd call in backup.

Not to mention the fact that Asher was still on board. She hated to think that Craig might die–scumbag though he was–but if he did, Ben's twin might be able to make it off the boat without being detected and swim for help.

But Jade still had the gun, and for the time being, Grace, Katie, and Ben were at her mercy.

"Can you drive this boat, Grace?" the woman asked again, her voice dripping with scorn as she drew out each word longer than necessary.

"I know the basics, yes," Grace said, swallowing hard.

She didn't bother to explain to Jade that she used to spend time on the Hinton Logistics company yacht, learning from the crew that her father had employed for over a decade. The Lumeneer wasn't the exact same model of boat, of course, but it was close enough.

She doubted that she was equipped to handle any malfunctions or major changes to the automatically controlled settings, but she had no plans to stick around long enough to find out.

No. There had to be a way out of this. Maybe if she did as Jade asked, an opportunity would present itself.

After waiting for Jade's nod of approval, she stepped forward, taking her place in front of the sprawling array of controls.

She glanced over the GPS screen, the throttle settings, and the controls for the auto navigation system. She could see the radio controls that

Katie had missed, but couldn't reach them easily, even if she decided to take a wild risk and tried to call for help.

"Give her some room," Jade ordered Katie, who was still sprawled in the central captain's chair, blocking her access to the ship's manual steering wheel.

Grace felt her heart aching as Katie walked across the smooth floor to go and stand a few feet away from Ben. All she wanted was to be with him now. The brief embrace they had shared upon her initial rescue hadn't lasted nearly long enough. Now she wondered if she'd ever have the chance to rest in his strong arms again.

No. She couldn't think like that.

Even in the midst of the chaos swirling around her, the quiet voice of the Holy Spirit uttered silent words from the Psalms that she knew by heart.

Wait for the Lord; be strong, and let your heart take courage; yea, wait for the Lord!

Waiting again.

She could do that, even if it felt impossible.

She tore her eyes away from Ben, forcing herself to look back down at the array of screens and switches, trying to get her bearings before Jade issued her next command. The gun was the most immediate threat to their lives, but even a large ship like this could be badly damaged in a collision.

According to the display, the ship was more or less resting in place without its anchor. Though it was drifting slowly near the shore of Mexico, they were still far enough away that their GPS didn't show any other vessels in their immediate vicinity. Good.

"Start heading away from shore," Jade demanded. "Get us out into the open ocean and then I'll figure out where we're headed next."

Grace nodded, wiping her sweating palms against the dress she'd been wearing since yesterday morning. As she looked at the controls, the dozens of different buttons and switches seemed to swirl together into one confusing mess.

She heard Jade's footsteps behind her, and a moment later, she felt a jolting pain in the back of her head as she jabbed her with the gun.

"I thought you knew what to do."

"I–I do," she stammered, reaching for the GPS control wheel and scrolling across the map.

"Maybe if you stop pointing a gun at her she'd be able to focus!" Ben snapped from his place near the door.

Jade scoffed. "Fine. But you'd better get this thing moving. And I want to see some speed."

Chapter 41

Gabe

Gabe raced toward the beach, no longer bothering to be discreet now that the gunshot in the distance had sent the kidnapper's lackey running. The humid summer air felt thick in his lungs as he tried to close the distance between himself and the Hintons, who were both still standing near the dock, looking panicked.

He couldn't hear if they were saying anything to one another over the rest of the background noise. Fortunately, it was better for them to stay put for the time being. They needed a game plan, and he didn't have time to chase Grace's parents through a crowd of terrified locals and tourists.

Before he could even make it onto the beach, however, he noticed that the yacht had moved.

After a few more strides brought him to a patch of concrete free of people, he paused for a moment, trying to catch his breath.

The location of the Hintons had suddenly become the least of his problems.

He watched in horror as the huge craft finished its turn and now faced the open water. With barely a minute's hesitation, the ship proceeded to pick up speed and rush off into the Gulf.

This was really, really bad.

Ben and Asher had been right. He had let this mission fall apart. It was his fault, and now some of the people he cared about most in the world might pay the price.

His leg muscles burned as he fought through the thick sand at a run, dodging other people who were heading away from the sound of the gunshot rather than toward it.

He never should have let the Hintons handle paying the ransom on their own.

He should have realized that a supply chain baron and his self-proclaimed trophy wife weren't going to be able to take the heat when their daughter's life hung in the balance. Whatever other option he might have tried, it was too late to do anything about it now. He'd beat himself up over his stupidity later.

To his surprise, Isla Hinton had mostly calmed herself by the time he reached the dock. The terrified cries for her daughter had been replaced by a look of steely determination on her lacquered face.

"Gabriel," she called, sounding breathless, as though she'd been the one who had been running. "We're not just going to let them get away. We need to go after them!"

It was all Gabe could do to keep his mouth shut instead of reminding them just how badly they'd failed to obey his directives.

Not that it mattered.

It was his op, and therefore his responsibility. He would have told his brothers the same.

Fortunately, Robert spoke before he could attempt to shift the blame off of himself and make his clients feel worse than they already did.

"How, dear?" he demanded. "You gonna dive in?"

Isla peered over at the crystal water for a moment before shaking her head. The boat was still well within sight, but it was growing smaller with each passing minute. "Don't be ridiculous. No. We're going to get in one of those little speedy boats and follow them."

"We don't have one, Mrs. Hinton," Gabe said carefully. "We were trying to come quietly by car and avoid detection."

Isla gave a dramatic eye roll, suddenly looking very much like Grace.

Gabe missed her. Even if he was usually the one stuck on the other side of her more dramatic mannerisms.

"Really, Gabriel," Mrs. Hinton scolded. "I'd expect a man of your expertise to know when it's time to think outside of the box."

Without giving her husband or Gabe any time to respond, she stepped off the dock and set off along the beach, her blonde bob bouncing in the breeze as she began to jog.

"Ma'am! Please be careful!" Gabe called out, striding quickly after her as she climbed onto a rickety dock a little ways down with Robert at his heels.

There were several men standing around talking, their boats bobbing in place nearby.

Dozens of people had already begun making their way back onto the beach, no longer concerned about the single gunshot, though these men didn't seem to have fled in the first place. They could be dangerous, perhaps even accomplices to the kidnapper, but he couldn't exactly shout as much at Isla. He wished she was wearing an earpiece.

Not that she would have listened to him anyway.

"Wait," he said, sticking out an arm to restrain Robert as his wife began speaking to one of the men sitting next to an old but admittedly quick-looking speedboat.

He didn't need the tiny speakers in his ears in order to hear Mrs. Hinton's horrendous attempt at Spanish. Gabe spoke the language decently himself, but he didn't want to jump in and take over. He was a tad more intimidating than Grace's bumbling mother.

"Hola! Por favor? Boat, por favor? Señor? My hijo...hija? Perdida! Ola...rapido."

She was pronouncing each word with what sounded almost like a French accent, and nothing resembling an actual sentence emerged.

The man was staring at her with an expression of pure bafflement, holding a hand to his forehead to block the sunlight.

"Por favor?" Isla added, as though that might clarify things.

"Lady, please speak English," the man said after a moment, his tone friendlier than Gabe would have expected after witnessing the massacre of his native language. "Por favor."

"Oh, thank goodness," Isla said, her breath escaping her lips in a dramatic sigh. "I took high school Spanish a few years ago now. A person forgets the little details. Though it wasn't really that long since–"

"Your daughter is lost at sea?" the man interrupted her. "Yes, I am happy to help."

Relief flooded Gabe's chest as he gestured for Robert to approach his wife and the stranger on the dock.

Like mother, like daughter. Grace had a little more tact than Mrs. Hinton, but she, too, had a way of getting people to like her and to do what she asked. Her sunny attitude often drove him and his brothers crazy, especially Ben, but at the moment, Gabe was thankful she had inherited it from her mother.

"Thank you, sir," Robert interrupted before his wife could say anything more. "Actually, my daughter has been kidnapped by some unnamed thugs and we suspect they're on board that ship."

He pointed in the direction of the yacht, which was now little more than a white dot bobbing along the blue horizon. They were running out of time.

The man held up his hands. "I am not sure I can help, then," the man said, eyeing the craft. "I do not have a gun. Such criminals are dangerous. We can contact the local police–"

"Oh, never mind all of this," Isla said, reaching her hand into the front of her buttoned blouse. "Let's handle this the old fashioned way."

Her husband blanched, and the man on the dock crossed his arms over his eyes as though warding off evil.

Before Gabe could attempt to avert his own eyes, she had yanked out the small money belt that he'd advised her to wear and, fortunately, nothing else had been exposed.

She gathered up more than half of the veritable pile of bills, a mix of dollars and pesos, and shoved them in the direction of the stranger.

"May we borrow your boat, please?" she asked.

The man stared at the clearly ridiculous sum and nodded without a moment's hesitation.

He reached into the pocket of his cutoff denim shorts and procured a set of keys on a neon green rubber fob.

Mrs. Hinton beamed at him, taking the keys from his fingers and tossing them to Gabe.

"You drive."

"Isla, you can't possibly think you're coming," he argued. "It's not safe–"

She stared up at him from her impressive height of five-foot-two, her bright blue eyes snapping.

"Gabriel, you drive. Is that clear?"

He sighed. Robert was already climbing on board.

"Yes, ma'am."

Grace

Grace could still feel the barrel of the gun biting into her skin.

After taking a couple of deep breaths to steady her mind, she started flipping switches and pressing buttons, guided by the memories of days at sea on her father's company yacht.

The engine began to hum below their feet, and Grace took hold of the slick metal steering wheel.

No one spoke as the craft began to slip through the water, turning smoothly until the bow of the ship faced away from the shore. They were picking up speed now, moving farther and farther from the beach and from the possibility of getting help.

Who would see them here? What could she do aside from keeping the boat moving?

Grace tried to focus on the expanse of blue, but she could barely see it through the bright sunlight that was coming from somewhere on her left. She blinked several times, trying to stop her eyes from blurring as she fiddled with the controls, but it didn't work.

Her eyes filled with tears as quickly as she could blink them away, and she wondered if all of them came from the sun in the first place.

Forcing herself to ignore the pressure of the gun against her head, she turned slightly to glance in the direction of the offending light. If she couldn't get rid of it, she'd have to adjust their heading in order to see properly.

Sure enough, the position of the ship now ensured that the window to her left lined up perfectly with the burning midday sun.

But that wasn't all she saw.

She closed her eyes as she turned back toward the controls, the backs of her eyelids exploding in white firecrackers as the searing light faded away from her vision.

She understood now why God had told her to wait.

He had a plan all along.

Chapter 42

Ben

For several long minutes, all that Ben could hear was the humming of the engine.

Katie was leaning against the wall, her eyes filled with tears. Though Ben was just a couple of feet away from her, he didn't dare reach out to comfort her.

He thought of Asher, waiting with Craig closer to the stern. Was there another phone on board somewhere that he could use to call for help? Was help already on the way?

He dismissed the thought. Craig had been in bad shape, sure, but it seemed that Asher's t-shirt was more or less stopping the bleeding. Whatever the man had done, Ben knew that his twin wouldn't leave him to die. So long as he was still alive, it was safe to assume Asher was still with him, trying to help.

Which left Gabe.

Who was somewhere on the beach in La Pesca, soon to disappear into the distance as Grace drove them out to sea.

He looked over at the woman he loved, no longer afraid to let that frightening word fill his thoughts. He did love her, but he knew that he didn't deserve her love in return.

Ever since the terrifying flight that had brought them to South Padre Island, he'd been failing her over and over again.

He wanted to believe that he'd changed since losing his job as a police officer, but had he, really?

Then as now, he had tried to protect the people he cared about from getting hurt, and in the end, he'd only made things worse.

Was that why Mikayla had betrayed him?

He no longer missed her, but the weight of his own faults still felt heavy.

He swallowed hard, surprised at the emotion he felt. He'd gone through life with his walls up, always trying his best to stop himself from letting himself feel too much. It only led to trouble.

Grace was the one who held her heart out in the open, believing that God was good and that the people she met had potential. Even when she'd learned in the most traumatic way possible that some people still chose to sin in the most violent, horrifying ways.

She should have been terrified.

And yet here she was, single-handedly piloting a huge boat carrying three of her friends, a dying man, and a gun-wielding psycho out into the Gulf of Mexico.

She didn't look anywhere near as scared as Ben felt.

No. He knew Grace Isabella Hinton well, and the

only emotion he could detect on her angelic face was immovable determination.

"We need to go faster," Jade demanded.

Grace didn't say anything right away. Ben watched as she looked over the controls, reading a small screen filled with numbers he couldn't begin to figure out. He was sure the yacht could attain higher speeds with a full crew on board, but it was clearly not designed to be manned by a single person.

"I thought you knew what you were doing," Jade said impatiently, giving Grace another one of her withering glares. "Or has all of that bleach leached into your brain?"

Katie glared at the back of Jade's head, opening her mouth as though she was going to defend their friend before thinking better of it.

Ben caught her eye, wishing she understood his unspoken gestures as well as Asher or Grace would have. As far as he was concerned, the more Jade underestimated Grace, the better.

"I'm just waiting until we pass over this shoal," Grace said. "I don't want to blow the propellers if we hit a rock or something."

Jade said nothing, but Ben could tell by her expression that she was not pleased with the delay. Or perhaps she was just bored because she couldn't scroll on TikTok while holding a gun to a hostage's head.

Several minutes passed, and the bridge was quiet now that they were moving more slowly. The sound of the engine had been reduced to a low, rhythmic hum.

Grace continued to stare at the various screens and instruments, not offering so much as a glance in Ben's direction. From what he could discern on the sonar screen, they seemed to be approaching deeper open water once again.

He released a breath. They hadn't hit anything—that was good—but the beach already felt very far away.

Grace's calm voice broke the silence.

"Jade?"

She rolled her eyes, and Ben could see her grip tightening slightly on the pistol.

"What?"

"I'm about to hit the throttle," Grace said. "But I can't really see very well with the sun in my eyes. Can we fix it?"

"Whatever," Jade repeated.

"Ben," Grace said. "Please close the curtains on the window to your left."

Something about the deliberate, almost robotic way that she made her request made Ben hesitate.

Her blue eyes caught his own, and time slowed even as she gave him the most imperceptible of nods.

A second passed, one millisecond at a time.

She was trying to tell him something, but he had no idea what. Was he supposed to tackle Jade and go for the gun? Was she going to do something with the controls and cause some sort of distraction?

His mind hurt as he tried to sort through the possibilities using time they did not have.

At last, he yanked his gaze away from Grace and moved toward the curtain.

And as soon as he saw the window, the unspoken message became clear.

"You gonna do it or what?" Jade snapped, using her free hand to shield her eyes from the glare of the sun. "I can't see, either."

"Sorry," Ben said quickly.

He allowed himself one long breath. There wasn't enough time to say a prayer, but he hoped that the Lord would be with him now just the same.

He lunged for the window.

For a moment, the bridge was flooded with even more light, momentarily blinding Jade.

Before she could figure out what he was doing, Ben gripped the curtain rod he'd yanked free, and swung it as hard as he could.

Grace

The sudden rush of sunlight forced Grace to shut her eyes.

Barely a second passed before chaos broke out.

The two other women screamed and she turned around, blinking away the remnants of the blinding light from behind her eyelids. She heard the sound of metal clattering against the smooth wood of the bridge's floor.

She moved to reach for the gun, but Ben was faster.

He held the weapon with both hands, taking a couple of steps until he was standing over Jade. She was sprawled out on the ground, clutching her knee and howling in pain.

"Do me a favor and stay where you are. I don't want to hurt you for real, but I will if I have to," he said, kicking the curtain rod out of her reach. Grace listened as it rolled across the floor, finally coming to a stop at Katie's feet.

She stepped back quickly, as though the long piece of hollow metal was a snake or a large insect. Her eyes were damp with tears, but before Grace could go to comfort her, she heard an annoying beep from one of the boat's control panels.

"Katie, it's gonna be okay," she said instead. She turned away to return her attention to driving, easing the throttle back until they were bobbing in the water. If Craig was still alive, they'd have to get to land in a hurry, but for the moment, all she wanted was a chance to breathe. "We're gonna get you home."

She heard Jade's bitter laugh behind her.

"Katie probably won't want to be under her dad's roof ever again after this."

Grace felt sick. It was true. Ultimately, it had been Donald's illegal actions that had led to Katie's abduction. Whatever his reasons were, his daughter had been the one to bear the consequences. At least until now.

"I'm the one with the gun now, Jade," Ben said, his deep voice filled with venom.

"And it changes nothing," Jade countered. "You're still not gonna shoot me. You're the good guy, right? The muscle of the family with a heart of gold?"

Ben ignored her, sticking the gun into a holster at his waist.

"I doubt you can walk with that knee anyway," he said. "I'm sure Katie will let me know if you move."

Katie was leaning against the wall now. She still looked shaken, but she gave Ben a firm nod. "You can count on it."

For once, Jade didn't offer a retort, and Ben crossed the bridge in a couple long strides and placed a hand on Grace's shoulder.

"Hey," Ben whispered near her ear, leaning in and giving her a kiss on the cheek.

Grace punched a few buttons on the ship's auto navigation system, keeping their position stable. The feeling of his lips and slight stubble against her skin made her stomach leap in the best possible way.

"She's right, you know," she said quietly, though she was sure that Jade could still hear them. "You are the good guy."

His eyes darkened at her words, and he said nothing.

Even after all that they had been through together, were there still secrets he wasn't ready to bring into the light?

She gave him a small smile and tilted her head back, inviting a kiss. He took it, leaning over her easily until his lips met hers upside down. Even the brief peck was enough to send her already pounding heart racing even faster.

She loved him. And if he loved her back like she thought he did, she trusted that he'd open up to her when he was ready. Right now, they needed to figure out their next move.

She was about to ask Ben whether he wanted her to set their heading or go and find Craig and Asher while he watched Jade, but before she could, she noticed a small boat had appeared in view of her windshield.

It was moving fast.

Was it possible that Craig and Jade's other associates were coming back to the yacht?

As it got closer, she could see that it was a speedboat with three people on board. It certainly didn't look anything like a Coast Guard boat, or the Mexican police.

Ben squinted toward it. "Wait, is that–"

She felt a smile spreading across her face as relief flooded her.

Gabe was driving, her father was standing next to him, and her mother was clinging to her seat for dear life, her blonde bob held back with a baseball cap she normally wouldn't be caught dead in.

Finally, backup had arrived. It was over.

Chapter 43

Ben

Ben rested his forearms on the railing of the yacht and stared out at the water, glad that the sun had begun to lower a little in the sky. He could see the back of the speedboat as it raced toward the coast with Gabe, Katie, and Craig on board.

The man had been badly hurt by Asher's gunshot, but thanks to his twin's determination to stay with him and keep him from bleeding out, they were confident he'd survive. Gabe had radioed for help, but in the end, they'd made the call that taking the injured man by speedboat down to Tampico hospital along the southern coast of Mexico would give him the best chance.

To Ben's surprise, the shaken Katie Fairman had volunteered to go with Gabe, allowing Asher to take a break from keeping the man who had abducted her alive. Apparently, she'd been a lifeguard for several years and had a lot of First Aid training.

Ben felt ashamed for just how much he'd underestimated Katie. He hoped he'd get a chance to apologize when she returned to the states.

"Think Gorsky is gonna make it?" Asher asked from somewhere at his back, startling him.

"You scared me, man," he muttered. "I'm gonna buy you a bell."

Asher leaned on the railing beside him and stared out into the distance as the borrowed speedboat disappeared over the horizon. He shrugged, rubbing his short blonde beard with his fingertips. "I'm not scared of you. Grace has your gun, remember?"

He did. She was still at the bridge, keeping one eye on the yacht's controls and one eye on Jade.

As much as he wanted to debrief the case with her, however, he'd needed a few minutes to get some air after helping Gabe and Katie load Craig into the speedboat.

Ben offered his twin a muted punch on the arm. "I could break you in half, bro, gun or no gun. Be real."

Asher said nothing, and for a moment, they just watched the white foam bubbling on the ship's wake.

"He's going to be fine," Ben said at last. "And even if he isn't, you can't beat yourself up over this. You were doing the best you could in the heat of the moment. Sometimes you have to make a call, even if it ends up being wrong in hindsight."

His words hung in the space between them, and immediately, he wished he could take them back. His twin always knew how to read the secrets he kept hiding in between the lines.

But if he knew that, why did he say anything at all?

"Have you ever considered taking your own advice?" Asher asked, giving him a pointed look.

"You know I told Josiah the same thing I'm telling you," Ben growled back. "That thug was gonna kill us both, and he made the call. It just happened to be a bad one."

Asher shook his head. "I'm not talking about your old partner. I'm talking about you."

"I didn't shoot the suspect."

"No, you didn't. But you're the king of beating yourself up, anyway."

It was true, and they both knew it. Ben hid his guilt, but it was always there. He hadn't been able to shake it in the seven years since he'd left his job as a beat cop with the San Antonio police.

"I'm fine."

He didn't sound convincing even to himself.

"You gonna tell her?" Asher asked.

Ben sucked in a breath. Grace knew that something had happened to him on the job that had led to him leaving the force, and anyone with a functioning brain could see he had trust issues, but that was all. She didn't know about the betrayal he'd endured.

"If you're gonna be with her, she needs to know the whole truth," Asher continued.

"I thought I was supposed to stop beating myself up."

Asher chuckled. "Dad would say that we only get to stop reflecting on our sins once we tell God we're sorry for committing them. I think telling the woman you love would fall into a similar category."

"Fair enough."

Asher pulled back from the railing and stretched his arms over his head. "I'll take Jade downstairs and keep an eye on her. You should talk to Gracie. No time like the present."

Ben didn't argue, but he'd already pushed his regrets back down deep.

He would tell her. But not yet.

Alone again, he closed his eyes, feeling the warmth of the sun on his cheeks as he listened to the gentle shushing of the yacht moving through the water, heading steadily toward Texas.

Asher's words repeated in his mind over and over.

Maybe he had a point about God. Well, maybe their father did, at any rate.

Ben had been going to church every Sunday for years. He believed. But when he looked at Grace's faith, he couldn't help but notice what was missing in his own.

Even when things seemed dark and painful, Grace chose to trust Jesus.

Ben usually chose to trust in himself.

He blew air out of his nose, resting his head in his arms along the railing of the ship. He couldn't deny that it was true. But was it too late for him to ask Jesus to change his hardened heart?

Before he could figure out the answer, he felt a hand on his back, startling him for the second time.

"Asher," he snapped, "I swear–"

Grace was standing there, her blonde curls swept back by the gentle breeze as the cheerful afternoon sun made her blue eyes sparkle.

"Sorry for scaring you," she said, a smile teasing at her full pink lips. She didn't look sorry at all.

"You don't scare me, Hinton," he said, leaning back against the railing.

Her eyes lingered on his. Like Asher, she saw more than he revealed. She had questions, but unlike Asher, she didn't pry. But nonetheless, she deserved answers, and he'd give them to her– just as soon as he'd had the chance to have a long talk with Jesus.

If he wanted to learn to trust, he was going to have to let go of the bitterness he carried.

His father was right. God would not only forgive him; He'd cast his sins into the sea. That was where his healing had to begin.

He cleared his throat. "Where's Jade?"

"She's still tied up on the bridge for now," Grace said, fiddling with a lock of her hair. "Asher offered to give me a break from listening to Princess Gorsky complaining about us meddling kids. And from captain duty."

Ben's eyes narrowed. "You do realize I barely trust him to operate my car, correct?"

Grace rolled her eyes, but her pretty smile stayed in place. "Oh, be nice. The auto navigation is set. We're far enough out that I don't see us running over any wayward fishing vessels, and if the radar beeps, he knows to come running for my assistance in a fit of panic."

Something about the teasing look in her eyes made his heart pick up speed.

She hadn't moved any closer, hadn't even tried to walk up to the rail and look out at the view beside him. She wasn't going to make a decision for him.

There were so many serious words left to say. So many apologies he still had to make. So many ways he'd failed to protect her.

And here she was, standing there like some kind of tropical angel, waiting for him anyway.

He stood up straight and closed the gap between them in a single long stride, his hands finding her waist. She looked up at him and then let her eyes fall gently shut, as though the angel had gone to sleep, completely trusting the man she had chosen to bless with her love.

He leaned down, pulling her in close to his chest as their lips connected, wanting to feel her heart beating against his own.

He heard her humming gently as they kissed, clearly savoring each second just as much as he did. He shut his eyes as well, wanting to feel every sensation. Not like anything could distract him right now, short of the world falling to pieces beneath their feet.

Maybe not even that.

At last, she broke away, opening her eyes as though waking up from a good dream. She looked as though she was going to speak, but instead, she leaned her head against his shoulder.

She was waiting for him, and he knew it.

Should he pour out his heart to her, even with so many other things he still needed to explain?

Only God knew.

But today, he was stepping out in faith.

"I love you, Grace Isabella," he said gently into her hair.

The truth was, he was scared of her. Scared to see her face as he said it, as though those piercing blue eyes could see straight through to his flaws.

To his relief, she didn't move. Instead, he heard her taking a few slow breaths, the air warm against his neck as he held her tight.

"I've loved you always," she said simply.

He planted a kiss on her forehead and looked up at the water, listening to the cawing of the gulls and feeling the spitting salt spray on his skin.

For the first time since arriving on South Padre Island, he realized that he wasn't looking forward to going home to San Antonio. Even if Gabe had promised that he could take the train home instead of flying again.

Because going home meant loving Grace in the world they both shared. Loving her in the world where he'd spent years acting like a stubborn idiot, when the most amazing woman he'd ever met had been right in front of him all along.

He'd be forced to face his pride, his foolishness, his past.

His sin.

But by the grace of God, he'd get through it.

And though he'd be able to shower away the lingering salt, and forget the fear they'd faced together, he knew he'd never forget this little corner of the world.

It was where Jesus had helped a blind man to see.

Chapter 44

Grace

One Month Later

"So you're never going to fly again?" Grace teased as she climbed out of the passenger seat of Ben's sedan.

"And deprive myself of enjoying this incredible machine?" Ben joked, rapping on the top of the vehicle with his knuckles.

Even though the drive from San Antonio to Austin had only taken a little over an hour, Grace felt restless. She didn't want to admit it, but her brief time in captivity on board the Lumeneer had affected her a lot more than she expected. Most of all, she now treasured the feeling of having her feet on solid ground.

"Are you all set?" Ben asked, gesturing in the direction of the hospital's sliding doors as Grace stretched her arms high over her head.

She nodded, stepping beside him as they made their way out of the warm day and into the air conditioning. Without thinking, she moved to reach for his hand before quickly pulling it away.

He glanced down at her, giving her a look that made her want to ditch visiting hours and spend the time kissing him instead. She ignored him, though she was sure he'd notice the rising blush on her cheeks, just like he noticed everything else about her.

Today, they had to be discreet and professional.

They were representing Forge Brothers Security, and perhaps more importantly, they had to uphold the good name of their liaison with the San Antonio police, Allie. She'd called a friend at Austin PD and pulled some strings, and the department had allowed them to conduct their own interview with Craig Gorsky while he remained in custody. Assuming he was willing to speak to them.

As they meandered toward the information desk, she was struck with an uncanny sense of deja vu. It was hard to believe that only a month ago, she and Ben had been visiting Reilly and Lauren's twins, unaware that their relationship was about to change forever.

Katie Fairman was home safe–though as Jade predicted, she was furious with her father for what he'd done, even though he'd had nothing to do with her actual kidnapping. Donald was under house arrest, where he'd remain until the date of his trial. Grace hoped he'd face some jail time, but it was hardly a guarantee. Somehow, white collar criminals often seemed to get off easy.

Grace had resolved to stay in touch with Katie, and her parents had promised that the young woman was welcome to stay with them any summer, Christmas break, or weekend away from university that she liked. Now that Katie's father had been officially removed from the struggling AveroTech, her lifestyle was going to change, but unlike Jade, Katie was humble along with being smart. Grace was confident that she'd create a solid future for herself despite her difficult circumstances.

"Good morning, how can I help you?" a pleasant looking woman at the front desk said, snapping Grace out of her thoughts.

"Hi. I'm Benjamin Forge, and this is Grace Hinton. We're here to see a patient who is currently in police custody."

The woman looked up at them conspiratorially through eyelashes thick with mascara. "Mr. Gorsky, I assume?" she said in a stage whisper that was more attention-grabbing than saying his name aloud would have been.

"That's right, ma'am," Ben said at normal volume. "Austin PD knows we're coming."

"I'll page the floor and have them let the guard officer know you're here," she said in a hurried whisper, picking up the corded phone and tapping a few buttons.

"Which floor?"

"Floor seven. Just swing left, and then he'll be at the end of the hall."

Ben thanked her, and Grace followed him into the elevator.

Fortunately, it was quiet enough on a Friday morning that they were alone.

As soon as the doors slid fully shut, Ben pulled her toward him, catching her lips with his before she had a chance to breathe.

Not that she minded.

He deepened the kiss ever so slightly, and Grace was thankful that they only had a few more seconds before a ding sounded, signaling they'd reached their desired floor. It was hard enough to avoid temptation when other people were around. Being truly alone would be downright dangerous.

"Thanks for that," she said, wiping a smudge of mascara from under her eye and fluffing her curls. "Trying to get me all flustered before we play good cop bad cop with Craig?"

"Never."

"You'd better be careful, then," she teased. "We have our virtue to think of."

"All right, I can take a hint. You want me to buy you a giant, ridiculous Tiffany engagement ring covered in diamonds and get on with it."

His words were light, but she could see the desire for what a wedding would entail hidden deep within his green eyes, and it sent a shiver running down her back.

"Don't be a butthead," she said, laughing. "I'd totally settle for just one diamond."

"How magnanimous of you."

He planted a final kiss on her cheek as they stepped out of the elevator and started walking down the hall, and Grace's heart warmed.

Even though they both knew the whole shotgun-engagement thing was more Reilly's style than Ben's, it was hard to believe that he was even joking about the idea. Though Grace had daydreamed about it for longer than she'd ever be willing to admit.

It didn't take the two of them long to find where Craig Gorsky was recovering. They passed several shared rooms along both sides of the hallway, finally reaching the end, where a plainclothes police officer was sitting on a red plastic chair and keeping watch. He didn't look particularly worried that the gunshot victim was going to jump out of his bed any time soon.

"Officer Harlan Dawes," the man drawled, getting to his feet and extending a hand. Ben and Grace shook it in turn. "They told me you were comin' up."

"Yes, Officer," Grace said, giving him her most charming smile. Though the man looked to be in his thirties, there was something about his accent and mannerisms that reminded her of an old-school, middle aged rancher. The only thing missing was the cowboy hat and boots.

"I took the liberty of letting Gorsky know you wanted to speak with him," the man said, each word pouring out slowly like water cutting through sand.

"Thank you," Ben said. He was polite, but Grace could tell by the slight edge to his voice that he was eager to get on with it.

"If you need anything, I'll be right here where you left me. I don't anticipate much action from the suspect."

"Maybe we can grab you a coffee when we get back," Grace offered before Ben could sweep past him and into Craig's room. "Since you're pretty well trapped in place."

"I'd appreciate it, thank you, ma'am," Officer Dawes said, settling back into his chair.

Craig was awake in bed when they entered the hospital room, sipping at a plastic cup of water with a straw.

"How're you feeling, Mr. Gorsky?" Ben asked, settling into a chair near the bed. Grace did the same, noticing that the cushions were comfortable and the room was almost pleasant. Jail would be a whole lot worse.

"Your brother is a good shot," he said. "But fortunately, not a perfect one."

"Asher wishes things had gone differently," Grace said quickly. "He wants you to know he's praying for your recovery."

Craig leaned back against his pillow and closed his eyes for a long moment, chuckling to himself.

"The man I assaulted offers mercy, and the

daughter I raised hardly cares if I live or die. Go figure."

Grace felt a pang in her chest. He wasn't wrong. Despite all that Craig Gorsky had done, she pitied him. All of the money and power on earth mattered little if your own flesh and blood didn't even love you. Worse, it didn't seem like he trusted in the love of God, either.

"Where is Jade now?" Ben asked.

"The police told me she's in custody," he said flatly. "I've been writing her letters, but I'm not sure I'm ready to send them just yet. To think, I did this for her. And because of her."

He mumbled the last few words, but Grace wasn't about to let the question of Jade drop just yet.

"Jade admitted that you cooked up an insider trading scheme with Donald Fairman because his company, AveroTech, is in the toilet. He paid you a monthly fee, you gave him the information about Lumen's acquisition of Senera Pharmaceuticals so he could buy stocks early, everyone wins."

"That's correct."

"But why?" Ben cut in. "Why take the risk in the first place, let alone kidnap Katie Fairman in order to keep the ruse going? I'm just not getting it."

Craig paused for a moment, adjusting the pale green blankets around himself. Somewhere down the hall, Grace could hear the busy chatter of the nurses and other hospital staff, interrupted by the occasional beep of machinery.

"You know about my wife," he said. "You're in private security. I'm sure you looked into me."

"We did," Grace answered. "And Jade told us about her death. She said that Senera killed her, and that you weren't willing to work with them when Lumen bought them out. What I don't understand is why this seemed like the only way you could escape."

Ben gave her an approving glance, and she felt herself blushing with pride. She'd learned a lot about field work on this operation, and as it turned out, she quite enjoyed interviewing suspects.

"I had a strict non-compete clause in my contract, first of all. I'd basically be forced out of my field. I was willing to retire, but I'm not old enough to take my pension."

He moved to cross his arms over his chest, only to remember the bandaged gunshot wound was still there. He sounded defensive.

"So instead of just doing some other type of work, you decided to break the law?" Ben demanded. "Real mature of you, Craig. Great example for your daughter."

Grace said nothing. Ben's words were harsh, but she couldn't say she disagreed with him. Craig's greed had put multiple lives at risk and had nearly cost him his own. Now, he faced the possibility of retirement in a jail cell–especially if he refused to tell them where her parents' ransom money had ended up which, so far, was information he'd withheld from the police.

Craig looked as though he was going to argue, but all at once, his arms slumped to his sides and he shook his head, defeated.

"I keep trying to protect her. But I'm not sure there's a point any more."

"Protect Jade?" Grace prodded.

"She told you the truth. I wasn't willing to work with Senera, and I did feel trapped."

"But?" Ben added gruffly.

"I couldn't just get another job," Craig admitted. "I'm in debt."

"Half of America is in debt," Grace said. "You consolidate, you make payment plans, you sell assets–"

"Millions, Miss Hinton."

"–you declare bankruptcy," she finished firmly.

"I know. That's what I should have done, hundreds of thousands of dollars before now. But I was weak. I couldn't tell her no."

Ben rubbed at his temples. "Jade was spending all of your money."

"And you were letting her, because you felt guilty. Because she no longer had a mother, and you were working all the time, and you thought taking away her life of luxury would be just too cruel," Grace finished for him.

Craig didn't look particularly surprised by their analysis. "Cliché, isn't it? I know I should have dealt with it when it was manageable, but I didn't. I know the trading scheme was wrong, but in my mind, I justified it. I was trying to fix things, and I guess I figured that Donald making the money off of Senera felt like less of a betrayal of Amira's memory. At least I'd be helping an old friend. Well, that didn't turn out like I wanted it to."

"And I assume you weren't going to be able to flip the shares yourself," Ben put in.

Craig nodded. "Correct. There was a blackout period and other safeguards. It was too much of a risk even if I'd wanted to get that close to Senera's money. I was making some progress on the debts. I was digging my way out, but Donald was paying me in installments, and it would take time. Time I had, until Katie Fairman caught wind of what we were doing and threatened to talk. I absolutely could not allow that to happen. You have to understand. I was in too deep."

Craig swallowed hard, and his eyes were haunted by what his words left out.

Grace caught Ben's glance as alarm bells sounded in her mind.

"The 1.8 million dollars," Ben said flatly. "You weren't paying off a Sephora card, were you?"

Craig winced in pain as he tried to sit up a little further in bed. "The debt started that way. The house, her car, my car, her designer bags, vacations, going out to eat, all of that. I thought I could stay on top of the minimum payments, but we were drowning. I needed a loan to cover my loans."

"A loan you weren't going to be able to get when you left Lumen. Not with every bit of credit you had available to you maxed out," Grace said.

"Nope. I had to find a–shall we say–alternative lender. I regret that decision."

He smiled as he said the words, but there was no happiness in his eyes.

Ben shook his head. "I get it. You really did feel you had to kidnap Katie. You owed dangerous people a bunch of money."

"We would have gotten out of it in a year or so, but not if Katie talked."

Grace bit her lip, trying to put the remaining pieces together. "You aren't a hardened criminal.

When she threatened to expose you and Donald, you panicked. You just wanted to take her and keep her quiet, hoping that even if she was missing, her father would keep paying up so you could save your own skin."

"And my daughter's life," Craig clarified. "I wasn't about to let her get killed over the money we borrowed. And believe me, these sharks threatened to do it."

Ben snorted. "Glad the compassion went both ways. I have a feeling Jade was ready to kill Katie from the start. She knew that keeping her prisoner for months was a stupid plan."

Craig said nothing, setting his lips in a firm line, but Grace knew that was no denial.

"And let me guess, you didn't ask for ransom for Katie in the first place because you knew that Donald didn't have that much money up front? I take it he was using corporate funds to buy the Lumen stocks?" Ben asked.

Craig sighed. "Right on both counts. He was still taking a company salary, but it wasn't much. AveroTech was struggling, but considering that he knew for a fact that Lumen's stocks were about to skyrocket, he'd been willing to make a big bet on investing in it. I assume his influence was enough to convince his team that it was the right call."

"And then we showed up and made a bad situation worse," Grace said.

"Pretty much."

"Donald never told us anything," Grace mused aloud. "Even though his own daughter was still missing, he never said a word about the crime he was committing. No wonder he wanted to hide out in China."

Of course, he was back home on American soil now, awaiting trial. At least he'd had the decency to come quietly.

"So," Ben said, his face clouding with anger that he scarcely bothered to hide. "Is this when you chose to assault and kidnap Grace?"

"My associates," Craig corrected. "But yes. I gave the orders. And yes, I told the police their names."

So much for honor among thieves. Or, in this case, kidnappers.

"You knew Ben and I were going to solve the case eventually, and it wouldn't have taken much research to figure out that my parents had the money to pay for my safe release."

"Yes," Craig admitted. "I did a bad thing. But I felt trapped. I didn't want to hurt Katie. I was trying to find a way out of the mess I got myself into without causing any more harm to anyone else."

"Abducting Grace caused harm, Mr. Gorsky," Ben said, his voice dangerously low. Grace reached over and rested her hand on his arm. Despite how angry she should be at Craig for what he'd done, she believed him. In his own way, he had been trying to protect her, Katie, and Jade.

"That offshore bank account where my father sent the money–it went straight to the guy you borrowed money from, didn't it?" she asked, trying her best to keep her tone neutral.

Craig looked pained. "That's right. I can't get it back. I don't even have a name to offer the police; the guys I borrowed from were too careful. I've been telling the cops as much, but they won't believe me. I assume that when I'm imprisoned and my assets are sold off, your parents will see some restitution, but it won't be the full amount. I'm sorry, Grace. For that, and for everything else."

For a long moment, Grace considered his words. She had no doubt that he was sincere. The man had made catastrophic mistakes, but they were mistakes borne out of grief.

She wasn't angry with him anymore. All she felt was sadness.

She glanced at Ben, wondering if he was thinking the same thing. He'd lost his mother. He understood Craig's pain better than she ever could. And Jade's, for that matter.

"Have you ever read the Gospel of Matthew, Mr. Gorsky?" she said at last.

Craig looked puzzled. "Maybe a long time ago. Why?"

"Read the eighteenth chapter. You can start around verse twenty-one, if I'm remembering right," she said, unable to contain the smile that was rising on her lips. Ben raised his eyebrows, but said nothing.

"I'd be happy to. I owe you that much and a whole lot more," Craig said carefully. "But again, may I ask why?"

"Because God has forgiven me a whole lot more than 1.8 million dollars' worth of sins," she said. "The money is gone. My parents weren't even supposed to transfer it until I was safe, and they went ahead and did it anyway. I already talked to my dad about it. You can consider your debt to me and to my family already paid."

Grace felt Ben stiffening beside her, but she didn't turn to see the look on his face. The tears that had begun to run down Craig's ochre skin had captured all of her attention.

She reached for his hand as the man wept, his wounded body shaking with sobs beneath the sheets and layers of bandages that covered his chest. More than once, he tried to speak, but Grace hushed him softly.

Ben moved closer to the bed, resting his own hand firmly upon Craig's shoulder.

She looked up at him, seeking answers in his perfect green eyes, but she could see nothing.

She let out a breath, squeezing the suspect's hand more tightly within her own as the man continued to weep. Justice would be done, but she had a chance to extend forgiveness.

That opportunity didn't always come.

After the bombing in Indonesia, she'd tried to offer forgiveness to her enemy in her heart. But it wasn't complete. Not when the terrorist's body had been blown to pieces and scattered among the rubble.

Craig Gorsky was here. She could look into his tear-filled eyes, and she could see the remorse written there.

Would Ben understand that her love for Jesus demanded she offer mercy?

And would she still feel the same about him if he didn't?

Ben

Despite the heat and the smell of the city, the fresh morning air felt glorious as it filled Ben's lungs. Grace stood beside him as they stepped out of the hospital lobby and into the sun, but their bodies didn't touch.

Witnessing the mercy that Grace had shown had made him love her even more, and yet, he felt as though her act had raised a veil between them, heavy with unspoken words and buried secrets.

Oh, how he wanted to take her hand, to kiss her, and to hold her close. She looked so beautiful in the light, her eyes even more blue than usual as they reflected the cloudless sky.

But he couldn't. Not yet.

Not until she knew everything about him, and the kind of person he really was.

"Grace," he said, stopping abruptly on the sidewalk. He didn't want to wait any longer. The thought of telling her the whole truth was terrifying, but he knew there would be no rest for his heart until he did. The time to have this conversation was now, no matter how imperfect the setting was.

"Are you okay?"

He swallowed hard. "Yeah, let's just sit down for a minute."

She raised an eyebrow but said nothing as he led her over to a bench with a view of the ambulance bay. Fortunately, it seemed to be a quiet morning, and there were no blaring sirens to distract him from what he needed to say.

"You know that I got fired from San Antonio PD," he said quickly, before his courage could dissipate.

Grace nodded without missing a beat. "Yes. You never would tell me why, just that it had something to do with trying to protect your former partner."

His cheeks burned with shame. He should have told her the whole truth a long time ago. His brothers knew, and they still loved him, so why did he fear that Grace would rip her heart away from him when he lowered his walls?

"My former partner's name is Josiah Everett, and he's a good man," Ben said firmly.

Grace let out a sigh of relief. "Present tense. Good. You had me nervous that you accidentally shot him or something."

"Thank God, no, I did not shoot him. He's alive and well, last I heard."

"Do you guys still talk?"

Ben's chest felt tight. That was a complicated question.

"No, but I wish him well."

"So what happened?" Grace asked. "Why'd you get kicked off the force?"

"We responded to a call at a trailer park. Old lady heard a neighbor woman screaming and called 911."

"Domestic?"

He nodded. "The guy answered the door, hammered drunk. We could hear a woman sobbing inside and we demanded he let us in to check on her. He refused, screaming about a warrant, the usual nonsense, no matter how much we explained to him what his actual rights were when we were facing an immediate threat to another person. The suspect was unpredictable. He slammed and locked the door without warning, and we heard the woman screaming again."

Grace reached over and placed her hand on top of his as a patient in a wheelchair rolled past them. Ben was glad for a moment to breathe. The memories of that night still bothered him, even after all these years, but now that he was talking, he realized that it felt good letting the story out. Grace of all people would understand.

No matter what she went through, she never allowed darkness to dampen her light. She hadn't let her trauma build walls around her heart.

"I started trying to break down the front door," he continued. "Josiah ran to the back and started trying to get in that way. I could see the windows were all covered with planks. The glass was long gone. The woman was crying and begging for her life, and I was starting to panic a little. We both were. We should have grabbed him right away, but we didn't."

"Why didn't you?" Grace asked, her face twisting in puzzlement. Ben didn't blame her for being confused. He and the rest of his brothers generally knew how to act with conviction when necessary. Second-guessing wasn't really their style.

He wanted to explain, but he didn't want to make excuses. Not any more.

For years, he'd tried to blame everyone and everything but himself and Josiah, but the truth was, he'd let worries about his reputation and his career override what he knew was right in the moment. And in the end, he was worse off than he would have been had he just shoved the man in cuffs from the jump.

"You've seen how the police are treated by the media and by the general public when mistakes are made," he said carefully. "SAPD saw the writing on the wall. Diversity training, sensitivity training, de-escalation training–some of it was helpful, some of it wasn't, but it sent a message to me and my fellow officers: if you screw up out there, we're not going to have your back.

"The suspect that night happened to be a black man. We both knew that we had to tread carefully, so we did. We talked to him at the door. We tried to de-escalate. Later, of course, with time to think, we realized we hadn't even followed the training as well as we might have, but in the moment...it's a lot harder than people realize to make the right call."

Ben felt gooseflesh rising on his skin as he remembered. The pounding on the door. Wiping sweat from his brow. Shouting at the man as his girlfriend sobbed in fear. Not knowing where exactly his partner was. Calling for backup that wouldn't make it in time anyway.

"At the end of the day, we both used poor judgment. The man was in that trailer with the woman he'd been beating up, and we were on the wrong side of the wall."

Grace hadn't taken her hand off of his, and he drew strength from her touch. At least she'd know the truth, whatever she felt about it. Or about him.

"I heard glass breaking, and I gave up on the front door and ran around to the back. I made it through the door to the laundry room just in time to hear one gunshot, and then another. I remember how my heart was pounding. I could hear the girlfriend screaming, and I guess I was yelling too, but I don't really remember what I said."

Ben paused, pressing his eyes shut for a long moment as Grace squeezed his hand tighter. Usually, he didn't think about that night. He preferred to push it down deep, where the what-ifs and the could-haves lost their power to paralyze him. But just like his panic attack on their flight to South Padre Island, sometimes fear had a way of forcing you to face it.

"The suspect was on the floor of the living room, bleeding out. Josiah was trying to revive him, but it was very obvious he wasn't coming back from two shots to the chest at close range. The girlfriend was hysterical."

"Did Josiah explain what happened?"

"It wasn't until later that we got a chance to talk about it, and by then, the investigation was underway, the media had shown up, and it was obvious nothing looked good for Josiah. The guy's girlfriend was covered in bruises, and the situation was chaotic. Josiah was yelling at him to put his hands up, and the suspect didn't comply. He thought the guy was reaching for a weapon."

Ben swallowed hard.

"Josiah was scared for his life. He did what he felt he had to do."

"The guy wasn't armed, was he?" Grace asked.

"No. No weapons were found in the trailer at all. Just a small amount of dope, and of course, his obviously injured girlfriend. Like I said. Didn't look good for my partner."

Grace pulled a face. "I don't understand. It sounds like it was an accident."

"The guy's girlfriend threw us under the bus, but she didn't actually tell any outright lies. Nothing that would contradict the bodycam footage. From her perspective, we butted in on her private business and got her man killed."

"Wait. There was proof of what Josiah saw? On camera?"

Ben no longer felt relieved to be telling the truth. No, this was the part where he would have much preferred to let Grace go on loving the person she thought he was.

"There was video footage, yes. Mine lined up with both of our statements."

"And Josiah's?"

"Josiah told the police that he saw the suspect reaching for a weapon. Told them that the guy was moving toward him, and that he was certain he was about to be shot."

Grace's brow furrowed.

"I don't get it. He lied?"

Ben let out a breath. "To this day, I don't think he did. I think that Josiah really did believe he was about to be shot. I think that the suspect played a stupid game and won a stupid prize, and the idea that he gets to be a martyr is ridiculous. And don't even get me started on his girlfriend and her Stockholm syndrome."

He had tightened his free hand into a fist as anger welled up in his chest. He was thankful that Grace was on his other side, stroking his thumb with her own. It was too late for his indignation to mean anything. The situation had been what it was, and his dumb decisions were his own.

"I went home that night and logged into the SAPD system," he said quickly, half-hoping that Grace would let the statement pass.

"Illegally, you mean. You hacked your way in."

Her glare was about as intimidating as a chihuahua guarding a chew toy, but still, he hated disappointing her.

"Yes. Look, I know it was wrong, but I was worried. Josiah was freaked out. His face was on the news already. People on social media were accusing him of being a racist for shooting an unarmed black man. He was my partner. I felt that I had to look out for him."

Grace raised her eyebrows at him, but made no further comment, her manicured fingers still resting lightly on his own.

"The bodycam footage was bad. Really bad. It was blurry and chaotic, but just clear enough that I could tell the guy wasn't reaching for a weapon. Josiah let his panic cloud his judgment. He went against our training in a chain of bad decisions. He shot and killed a man. But I still couldn't bear the idea of his life being ruined over it. It was a mistake. It felt so unbelievably unfair.

"So I did what I thought was the right thing. I downloaded the footage, did some tinkering, and reuploaded it. By the time the investigation team got a chance to look at it the next morning, it looked like a corrupted file. They couldn't see anything. And in the end, he kept his job, and at least some of his reputation once the news cycle moved on."

"I'm confused. Your bodycam footage didn't show you doing anything shady, so why did you get fired?"

"I wasn't the computer genius I am today, I guess," Ben joked without mirth. "They figured out that someone destroyed the footage on purpose and they traced the hack to me. I was fortunate I only lost my job. I guess the SAPD knew it would make the whole shooting fiasco look even worse if they let the story get out."

"I guess you deserved that," Grace said flatly. "We can't do wrong in hope that something good will come of it."

"Oh, that wasn't the worst of it. After I got fired, the fellow officer that I was planning to propose to, Mikayla? She dumped me. She was moving up the ranks on the force, and me getting fired didn't exactly look good on her."

"Okay, maybe you didn't deserve–"

"Did I mention that about a week after she

dumped me, Josiah swooped in and they started dating?"

Grace's shocked expression immediately shifted to guilt.

"I still deserved it. Yeah, it was not exactly up to bro code, but it's not as bad as you think," Ben said quickly. "He never actually found out that I was the one who probably kept him out of jail by messing with that footage. SAPD fired me quietly. After that night, I was feeling pretty messed up. I thought Josiah was, too, until I realized he was drowning his sorrows with a new relationship. We didn't discuss it again. And then we fell out of touch, and that was that."

He let the last few words escape in a rush. It was all out on the table now. Even if he didn't get mushy about how he really felt–and he wasn't planning to–Grace was smart. She'd read between the lines and see the hurt that he tried to pretend wasn't there.

At least, he hoped she would.

Would she see the same remorse that Craig Gorsky had shown her, even though his own eyes held no tears? Would she realize that he wanted to trust her with all of his heart, even though it scared him?

He listened as an ambulance roared into the parking lot, sirens blaring as the blue and red lights competed with the sunshine.

Either she'd understand, or she wouldn't.

All he could do now was pray that God would give him one more chance.

Losing Mikayla had hurt for a while.

But losing Grace would hurt for the rest of his life.

Grace

Grace felt Ben's hand shift beneath hers. The movement was almost imperceptible, but it was there.

After everything he'd told her, was he really going to pull away?

Again?

She turned to face him.

"So that's it?" she said, forcing a harshness into her tone that she wasn't sure she felt.

Ben drove her crazy, but she'd known that forever. He wasn't vulnerable about much, and she knew it must have been difficult for him to tell her the truth. But this was it. She wasn't going to sit around waiting any more. Either he was going to give her his whole heart, or she was going to walk away again. And this time, it would be for good.

"I've pushed through all of your brooding, and all of your I'm-too-broken-for-love crap, and that's the deep dark secret?"

Ben looked so shocked by her words that she almost gave in and kissed him right there.

She wanted to dive into his arms and tell him she loved his infuriating, stubborn, handsome, stupid face. But that could wait.

"I mean, it's not up to par with surviving a suicide bombing," he said, his voice taking on the growling tone that always pulled her in. "But yeah. I lost my job. The woman I was going to propose to broke my heart. One of my best friends betrayed me."

Grace leaned back a little on the bench, pulling her hand away from his and crossing her arms over her chest expectantly.

"And?"

Ben looked a little bit mad, but she could read those eyes. He wanted to kiss her and shut her up. Go back to the easy banter and the chemistry that neither of them had ever been able to fully hide.

Well, too bad.

"What do you mean, and?" he argued, mirroring her gesture, though his thick arms looked a tad difficult to cross properly.

She forced her face to remain impassive.

"You know what I mean, Benjamin Melchizedek Forge."

"I thought you swore that you would never use that name in public."

"I'm not sure that a lonely bench in front of a hospital a hundred miles from where you live actually qualifies as public."

He was staring at her lips again.

She cleared her throat. "Anyway, don't change the subject."

"Which was what, exactly?"

She let out a sigh, shaking her head. He wasn't making this easy.

Or maybe he was more clueless than she thought.

"We've all had bad things happen to us, Ben," she said, allowing a hint of her usual gentleness to come through. "We're all sinners. We're all broken. The fact that you are too isn't exactly some big revelation."

"What do you want from me, Grace? In case you missed it, the reason I got fired isn't exactly common knowledge. I'm trusting you. Do you have any idea how hard that is for me?"

As the last few words escaped, realization flickered in his eyes.

"That's what I want," she said.

"What? For me to trust you?"

She offered him the hint of a smile.

"If we're going to do this, yeah. I need you to trust me. But more than that, I need you to admit that you struggle to trust. That you struggle to love. That Mikayla and Josiah caused not just anger, but pain. Just because you're good at putting up walls doesn't make you invincible.

"And it's not just me you've been holding at arm's length. I can see the way you struggle to let God in. You're determined to do everything yourself so that you don't have to risk anyone letting you down. I can't promise I won't fail you or hurt you if you choose to trust me with your heart. But I know for a fact that Jesus never will. You need to let him in, Ben. All the way. You can't hold anything back."

She let her words hang in the air as silence filled the space between them.

Ben looked down at his crossed arms and then let them fall to his sides, as though realizing that he was putting up barriers even as they spoke.

She pressed her palms against the rough wood of the bench and closed her eyes, letting the sun warm her face.

God was the one who softened men's hearts. She'd done her best to be a worthy instrument. The rest was–

Ben's lips found hers.

She kept her eyes closed as he shifted her into a more comfortable position on the hard bench, pulling her in closer as he deepened the kiss.

Another siren blared, but it sounded far away. Everything was quiet and loud all at once, like fireworks bursting under water.

His skin felt warm beneath her fingers as she wrapped her hand around his neck, feeling the slight scratchiness of his beard as she drew herself ever closer.

For the moment, she wasn't looking for any more answers. His touch, the softness of his breath, the pounding of her heart beneath his t-shirt, everything about the moment was speaking already.

At last, he allowed his lips to fall away, his fingers tangled in her curls as he nestled her face against his neck. "We need to be careful."

"It's you I'm worried about," she joked, giving him a quick peck along his jawline.

"You've been in love with me for years. Pent-up attraction is a dangerous thing."

She swatted his shoulder. "So is stubbornness and denial, but that's never stopped you."

He pulled back a little, until their faces were mere inches apart.

He caressed one of her cheeks beneath his thumb, looking into her eyes with such intensity that she almost flinched, as though daring her to close the distance between them again with another perfect kiss.

"Grace."

"Ben," she raised an eyebrow, but he didn't smile.

His green eyes were filled with tempests once again as longing mingled with fear.

"You're right, you know. About everything. I am a coward, and worse, I'm a coward who is too proud to admit that he is one. So I guess that's step one."

He paused for a moment, drawing a breath before continuing without letting his gaze slip away for even a moment.

"Grace, I'm scared to love. Even you. Even my own brothers, half the time. Even my Savior. The only person I'm not scared to love is myself, as though I'm even remotely capable of always getting everything right. That's the whole ugly truth."

She smiled, reaching up to fix a strand of his hair that had fallen onto his forehead.

"And?"

"And it doesn't matter. It doesn't matter, because it doesn't change how I'm going to choose to live my life."

Grace swallowed an unexpected lump that had arisen in her throat. She felt his fingers twining with her own, capturing her as firmly and securely as an anchor at harbor.

His eyes weren't filled with fear any more. The storm had finally calmed.

"I love you, Grace. I'm done holding back. I want you to have my whole heart. All of it. Stomp it to pieces, bury it in the dirt, toss it into the Gulf of Mexico–so be it. It's yours."

* * *

I hope you enjoyed *Forged in Secrets*!

Forged in Deception is coming soon. I can't wait to share Asher's story with you. Keep reading to find out how to get your free prequel novella.

If you enjoyed this book, please take a moment to leave a brief review — it helps more people to find my books. Thank you!

Get Your Free Prequel

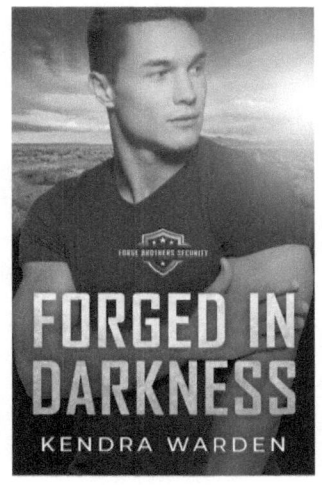

Find out how Reilly and Lauren met with a FREE novella!

Just head to www.kendrawarden.com/newsletter to sign up for my latest updates and download your copy. :)

About the Author

Kendra Warden writes romantic suspense with real danger and fearless faith. She lives in Ontario, Canada, with her husband, three young children, two cats, and a whole lot of books. She's passionate about (very) early mornings, long walks, and buffalo sauce.

https://www.kendrawarden.com